FATHER'S SHADOW

"An emotionally-consuming novel of strength, growth, and love that will leave you with a dizzying book hangover." - Jennifer Donovan, Discovery Reviewer

"Wow, what an awesome book. This is the first time I've read a book by Quinn Avery. I couldn't put it down. It's a great thriller. " -Goodreads

"Well written by an author, Quinn Avery, that I am excited to read more of, her words did not allow for me to put this book down from the moment I began. I regret nothing. Absolutely stellar writing, completely awesome novel." -Amazon

"With equal parts in romance, mystery and thriller, this story had me all twisted and tied up on the inside." -Amazon

Praise for The Dead Girl's Stilettos

"Bexley is a great leading lady who, with a little sass, just enough self-doubt to make her relatable, and plenty of intelligence, will have readers coming back for more." -InD'tale Magazine

"Author Quinn Avery seems on the verge of creating her own sub-genre of crime fiction, delivering a clever protagonist with serious emotional heft that does her best work amongst the playgrounds of the super rich and famous. Fans of Willow Rose will love this novel, but Avery is an original." -BestThrillers.com

"I absolutely devoured this book! I loved all the twists and turns, it definitely kept me on the edge of my seat. This was my first Quinn Avery book and it definitely will not be my last!" -NetGalley

"I can't say enough about this story and these characters. Really looking forward to what comes next for Miss Bexley Squires!!" -NetGalley

IN HER FATHER'S SHADOW

QUINN AVERY

BOOKS BY QUINN AVERY
www.QuinnAvery.com

BEXLEY SQUIRES MYSTERIES
The Dead Girl's Stilettos
The Million Dollar Collar
The Guard's Last Watch
The Skeleton Key's Secrets
The Notebook's Hidden Truths

STANDALONES
What They Never Said
In Her Father's Shadow
Woman Over the Edge
Deadly Paradise

TIKI TROUBLE COZY MYSTERIES
Moscow Mules & Murder

STEAMY ROMANCE BY QUINN AVERY
WRITING AS JENNIFER ANN
www.authorJenniferAnn.com

KENDALL FAMILY SERIES
Brooklyn Rockstar
Midwest Fighter
Manhattan Millionaire
Oceanside Marine
Kendall Christmas
Miami Bodyguard
American Farmer

ROCK BOTTOM SERIES
Outrageous
Notorious
Courageous
Ferocious

STANDALONES
Broken Little Melodies
The Secrets Between Us

FALLEN HEROES DUET
Saving Phoebe
Saving Alexa

NYC LOVE SERIES
Adam's List
Kelly's Quest
Chloe's Dream

This is a work of fiction. Names, characters, business, events and incidents are the products of the author's imagination. Any resemblance to actual persons, living or dead, or actual events is purely coincidental.

No part of this book may be reproduced in any form or by any electronic or mechanical means, including information storage and retrieval systems, without written permission from the author, except for the use of brief quotations in a book review.

Any trademarks, service marks, product names or named features are assumed to be the property of their respective owners, and are used only for reference. Namely: The Cars, Volvo, *Jurassic Park*, *Alien*, *The Goonies*, Def Leppard, *Donny Darko*, *Dawson's Creek*, YouTube, *Evil Dead*, Google, Jeep, Gucci, New York Times, Wikipedia, Tiffany's, Aerosmith, Nutella, *Will and Grace*, Range Rover, Mercedes, Fleetwood Mac, Instagram, Cheshire Cat

In Her Father's Shadow

(formerly *Purpose*)

Copyright © 2021 by Jennifer Naumann writing as Quinn Avery. All rights reserved.

Cover: Najla Qamber Designs

www.QuinnAvery.com

ISBN: 9798499838556

For SJN and OBN who constantly inspire me to be a better person

PART 1
CHILDHOOD INTERRUPTED

"We don't even know how strong we are until we are forced to bring that hidden strength forward. In times of tragedy, of war, of necessity, people do amazing things. The human capacity for survival and renewal is awesome." -Isabel Allende

1

Sienna Rivers was eleven when both her hopes for a normal childhood and her father's career as a serial killer came to an abrupt end.

The night began innocently enough as Sienna packed for her first sleepover. She'd never been invited to even *visit* anyone's house before, and deep down she knew it was because she wasn't anything like the other girls. She'd witnessed them during enough lunch periods to understand being forced to adhere to a strict diet rich in vegetables and protein was abnormal. She listened in on enough conversations to doubt any of them were made to run three miles on the treadmill every morning, or religiously care for their hair like it was a separate living entity. She noticed a few of them had started experimenting with basic makeup, like mascara and eyeshadow.

Sienna shuddered at the idea of someone seeing her freckles in public.

The invitation to Rowan Holloway's birthday party had been a spur-of-the-moment decision that occurred shortly after Stewy Rogers had called Sienna a "freak of nature" when she'd thanked the lunch lady for a generous helping of broccoli. With the exception of Rowan, everyone in the line around them had cackled with malice. Sienna, having been groomed to remain poised in public, held her composure until after she'd finished her lunch and could lock herself in a bathroom stall. Rowan had been in the restroom and overheard Sienna crying. She'd offered kind words to calm Sienna before the offer to attend the sleepover was made.

Sienna's family was as wealthy, if not *more* wealthy than the other families that attended the private elementary school in Brooklyn, yet her classmates had treated her like an outcast for as long as she could remember. She didn't believe it was because she was a reigning beauty queen, because she was certain almost none of them actually cared. She was also certain it wasn't because she was smart, or because she maintained the best manners of anyone in her school.

Whatever the reason, it only added to her

complex as someone who was taught to project nothing less than perfection. She longed to be accepted. She wanted to be surrounded by as many friends as Rowan Holloway. She wished boys would notice her for reasons other than her abnormalities. She yearned to snack on candy bars while drinking a can of soda like Rowan and her friends often did over the lunch hour. While she'd been presented with countless opportunities to try what her mom would deem "junk food" at school, she was certain her mother would notice if she packed on so much as a single pound. *"If you don't control your weight, it will control you,"* her mother was constantly reminding her. *"Discipline and determination are what make you beautiful, Sienna. Not genetics."*

While carefully folding her pajamas, Sienna's gaze skipped around the contents of her bedroom. What would Rowan think of her room, she wondered. The abundance of large pageant trophies and awards lining a wall of shelves would undoubtedly overwhelm someone unfamiliar with a lifetime of competitions. Aside from those, she wanted to believe it was a typical room for a girl her age, complete with a 4-poster bed and dainty nightstands. Knickknacks from her younger years filled a shadow box, mostly memorabilia from the cities she'd visited during competitions. In the windowsill overlooking their condominium's meticulous courtyard, a collection of shells and sand she'd personally harvested while visiting her aunt filled mason jars. Years prior, the bedroom walls had been painted the same soft lilac color as the dainty flowers in her duvet. At the same time, contractors had installed built-ins that now overflowed with countless books.

Reading was one of the few leisurely activities encouraged by her mother, and she'd amassed an impressive collection of paperbacks. She didn't favor any certain genre—women falling in love, dogs on adventures, aliens invading earth, pirates sailing the high seas—everything was fair game. Each evening after homework, exercise, and her daily beauty regimen were complete, she'd lose herself in a new adventure. Most recently, she'd discovered a tale about a boy living under a stairway who learned he was a wizard, and she was unable to put it down. She connected with the boy on a level she couldn't explain.

She'd admittedly outgrown the poster of baby kittens wearing little hats that hung over the cluster of pretty pillows on her bed, but her father had won the poster by throwing baseballs at bottles the only time he'd ever taken her to Coney Island. She refused to take it down as that trip had marked one of the last happy memories involving her father before his absence became the norm.

Sienna's father put in grueling hours as one of Manhattan's most successful financial advisors, and travelled often on business—or so Sienna's mother was made to believe. Sienna longed for the days when she'd been able to make him laugh in his deep voice. On the rare nights he was home before her bedtime, he'd sometimes allow her to watch his favorite television shows even though they were for grown-ups and the actors said bad words. Whenever he'd read her stories in animated voices, she'd giggle until her stomach hurt. She believed he was a good man with a big heart, like the time he showed up late to her kindergarten choir concert, and had apologized afterwards with a stunning bouquet of red spider lilies wrapped in a thick white ribbon. They were the coolest flowers she'd ever seen. Little did she know, the sight of spider lilies would one day chill her down to her core.

While she dug through her walk-in closet in search of her favorite sandals, shoving her collection of outgrown pageantry dresses aside, she shook her butt when Ric Ocasek commanded her to "shake it up." Her aunt Taylor had given her a stereo two

Christmases prior, and was constantly sending Sienna a vast array of music burned onto CDs. Although dancing in her closet seemed a silly thing to do, and most definitely something her mother would frown upon, the anticipation of the sleepover shimmered through her veins.

"What on earth do you think you're doing?"

The sound of her mother's stern voice from the doorway made her snap to attention with the precision of a soldier reporting to his commanding officer. As she turned away from her closet, she prayed the nervous quiver in her lips was undetectable.

Vanessa Rivers was a petite, strikingly beautiful brunette with piercing hazel eyes and flawlessly propionate features that were normally only achieved with the help of a plastic surgeon. As the wife of a wealthy man, whatever time wasn't devoted to Sienna was usually spent attending elegant luncheons and charity events. She wore designer labels, carried herself with the poise of a royal, and ensured she never had so much as a single strand of hair out of place. As she stood before Sienna in a pink cocktail dress, hair fashioned into a tight bun, several carats worth of diamonds dripping from her slender neck and delicate earlobes, she possessed all the favorable traits of a beauty queen.

Because her mother's childhood had always remained a mystery, for all Sienna knew, she'd participated in pageants too. Sienna had never seen a single picture of either of her parents taken before their wedding, and she'd never met either sets of her grandparents. When she'd once asked why her parents never wanted to visit their families in California, and why they'd never taken her there, her mother had simply stated family wasn't of importance to them.

With trembling hands, Sienna smoothed the creases on her white ruffled shirt. "I'm sorry, mother. I thought I was alone. I'm just listening to one of the CDs aunt T sent—"

"I'm not referring to your insolent behavior." Lips tight, one of her mother's french tipped nails gestured to the overnight bag on Sienna's bed. "I'm asking about *that*. Where exactly do you think you're going?"

"I'm going to Rowan Holloway's house for a sleepover," Sienna replied with a confident lift of her chin. Deep down, her nerves shook like maracas. "She invited me to her birthday party."

Vanessa's classically shaped eyebrows shot upward. "Is that so?"

Sienna nodded and flashed the pageant-winning

smile she'd spent hundreds of hours perfecting in the mirror. "Yes, ma'am."

"And what kind of activities do you expect to partake in while at this sleepover?" Her mother's voice was becoming sharper by the minute. "Do you have any idea what the other girls your age do in their spare time?"

"I...uh—"

"Do *not* stutter, young lady. It's almost as unflattering as that stupefied look on your face." With a huff of annoyance, Vanessa breezed past her daughter into the room. "I'll tell you what goes on at these sleepovers. They stuff their faces with junk food high in sugar content and stay up well past their bedtime while gossiping about boys—things unfitting for a young woman."

Panic swelled inside Sienna's throat. She was unaware of what really went on at such parties, but decided it sounded like more fun than she'd imagined. She had to convince her mother that she'd behave so she wouldn't miss out. "I'll watch what I eat, and I'll go to bed at the usual time. I promise."

Vanessa released a sharp laugh. "You will *not* be attending this party."

"Please, mother. The next pageant isn't for a few months. If I happen to slip up—"

"You won't, because you're not going." Her mother's lips pulled into a sneer. "My decision is final."

Sienna's excitement deflated with the precision of a needle on a balloon. "Why can't you trust me this one time?"

"Trust you?" Vanessa folded her arms tightly, glaring down the slim bridge of her nose. "Your father and I have invested *thousands* of dollars into transforming you into the beauty queen you've become. If you start attending these reckless parties, you may as well be throwing everything away. Those girls don't know what it takes to be a winner, and they'll only lead you down a menacing path." Eyes darkening, her body coiled. She'd never struck her daughter before, but Sienna wasn't so sure she'd hold back this time. It was like witnessing a cobra ready to strike. "Don't you appreciate all we've done for you?"

"I know you've spent a lot of money and made sacrifices, but have you ever stopped to think maybe I'm tired of competing?" Irritation rumbled through Sienna's insides, making her fists ball and her teeth chatter. She was afraid of what her mother might do in that moment. She was also fed up with the restrictions set on her for as far back as she could remember. "I'll be a teenager before long, and I don't have *any* friends. I want to attend sleepovers like the other kids! I want to watch scary movies and talk about boys!" Frustrated tears burned behind her eyes. She wanted to scream from the rooftop, or maybe even break one of her precious trophies. But the consequences would've been far too bleak. "I'm tired of watching what I eat and minding my manners! The kids at school think I'm a freak! If you don't let me go to Rowan's, it's just going to become worse!"

"How dare you speak to me that way!" Vanessa spat, rushing forward. "Who have you been hanging around? Who taught you this way of disobedience?" The palm of her hand struck Sienna's cheekbone. Both mother and daughter gasped.

"I'll run away," Sienna whispered, covering her stinging face. "I'll go to Aunt T's."

Her "aunt" Taylor wasn't actually a blood relative. The eclectic artist and her husband had lived in the same apartment building as Sienna's parents when they'd first moved to Brooklyn, and Taylor had befriended Sienna's mother on first sight. Taylor and Jason, a Brooklyn police officer, had inherited a cottage in the quaint coastal town of Blue Bay around the time Sienna was born—when the two women had become as close as sisters. The cottage's renovation took place over the next several years, halting when Jason was killed in the line of duty while attempting to deescalate a call for domestic dispute. Heartbroken, Taylor finished the renovation on her own, and moved to Blue Bay alone. Although Vanessa and Taylor had grown apart, every summer Vanessa sent Sienna to visit Taylor for several weeks.

"What's going on in here?" a deep voice rumbled, clipped with irritation.

Sienna's heart soared with the sight of her father in her bedroom's doorway. Jonathan Rivers was a man with an unmistakably large presence both in size and personality. He was an entire head taller than his wife and notably good looking, possessing the same shade of thick strawberry blond hair as Sienna's, same dusting of freckles across his broad face and long limbs, same almost colorless gray eyes. Sienna didn't miss the way other kids' mothers would look at him with interest, or the way he'd respond with a wink and a charming smile. Although there was something different about the terse expression that crossed his face as he entered her room, she decided he was most handsome when dressed in a suit for work like the black one he wore that day.

With a genuine smile that pulled at her belly,

Sienna crossed the room to snuggle inside his strong arms, mindful not to mess up her hair. Her father's earthy, sandalwood scent warmed her body and made her feel safe. Not only had she desperately missed him in the four days he'd been gone, she knew he'd take her side. He wasn't as passionate about the competitions as her mother, and was often telling his wife to let up on some of the rules. "I'm so glad you're back, Daddy!"

Across the room, Vanessa's slender fingers spread over her hips. She shot her husband an irritated look that reminded Sienna of a hornet buzzing around its nest. "I thought you weren't coming home until tomorrow night."

As Jonathan patted Sienna's back, she felt every muscle in his body tense. "Something...*unexpected* came up." His voice was gruffer than usual. Darker. "I have to grab a few things before heading out again."

Vanessa released a cold, forced laugh. "Well, your timing is impeccable as always. Your daughter is displaying a taste of rebellion."

Head tilted back, Sienna met her father's confused expression. "I just want to go to a sleepover."

"That doesn't sound so rebellious," he decided, tucking his daughter beneath one arm.

"You're never here, Jonathan. You don't know what it's like with her."

"How bad can it possibly be?" His voice hardened with irritation, vibrating through Sienna's bones. "You've trained her to behave like a goddamn robot, Vanessa. I don't see the harm in letting her attend a sleepover with her friends."

"That's because—" Eyes narrowed, Vanessa gestured to her husband's arm on the opposite side of Sienna. "Jonathan, you're *bleeding!*"

Sienna's eyes tracked blood trickling from her father's arm down to a small puddle at their feet. "Daddy, you're hurt!"

"Everyone can calm the hell down," he snarled, cradling his bleeding arm against his chest. "I nicked myself in the parking lot when leaving the office."

"That's an excessive amount of blood for a mere nick." With a single shake of her head, Vanessa's mouth pressed into a hard line. "What *really* happened? I've grown tired of your lies, Jonathan!"

"I caught my arm on a goddamn piece of metal, okay?" he barked, passing his wife a menacing scowl. The intensity of his words sent a deep, cold shiver through Sienna. She'd heard her parents argue plenty of times before, but she'd never heard the degree of anger reflected in her father's current tone.

When he bent to kiss the top of Sienna's head, she was unable to muster even the smallest of smiles. "Step back, pumpkin. I'll be back in a jiffy to clean it up." Then he threw his wife a callous look. "We'll talk more about this sleepover after I've cleaned up."

Sienna knew it was best to remain quiet as her father hurried from her room with her mother right on his heels. Something about this argument felt dangerously different.

2

With her overnight bag packed, Sienna crept over the wooden floor in the narrow hallway outside her room, careful not to make it creak. She perched on the top step of the stairway leading down to the first level of their condominium, and strained to listen. From that position, she could hear the dishwasher running in the kitchen down below as well as the sharp words her parents uttered from their master suite on the floor above.

The picture window overlooking the stairway above her boasted a cloudless blue sky among the London plane trees that lined their sidewalk. The only home Sienna had known was nestled inside an upscale Brooklyn community among a family park, immaculate cobblestone streets, and a cozy bodega run by a family of Greek immigrants. The succession of quiet streets made the neighborhood a popular place for biking and skateboarding. Most of its residents earned a 7 to 8 figure income, and owned multiple vacation homes around the world. It was a charming locale, known for being safe for children, and frequented by responsible dog owners.

Rowan Holloway lived in a similar neighborhood a handful of blocks down from their private school. From the backseat of the private car that drove Sienna home every day, she'd witnessed the darkhaired beauty entering the largest building on the block on numerous occasions. Sometimes Rowan was alone, sometimes she was surrounded by several of their classmates. Sienna hoped and prayed those girls would soon become her friends as well. Rowan's party could be the gateway to more invitations to sleepovers.

Caught up in the fantasy of things to come, she was blissfully unaware the events about to unfold would forever change her, molding her into the cautious and untrusting adult she would become.

All at once, her mother's breathy shriek echoed among the stark white walls and rich hardwood floors. It was a harsh, jarring sound that sent pin pricks shooting down Sienna's spine. As her parents remained quiet, she sat glued to the step, worried her bladder would let loose. What reason would her mother have to make such a wretched sound? The wild, staggered beats of her heart shook her entire body as she rose on wobbling legs.

"Mommy?" she called out, surprised that she'd uttered the name she hadn't called her mother in years. With a flinch, she chided herself for the slip-up, knowing her mother would not be pleased to hear her speaking in a childish manner.

"Sienna!" her mother shouted in reply. "Don't come up here! Just...go to your room! Lock the door until I tell you it's safe!"

"There's nothing to be afraid of, Si!" her father's gravelly voice volleyed, instantly soothing her frazzled nerves. "Everything's okay!"

Sienna let out the breath she'd been holding. She'd never seen her parents physically fight, but she'd also never heard her mother sound so afraid. Something wasn't right. Her mother's voice lowered as she said something, the words distorted through the distance. Sienna tiptoed up the next set of stairs to linger outside her parents' closed bedroom door.

"—dare you bring my daughter into this!"

"You need to see a doctor, Jonathan. There's no sign of an exit wound. The bullet could be lodged inside a vital organ."

Sienna winced. Her father had been shot?

"I can't just waltz into a hospital!" he snarled in reply.

"The way you're bleeding—"

"The blood on my chest isn't mine."

"What do you mean? Whose is it? Who shot you?" Her mother's voice warbled with fear. "Jonathan, what have you done?"

"Stop asking questions, you stupid bitch, and get me another towel before I ruin the goddamn floor!"

With the sounds of rushed movement and cupboard doors slamming inside the master bathroom, Sienna's bladder gave a little tug. She'd never heard her father call her mother anything other than "sweetie" or "hun." And there was so much anger in his voice that her blood had turned impossibly cold.

"I made a mistake is all," he muttered. "A stupid, careless mistake."

"I don't understand!" Vanessa replied. "What kind of mistake ends with you getting shot?"

"After you fix me up, I need to go away for a little while. They could be looking for someone who matches my description. If they come by here, tell them I'm visiting my parents in California."

"Tell me what's going on, Jonathan!"

"I wasn't expecting her husband to be home this

early. Asshole shot me from behind, caught me off guard. I took care of him after I finished her, but someone inside a running car was waiting in their driveway. I'm pretty sure he got a good look at me."

There was a sharp hissing noise. "I always suspected there was something going on with you. I thought maybe you were having affairs—but if you're talking about *murder*—"

"Don't look at me like I'm a goddamned monster! I'm still the same man who keeps food on your table and treats you like a fucking queen! I'm still Sienna's father!"

"Don't you dare come any closer! I'm calling the police!"

An anguished cry ripped from the master bedroom, then something heavy fell with a thud. The pressure of Sienna's bladder finally gave out. She sprinted down the stairway to her bedroom, quickly engaging the lock on her door. Through a blur of rapid tears, she spotted the portable phone on her bed. She'd intended to call her aunt after she'd finished packing to tell her all about the party.

Sienna didn't want to get her father into any kind of trouble, but something was horribly wrong. He was wounded, *shot*, and her mother sounded terribly afraid. As she dialed 9-1-1, she desperately tried to forget the fact that her mother had uttered the word "murder."

THE NIGHT of Jonathan Rivers's arrest, the entire precinct was gathered at the station for a mandatory training two miles down the road. Within minutes of receiving Sienna's distressed call, over a dozen officers arrived outside the family's building. The front door was smashed to bits with a Halligan bar, sounding like an explosion against Sienna's ears. Loud footsteps struck the stairway outside her bedroom. Among the ruckus, someone pounded on her door. "Brooklyn Police! Open the door!"

From the floor above her, the unrelenting shouting began. *"Down on the floor!" "Hands up where we can see them!" "Don't move!"*

From behind her locked door, Sienna was terrified by the commotion. With every harrowing beat of her heart, she became more and more afraid of what might be happening. What would the police do to her parents? She'd relayed every detail of their argument to the woman on the phone. Would they arrest her father merely because he'd been shot? What had he done to her mother? Was she hurt?

As the shouting from upstairs lessened, a female voice called her name from the other side of her door. "Are you in there? Is anyone with you?"

"It's only me," Sienna whimpered, swiping the back of her forearm over her wet face.

"Are you hurt?"

Shame rippled through her. What would her mother say once she discovered she'd wet herself? "I'm—I'm okay."

"My name is Detective Novak. I work for the Brooklyn Police Department. Everything's okay now, Sienna. Your mom and dad are both safe. Could you please unlock the door for me so we can talk face-to-face?"

Before opening the door, Sienna glanced in the full-length mirror hung beside her closet. Her mother would be angered by her less than presentable appearance. In addition to the dark patch of urine on her shorts, her hair was mussed and her mascara had run down her cheeks. "Can you please give me a minute?"

"I'd rather you open the door now. I want to see with my own eyes that you're unharmed."

Swallowing the large lump in her throat, Sienna gingerly dabbed at her eyes with the end of her ruffled shirt. She couldn't let anyone see her cry.

Unsure of what would happen next, she grabbed her overnight bag from her bed. If they were going to take her away, she'd at least have a clean change of clothes.

Shoulders squared, she disengaged the lock on her door and positioned her bag over her crotch before flashing a bright smile. Although she felt broken inside, she was still able to put on a good show. It was an ability that had been instilled in her since birth.

An athletically built blonde woman with warm brown eyes too big for her petite head and a sleek bobbed haircut greeted Sienna with a terse smile. In a black blazer with black pants and a crisp white button-down, she emitted both professionalism and style. Although the woman stood alone in the hallway, the gruff voices of several different men floated up from the floor below. "Hi, Sienna. Are you sure you're alright?"

Sienna eyed the gun and badge on the woman's hip before she extended her hand. "Hello, Detective Novak. It's nice to meet you." Her pageant-winning smile spread wider. "I'd like to see my parents now."

Firmly shaking her hand, the detective's eyes widened slightly. "It's nice to meet you too." She bent down, leveling her face with Sienna's. "They're taking your dad to the police station for questioning, and your mom is being looked over by paramedics. If it's alright with you, I'd like you to come back to the station with me to answer a few questions about what happened here tonight."

"Is my mother alright?"

"She appears to be, although there's a good sized bump on her forehead. Do you know anything about that?"

"My parents were having a disagreement. She cried out, then something heavy fell onto their floor." Sienna's stomach dropped. "Was that her?"

"I'm not sure, sweetheart." With another friendly smile, the detective held out her hand. "Let's take a ride to the station."

Sienna folded her arms tightly over her stomach. "I'd prefer to wait here for my mother."

"As soon as she's cleared by the paramedics, she'll be coming to the station too." The detective's eyes remained kind as her lips tightened. "It could be a long night for both of your parents. We'll arrange to have someone come get you after I'm done asking questions—another family member, or family friend."

"My aunt's the only one you can call. She lives in Blue Bay."

Detective Novak smoothed a hand over Sienna's shoulder. "We'll figure out how to get her here as quickly as we can. I promise you that. Until then, there's a comfortable spot where you can wait at the station after you and I have had a little chat." Her hand slipped down Sienna's arm to wrap around her hand. "Right now I need you to be brave, Sienna, and keep your eyes on me. Can you do that?"

Nodding, Sienna pressed her quivering lips together and left the safety of her bedroom. They moved quickly down the steps, past the officers gathered in the kitchen, out the front door, and down the stoop. Among a handful of police cars and ambulances flickering bright emergency lights into the darkening sky, Sienna frantically searched for her mother. The detective tugged on Sienna's hand, urging her to hurry, but she was unable to spare Sienna the trauma of seeing her father being lifted into the back of an ambulance, both wrists cuffed to the metal gurney. Dried bloody fingerprints covered his bare chest, and his injured arm had been wrapped in gauze. He snarled and spit like a wild cat toward the uniformed officers at his side.

Sienna fought against the detective's hold, wanting to run to him. "Daddy!"

The sharp look her father cast her was cold and

dark. She didn't see any sign of the beloved parent she knew in the gray eyes that matched hers. It sent debilitating chills down her spine, making her teeth chatter. "*You* did this?" he roared. "You called the cops on *your own father*? You little bitch! After all I've done for you, this is how you repay me?"

Tears of horror burned Sienna's eyes. That couldn't be her father. It couldn't be the same man who called her "pumpkin," and told her that he loved her more than anyone in the world whenever he was around to tuck her in at night. What was wrong with him?

Detective Novak jerked her away with a firm grasp. "Don't listen to him, Sienna. He's not in his right mind."

Sienna blindly climbed into the backseat of a black SUV with the detective. She was convinced none of it was real. It had to be a nightmare. But she felt the press of cold urine against the back of her legs, smelled the rich leather of the car's interior, and the blast of cold air from vents dried the abundance of moisture building in her eyes.

Behind the steering wheel, a grayed-hair man in a dark suit turned to them. His steely eyes swept over Sienna before landing on Detective Novak. "Everything good?"

"All set," she answered with a curt nod.

The SUV pulled away from the curb, casting red and blue lights against the shocked faces of the neighbors gathered outside. Sienna's stomach cramped so hard that she was certain she'd throw up all over the leather seats. The detective held her hand on the short ride to the station, continuously assuring her that everything was going to be okay. Sienna was certain it was a lie.

3

The 2-story police station was alive with the shrill ring of telephones, the din of frenzied voices, and a flurry of movement. Dozens of uniformed officers and others dressed similar to Detective Novak hustled throughout the building, some casting Sienna curious glances. The elevated sounds added more pressure to Sienna's already pounding headache. She simply wanted to take a couple of aspirin, and lay down in the comfort of her own bed until the spinning stopped.

Detective Novak steered her past intake and toward a complex cluster of desks where her mother stood alongside a set of burly men, still wearing the same party dress as earlier. The festive bubble gum pink linen was a sharp contrast to the grim uniforms and suits all around them. Sienna's breath caught when her mother turned her head. The gruesomely deep shades of violet and yellow surrounding her mother's right eye were alarming. The lack of affection in Vanessa's dismissive frown, however, was expected.

She clamped a stern hand down on Sienna's shoulder, applying firm pressure. "Don't lose your composure, and don't tell them any more lies," she hissed. "This is all a big misunderstanding. We'll be back home with your father by morning." Her frown deepened into a scowl as her sharp eyes assessed her daughter's condition. "For god's sake, Sienna. Fix your face! Don't let them see you cry!"

Sienna wasn't surprised when her mother didn't offer the comfort of her arms. She was merely grateful her soiled pants seemed to go unnoticed. "Yes, ma'am," she answered, eyes trailing to the tiled floor.

At her side, a dark-haired man with a thick mustache, gray suit and red tie, nudged the back of Vanessa's arm. "This way, Mrs. Rivers."

Irritation flickered over Detective Novak's expression as they walked away. Before she turned back to Sienna, her eyes warmed with compassion and more pity than Sienna could stand. "Let's get you somewhere private where you can freshen up."

Inside a serene room filled with miniature furniture and toys intended for small children, Sienna's chest rose and fell with a deep inhale and exhale. Behind the closed door, the noises from the other room had ceased.

"The bathroom's back there," Detective Novak said, pointing toward an open door. "Take your time, sweetie. I'm going to grab you a soda and something to snack on. Is a cola okay?"

Dread tightened Sienna's stomach muscles. If her mother were to catch her snacking on anything unsavory, her impending punishment would only worsen. "If it's not too much trouble, I'd prefer a mineral water and vegetables."

"I'll see what I can do." The detective patted Sienna's back. "You're safe here, Sienna. You can relax. I'll be back shortly."

Inside the small half bathroom with jungle animals painted on the walls, Sienna deposited her shorts and underwear into the wastebasket. She didn't want anything to remind her of the worst night of her life. After she'd changed into clean clothes and washed her face, she brushed her long blond hair and stared numbly at her freckled reflection in the mirror. She was horrified her mother had witnessed her in a less than favorable condition—

their neighbors, too. Considering the size of the crowd who'd observed her father's arrest, she imagined it wouldn't be long until Rowan caught wind of what had happened. Any chance of being accepted by Rowan and her friends had been destroyed. Worse yet, she doubted she'd have the courage to face any of her classmates ever again.

Detective Novak returned nearly half an hour later with a plastic container of carrots and a generic bottle of water. A stout brunette woman in a less fashionable tan suit entered the room right behind her, introducing herself as "Captain Stone." While Sienna sipped the water, the two women took turns firing questions her way.

What kinds of things did she do with her father? What did he talk about when they were alone? Did he ever mention his work trips? Did he ever say things that made her uncomfortable? Had her father ever harmed her in any way? Had he hurt her mother before?

The interrogation felt never-ending as Sienna's eyes grew heavy and her bones grew weary. Any questions she asked about her father and what would happen next were smoothly deflected with promises to explain everything at a later time. She just wanted to go home, and hide beneath her blankets until the rest of the world disappeared.

Once the two women finally left her alone for a few minutes, exhaustion took over. She dozed off in a little rocking chair, waking with a start to the sound of her name.

"Sienna. Oh, my sweet, sweet Sienna." Her aunt rushed into the room, beloved West Highland Terrier tucked under her arm, and Sienna's resolve broke with the force of a cracked dam. All her fears came to the surface as Taylor wordlessly set Scotch onto her lap and wrapped Sienna inside her arms. Clinging desperately to the dog, Sienna finally allowed herself to let out a deep, soul-wrenching cry that would've disgusted her mother.

"I'm here, sweetheart," her aunt whispered, rocking her. "I'm right here."

Taylor Brooks, a 31-year-old widow, possessed cat-like hazel eyes beneath fierce eyebrows, and frizzy brown hair. Despite a haphazard diet and lifestyle, genetics made her impossibly slender. She claimed it was because she constantly vibrated with positive energy. Her wardrobe staple involved bright, flowing materials, and she always wore an excessive amount of jewelry that tinkled and chimed with her every move. The scent of mint and lanolin usually clung to her skin as she was always making homemade soap and other handmade items to sell at the local market. That night, as Sienna breathed in her aunt's familiar scent, she felt the first wave of comfort since being torn from home.

"Everything's going to be okay, Si," Taylor promised, dropping kisses against her niece's head. "I'm taking you home with me. Your mom will join us as soon as the police are finished asking her questions."

While Taylor carried on a short conversation in hushed tones with Detective Novak, Sienna stroked Scotch's thick white fur, laughing a little when he eagerly licked the salty tears off her face. She still didn't believe anything was going to be okay as everyone kept telling her, but at least her aunt was rescuing her from the nightmare by taking her to Blue Bay.

Visits to Taylor's cottage equaled countless hours spent barefoot in the sand and frolicking in the Atlantic Ocean, hunting for pretty seashells they'd later use for arts and crafts, chasing Scotch around the neighborhood, games of tag near the abandoned lighthouse, and roasting marshmallows over a campfire while her aunt's neighbor plucked out silly songs on his banjo. Sienna cherished the trips to Blue Bay, especially after she'd become close friends with the neighbor's daughter in recent years. But as she buckled herself into the passenger's seat of Taylor's ancient Volvo with Scotch still in her lap, she worried the elation of visiting Blue Bay would never be the same as the twinkling lights of the city grew smaller in the darkness.

"Kinsley will be so excited to see you again," Taylor said, reaching over to stroke the top of Sienna's head with a gentle hand. Her lips bent with a weak smile that fell flat against her hazel eyes. "We can plan a movie night on the beach tomorrow, with mattresses and everything...just like last summer. Of course Drake will have the final say in what we watch, as always—"

"Who shot my father?" Sienna interrupted. "Why'd they put him in handcuffs? Why didn't the police let my mother come along with us? What did *she* do?"

Taylor gripped the steering wheel with both hands, teeth clamped together. "How much did they tell you, baby girl?"

"Nothing. They told me absolutely nothing. And I'm not a baby."

"Of course you aren't."

"Then why won't anyone tell me what happened?"

"I will, I promise. It's just..." With a great sigh,

she met Sienna's gaze. "I wasn't able to talk with your mother for very long, so the facts aren't exactly clear. All I know is your father was injured while he was…hurting someone."

Tears stung behind Sienna's eyes. "He wouldn't hurt anyone!" Not her big, brave defender with the funny laugh and handsome smile. She balled her hands into fists around the sleeping dog. The same words her mother had told her just hours before spewed from her lips. "It's all a big misunderstanding!"

Taylor's eyes closed for a stuttered heartbeat before returning to the dark road ahead. "I know this is all extremely confusing, Sienna. I don't quite understand it myself. But worrying about things we don't know the answer to won't change the outcome, so it's best if we focus on the positives. Your mom is safe, and they said your dad's going to be okay. That's all that matters for now." She reached into the back seat and produced one of the blankets she'd crocheted. "Why don't you lay back with Scotch and shut your eyes for a little while? We'll be in Blue Bay before you know it."

Sienna had to admit sleep sounded like a good idea, even if she was more confused than before.

How could her dad be okay when he'd been shot? And what reason would he have to hurt someone? She was out before they'd left the city limits.

SIENNA WOKE to the sound of Scotch's persistent barking. A moment passed before her groggy, swollen eyes were able to focus inside the sunlit room. Tucked beneath the pretty sky blue comforter in the bed she'd slept in ever since she was little and surrounded by her aunt's oil paintings of whimsical sea creatures, an instant sense of ease washed over her. Stretching her arms up to the whitewashed ceiling, she inhaled the ocean air and felt her lips spread into a satisfied little smile. She was in her happiest of places where only good things ever happened. The entirety of the two bedroom cottage was decorated with bright and airy shades of blue in a seaside decor that Sienna hadn't seen anywhere else. Certainly not anywhere in Brooklyn. Each decorative item and piece of furniture inside the cottage was either vintage and refinished, or had been created by her aunt.

Then, the trauma of the previous night broke

through with a ferocity, and her stomach churned with sickening worry. With the memory of her father calling her names, her sore eyes stung all over again. She refused to believe he would hurt anyone. But why had her mother mentioned "murder" during their argument? Why had he refused to go to the hospital? And why would anyone shoot him? She wanted to see her parents, wanted everything to be okay like everyone kept promising.

Fighting to keep her composure, she slipped down from the high poster bed to peer out the window. The welcoming sight of the old stone lighthouse across the bay started to loosen the knot in her stomach. Blue Bay was filled with only the best of memories, all of which cloaked her with the same comfort as her aunt's handmade blankets. Taylor's cozy backyard was a maze of exuberant blue and white flower bushes around a small stone patio where colorful old rocking chairs and worn cushions beckoned to be enjoyed. Beyond the patio was her aunt's art studio, its cedar shakes and gable roof mirroring the architecture of the cottage. Where her lawn of Kentucky Bluegrass ended, creamy tan sand offered a gentle slope down to the public beach.

Scotch was always barking or chasing something —her aunt said the hunting nature of his breed was to blame. But that morning, he was barking at her friends, Kinsley and Drake, as they threw sticks on the beach towards the roaring ocean waves for him to fetch.

Her heart warmed with the sight of the siblings. They were a gangly pair, much like their father. Kinsley had inherited Andy's red hair in the form of springy curls, while Drake's unruly shag was a shade closer to their mom's sandy brown. Like both of their parents, the siblings were always busting at the seams with laughter and genuine smiles. Although Drake—now a young teenager on the brink of manhood—had become notably taller and leaner since her last visit, she knew she could always count on them both to make her smile. She couldn't wait to be reunited with the only two people she considered to be her friends.

Moments after she'd showered and made herself presentable, she heard the roar of an engine outside. Her chest tightened with the strength of a rubber band as she ran to the front of the house to peer out the bay window. Her aunt was already outside, preparing to greet a private town car in the driveway. Although Sienna was ready to learn more details of the events that had unfolded the night before, she wasn't convinced she was ready to face the wrath of her mother. She didn't know that she would ever be.

The back door of the town car opened. Vanessa crawled out wearing the same pink cocktail dress from the night before with oversized sunglasses. She lumbered away from the car with the grace of a 90-year-old woman. Taylor rushed forward in time to catch her when she collapsed.

What had happened to her mother since she'd left the police station? With a dizzying rush of concern, Sienna dashed out the front door. Before she was able to join her mother and aunt in the driveway, however, she was ambushed by the Lewis siblings.

"Si!" Kinsley exclaimed, throwing her scrawny arms around her neck. She smelled of sunshine, sand, and suntan lotion. "I can't believe you're really here! Ohmygod, I've missed you like a crazy person! We have so much to catch up on!"

Aware that her mother might be watching, Sienna buried her own burst of excitement and politely patted her friend's back. "Hello, Kins." She eyed Drake over Kinsley's springy red curls. "Hello, Drake."

With his hands stuffed in his shorts pockets, Drake jutted his narrow chin in her mother's direction. "What's wrong with your mom?" He let out a harsh laugh. "She looks super wasted."

Sienna disengaged herself from Kinsley to flash them a pageant smile. Her mother drank wine on occasion, but Sienna didn't think she'd ever seen her drunk. Could Drake be right? She quietly prayed her friends didn't know anything about the night before, or the reason she was in Blue Bay. "She had a bad night," she told them.

Relief nearly brought her to tears when Kinsley and Drake's dad shuffled in behind them. Andy Lewis was a middle-aged carpenter, decently muscular from the labor required of his job, and well over six feet tall. He was known for his booming laugh and endless sense of humor. His copper red hair had receded since the prior summer, and his wire-rimmed glasses were also new. He greeted Sienna with a firm, but brief, hug. "Good to see you, kid." Drawing back, he then hooked both of his thumbs over his shoulders. "Lewis kids, let's finish setting up for tonight's movie and give Sienna and her mom some space. Drake, you can help me find the DVD."

Drake's coffee-colored eyes popped wide. "The first *Alien*?"

With a little shake of his head, Andy pushed his

glasses up his hooked nose. "No, the second one on your list, bud. *The Goonies*. We decided that 'R' movies are a little extreme for this crowd, remember?" He gently squeezed Sienna's shoulder. "We'll be around back if you need anything, kiddo. You're welcome to join us at any time."

"Thank you, Andy," she told him.

Kinsley's eyes made a dramatic roll in Sienna's direction. "Guess we'll catch up *later*." She reluctantly trailed behind her father before glancing over her shoulder. "By the way, you look even more fabulous than last summer!"

An earlier glance into her aunt's bathroom mirror had proven otherwise, so Sienna merely released one of her perfectly crafted smiles in response.

As her mother neared, she inhaled deeply in an attempt to muster a bout of courage. Eyes glossy, Vanessa reached out to cup Sienna's chin. The stench of something sour rolled off her breath. "Guess you did us both a favor, Sien'…callin' the p'lice and whatev'. You an' me prolly woulda been his next victims if ya hadn't."

Sienna froze, her eyes blinking in rapid successions. "His next victims?" she repeated.

"Your mom's exhausted," Taylor told her with a dismissive wave of her hand. "Go help the neighbors set things up, Si. I'll join you after I help your momma crawl into bed."

A sense of doom seized Sienna as she watched her aunt struggle to help her mother inside. Little did she know, her world was only beginning to fall apart.

4

The normally sleepy seaside community of Blue Bay came alive in the summertime. It was a popular destination for New Yorkers to escape with a quick hour and twenty minute train ride. The town was one of the less affluent areas on the East Coast, but was renowned for outdoor concerts, food festivals, and its idyllic lighthouse.

While Sienna's friends enjoyed all the town had to offer during those warm months, night terrors began to tear her from sleep on a regular basis. She'd wake Taylor with cries of, "he's coming for me!" and other eerie declarations of a "monster" that rattled Taylor's nerves. After Taylor disclosed Sienna's situation to a good friend who was also a psychiatrist, Sienna began therapy with Dr. Walters three times every week.

Although Sienna missed her parents terribly and didn't quite grasp the severity of her father's situation, she had accepted the fact that nothing in her life would ever be the same. Vanessa only visited her daughter twice during those hundred plus days. On both occasions, she'd slurred her words and had trouble standing much like the time she'd come to Blue Bay the morning after her husband's arrest.

One late evening in mid-August, Sienna was torn from yet another nightmare in which her father had killed her mother, and was chasing her around their condo with a knife. She splashed water on her face in the bathroom and padded barefoot into the kitchen for a drink of water. Much like the rest of the seaside cottage's decor, the cabinets were painted a soft shade of turquoise, and coordinating glass pendants hung over the large dresser her aunt had refurbished and transformed into an island. That night, the calming accents of the room were a sharp contrast to her distressed aunt pacing the tiled floor. Wearing the oversized Def Leppard t-shirt she often wore as pajamas, she held a portable telephone to her ear, scowling and swearing under her breath.

Despite the manners that had been drilled into her by her mother, Sienna hid around the corner to eavesdrop on her aunt's conversation.

"—did the doctor have to say? How long is she being committed?" Taylor's paint-splattered fingers combed through her frizzy curls, creating a wild halo around her head. "Mmm hm...yeah...okay. I'll need some time to meet with a lawyer and have them draw up the paperwork. I can promise you that Sienna will be well taken care of until then. Thank you for calling, Detective Novak. Please keep in touch."

Taylor ended the call with a flick of her finger and tossed the phone onto the counter, swearing some more.

Sienna's heart slipped into her throat. "Aunt T?"

"Shit, Si!" Redness spread over Taylor's round face as she pressed a hand over her heart. "What the hell are you doing out of bed in the middle of the night?"

"Were you and Detective Novak talking about my mother? They're *committing* her? Why?"

Her aunt huffed with a stiff laugh. "Not much gets past you, does it?" She opened the retro-style refrigerator and plucked a small pitcher of water off the wire shelf. Then she grabbed a set of glasses and slid onto one of the metal stools at the island, patting the empty stool at her side. "Come have a seat, Sienna. We need to talk."

Sienna's feet suddenly felt encased in cement. What would happen to her while her mother was gone? As she reluctantly shuffled towards the stool, Taylor gazed out the window with a faint smile pressed to her lips. Off in the distance, the lighthouse's powerful beam swept over the dark water at a hypnotic pace. "Whenever things get too hard, I see that light and I think of my Jason. He believed the purpose in our lives is what we create for ourselves." Her eyes shone with tears beneath the pendant light as she poured water into a glass. "He truly adored that lighthouse. Did I ever tell you he's the one who convinced the historical society to get it up and running again after it'd been dark for thirty years?"

Nodding, Sienna sipped from the glass of water as she thought of the tall building with little windows. She'd only met Taylor's husband a handful of times when she was young. She remembered him as being a handsome man with a thick neck and long arms, kind eyes, and someone who'd constantly made her laugh. "He gave me a tour of it when I was little. It wasn't what I'd expected...it was old, and scary...full of spiderwebs. But Jason said one day he'd make it into a castle fit for a princess like me."

Taylor smiled fondly. "He thought you were the

prettiest little girl he'd ever met. He never understood why your parents made you compete in beauty pageants your entire life." Her shoulders rose with a deep inhale. "Your mom and I were once really close, and I still can't say I ever understood it, either. Of course she's drastically changed since we met all those years ago." Taylor turned to Sienna, running a hand over her silky hair. "You're so prim and proper, Si. I haven't seen you cry again since the night of your dad's arrest. I'd give anything to see you let it out, or be a carefree kid like Kins and Drake." Her expression became heavy, filled with caution. "I promised I'd explain everything that's going on with your dad once his trial was over." She paused to wet her lips. "It's time we have that talk."

Sienna's fingers tightened around the thin glass as a deep sense of doom spread through her. She'd heard reporters on TV call her father a "serial killer", but she didn't quite comprehend the scope of his sins. Most of the reports accusing her father of murder had both angered and confused her, so she went out of her way to avoid television. The glass shattered inside her grip, painlessly slicing through one of her fingers.

"Oh, sweetheart!" Taylor cried, cradling the bleeding hand. "Let's get you over to the sink!"

Sienna crossed the room with her aunt, numbly watching the blood drip onto the white porcelain as Taylor ran tepid water over the wound before inspecting it closely. "There doesn't seem to be any glass left inside, and it didn't go deep enough for stitches. You should be okay."

"I heard them say on the news my father hurt a lot of people."

Taylor's expression paled. "Yes. He hurt many, *many* women."

Sienna shook her head, over and over. "They have to be wrong. You and Jason were once good friends with him, Aunt T. How can you believe he's capable of what they're saying?"

"They aren't wrong, Sienna. A judge and jury listened to all the facts, including proof that he was...*with* the women when they died, and they all agreed he was guilty. And your dad...he more or less admitted he was guilty when your mother went to visit him after the trial."

The start of a headache seared behind Sienna's eyes. "Why? Why would he do such a thing?"

"No one really understands why, sweetheart. There's a dark, ugly sickness inside him that people like you, and me, and your mom will never understand." Taylor wrapped the injured finger inside a clean towel, and covered it with both of her hands. "They're sending him to prison. He'll probably stay there for the rest of your life...or at least his."

The night of her father's arrest had been permanently etched into Sienna's brain. She wanted to erase those dreadful memories and be reunited with the loving man who had once been the defender of her universe. Dr. Walters had tried to explain during numerous sessions that the father Sienna loved may never return. She hadn't fully grasped that concept either. "Will I ever be allowed to see him again?"

"There's a small chance you'll see him again one day. Probably not until you're older. Prison visits, they're...hard."

Sienna squeezed her eyes shut, attempting to stop the building tears from falling. How could she have not known her father was a murderer? Had he wanted to hurt her and her mother, too?

"Your mom was committed because she's...not doing so well. She doesn't want to believe your dad could hurt those women either. She went to every last one of your father's hearings. After the judge showed some pictures at the trial, she blacked out and had to be escorted from the courtroom. She hasn't been herself ever since then. A few nights ago, she decided she wanted to...uhh...get away from everything, I guess you could say."

Holding her aunt's gaze, Sienna hiccuped on a sudden sob. "You mean she tried to *kill* herself?"

"Yes, sweetheart. I'm afraid so." Taylor blinked heavily, releasing tears from her thick eyelashes. "They're putting her in a hospital where they can help her feel better, but it's going to take some time. Likely several months." Her fingers squeezed around Sienna's, offering false reassurance. "Until she's healthy again, you'll stay here with me...and Scotch, and Kinsley. We'll get you enrolled in Blue Bay before school starts in a couple of weeks. I'm leaving for Brooklyn in the morning for a few days. You'll stay with the Lewises while I take care of some legal matters, and pack everything in your old bedroom. When I return, we'll fix up your room here however you'd like, make it feel more like home."

Heaving a great sigh, Sienna took a minute to think it all over. She'd decided months ago that she never wanted to return to Brooklyn where everyone would know her family's dirty secrets. The entire *world* probably knew of her father's evil deeds by then. As far as she was concerned, Sienna Rivers disappeared along with her ideals of a perfect family. "I want to change my name," she blurted.

Taylor's eyebrows rose. "Did you have something in mind?"

Sienna's heart tugged as she thought of the kind girl who had invited her to her first sleepover. "Rowan. Rowan Brooks. If I use your married surname, people will think I'm really your niece."

"Rowan's a pretty name. And Jason would've been honored to have you as his unofficial niece. I can enroll you under that name for school, but it's going to take some time before we can make it legal, and...there's no promise someone still won't recognize you as Sienna Rivers."

Breaking her aunt's stare to glance at the broken glass on the table, Sienna's stomach tightened. "I understand."

"You'll need to get your mom's permission, and that might be tough. She'll also have to sign papers agreeing to make me your temporary custodian until she's feeling better."

"I don't ever want to go back to Brooklyn, Aunt T. I want to stay here, with you, for as long as you'll have me."

Taylor's eyes lit with a hearty smile. "As much as I'd love to have you, we'd have to get your mom to agree, and I know how much she loves you. I don't think she'd be too willing to let you stay."

"You haven't seen how she acts around me in a very long time." Darkness wove around Sienna's heart. "What she *loves* is parading me around like I'm a living doll. She loves making the housekeeping staff dust the trophies in my room to remind them that they're in the presence of a national winner. She loves bragging to her friends about all my accomplishments. Beyond that, I'm not sure how she feels about me as an actual person...as her *daughter*." Tears sprung to Sienna's eyes. "My father is the only one who ever told me he loved me."

"Oh, Si." Taylor wrapped her inside a strong, warm hug. "I love you madly, sweet girl. I've loved you since you were a few hours old, the very first time I held you in my arms. I vow to show just how much you're loved from now until the day I die."

"I love you too," Sienna murmured, vowing she wouldn't let herself fall apart. It would be too easy to let her grief control her, making her weak and vulnerable to whatever else tried to destroy her. Instead, she wiped her eyes and straightened her spine, sitting taller and taking a deep breath. "There's something else I want to change."

When they parted, Taylor laughed and dabbed at her wet eyes with the back of her hand. "I'm already a gooey puddle of emotions, but let's hear it."

Sienna tugged on one of her own curly, strawberry blond locks. "I want to change my hair."

Hand held up between them, Taylor gave a resolute shake of her head. "I'm not sure about that one. All these other changes...they're going to be a lot for your mom to take in already. And your hair is so beautiful, sweetheart."

"I don't care. I'm done with pageants. In fact, when you go back to the condo, please leave all my trophies and dresses behind. I don't want to see another can of hairspray or another bottle of self-tanner for the rest of my life." Her heart gave a little squeeze as she thought of the kitten poster. "You can leave that poster over my bed behind, too." With her father still on her mind, she added, "I need a completely different look. It's bad enough I have his complexion. His *freckles*. I don't want his hair color too. I want something dark and short. Something that's not so hard to maintain."

"Okay," Taylor agreed, once again running a hand over Sienna's prized hair. "I'm sure Kinsley's mom will be up to the task. Steph is usually booked several months out, but I doubt it will take much convincing for her to fit you in while I'm gone."

THE VERY NEXT EVENING, while Taylor met with family lawyers in the heart of downtown Manhattan, Steph Lewis was able to clear her schedule at her popular salon on a nearly empty street of Blue Bay. The sharp, chemical smells and bright pink walls of the modern salon stirred an excitement deep in Sienna's belly. She was ready for a drastic change.

When she settled in the faux leather styling chair, pink polka dotted cape fastened around her neck, Steph produced a sharp pair of sheers and playfully snipped them through the air. She was a petite brunette with bright green eyes, and could always be counted on to wear pretty floral dresses to work. She was so tiny that Andy often joked he could fit her inside his pocket.

"Are you absolutely sure about this, Si? You have the most beautiful hair of anyone I've ever worked on, and there's no gluing it back in place if you change your mind."

Sienna shifted uncomfortably, glancing over each shoulder. Even though the other three booths were empty and the receptionist had left to give them complete privacy, Sienna worried the secret of her real identity would spread like wildfire if anyone were to learn she was Jonathan Rivers's daughter. Taylor had gone to great lengths to keep her sheltered from the community throughout the summer, and the Lewis family had been sworn to secrecy.

"Please don't call me Si or Sienna anymore, Steph. I'd prefer it if you could somehow convince Kins and Drake never to call me that again, either."

"Oh, sweetie, I'm so sorry." Steph lightly gripped Sienna's shoulder, and met her gaze in the mirror with a warm, sympathetic smile. "Your aunt told me about your name change this morning, and I already forgot. It was a really hectic day—"

"Don't worry." Sienna flashed a pageant-appropriate smile. "I understand."

"Alrighty, then. Let the transformation begin." Steph grabbed a comb, and went to work.

Several hours later, with a trendy hairstyle in a rich shade of nut brown, Rowan Brooks was officially brought into the world.

5

In another part of the country, the teenager curled into a ball on top of the dirty mattress, stomach painfully hard as laughter penetrated the thin walls. Every sound inside the once abandoned house was amplified, causing his heart to thud with a frantic beat. He reached beneath the stained pillow he'd rescued from a nearby apartment's dumpster, curling his fingers around the knife's wooden handle. He'd been beaten within an inch of his life by his peers in detention centers and inappropriately touched by enough foster parents in one way or another that he'd decided he was better off on the streets, fending for himself.

He'd been squatting in the house, deemed uninhabitable by the sheriff's department as stated by the paper tacked to the front door, for two weeks before he'd been joined by a set of junkies. The man and the woman mostly kept to themselves once they camped out on the other side of the rambler, but a few times they'd invited other junkies that weren't as peaceful. He'd since stolen the knife from a soup kitchen, and hid it behind a vent whenever he left the house.

"That gangly kid still around here?" a gruff voice asked.

Fear prickled against the boy's neck. He gripped the knife a little tighter.

"Yeah, but he's one of the good ones, so leave 'im alone," the female junkie's sing-song voice answered with a drug-induced slur. "Poor kid can't help it his momma's dead."

"Where's his old man?"

"Not sure he knows."

The gruff voice grunted. "A boy without a parent's gonna be messed up. Maybe I should teach 'im a thing or two about life."

"Leave 'im alone, Roy!" The woman's voice sounded dangerously close. "I mean it!"

Tears stung behind the boy's eyes as he watched the knob on the bedroom door jiggle. He'd braced it with an old wooden chair that was too fragile to survive much of anything.

He squeezed his eyes shut, crying silent tears as the female junkie and the gruff voice engaged in a shouting match in the hallway. He wasn't sure whether or not he had the courage to stab someone, but he sensed he was about to find out.

PART 2
BEGIN ANEW

"Life isn't about finding yourself. Life is about creating yourself." George Bernard Shaw

6

With a new name and a brand new look —including a fresh wardrobe void of formal dresses, slacks, or blouses— hand-selected by Kinsley, Rowan Brooks attempted to transition into her new life in Blue Bay with the grace of a beauty queen. She did her best to blend in with the other sixth graders, mindfully trying to shed the stern habits taught by her mother. She followed Kinsley's lead when possible, although she found it difficult to go against the manners instilled in her for life.

She finally experienced her first sleepover at Kinsley's in October, staying up past her bedtime to watch horror movies while gorging on junk food until her gut cramped in disagreement. Tragically, she was forced to return to her aunt's before dawn when the screams from her nightmares shook each of the Lewis family members to their core.

Although a grade older, Kinsley hovered over Rowan like a protective big sister when their classes merged during recess and lunch hour. Even Drake watched over her from the high school, picking a fight with anyone who started rumors over Rowan's sudden presence in Blue Bay. Somehow, miraculously, she remained a stranger to those outside of her tightly knit circle.

By Halloween, she'd slowly reverted back to the bulk of her old ways. She feared everyone noticed she'd put on four extra pounds, and began to run five miles every morning before school. She'd indulge in chips and ice cream in the presence of her classmates, then would later sneak off to the bathroom and jam her finger down her throat to rid herself of the calories. Simply because she wasn't competing for a title anymore didn't mean she had stopped obsessing over her appearance.

With the absence of her parents, she'd developed a severe paranoia that hindered her ability to spend time around anyone outside of school beyond her aunt and the Lewis family. The fear that the police would find a reason to break into her aunt's home like they had in Brooklyn sometimes paralyzed her.

She would often stay awake for hours after her bedtime, ice-cold claws of terror gripping her spine as shadows danced across her bedroom walls. Thunderous beats of her heart rattled against her ribs whenever she wondered if her father could be released prematurely, and come for her the way he'd gone after his victims. The memory of his final harsh words to her constantly lingered in the back of her mind, no matter how hard she tried to forget.

Whenever her nose wasn't buried in a book, she was most at peace when spending time with her aunt. They were always creating something with their hands—mediums from pottery and oils paintings to crochet and macrame. While they produced art, Taylor continued to introduce her to a wide variety of music—Sinatra, Cash, Joplin, Zeppelin, Joel, and everything in-between. Sometimes they'd invite the Lewis kids over, but it was usually just the two of them. Rowan's aunt schooled her on the ways of the world, teaching her the kind of things one didn't learn in school, and taboo subjects her mother had deemed inappropriate. They'd talk of relationships, money, education, politics, sex—nothing was off the table. Rowan was happiest when her aunt treated her like an adult.

She'd learned the value of a happy, healthy family

unit with the Lewises. She spent enough time at their house that Steph automatically set an extra place at the table for dinner every night, just in case Taylor was too deep into creating something to make dinner and Rowan came wandering over. She fought with Drake as if he was her biological brother. And once Dr. Walters prescribed the right mix of antidepressants and sleeping pills, Rowan was finally able to stay over with Kinsley more nights than she slept at her aunt's.

For Drake's 15th birthday in the spring, his parents gifted him the video camera he'd begged for all year. Ever since his dad had taken him to the premiere of *Jurassic Park* when he was little, he'd dreamed of extending his love for movies into his own creations. Although he'd long since deemed himself too cool as a high schooler to spend time with Kinsley and Rowan, he came up with a master plan the night of his birthday while they watched the recently released to DVD version of *Donny Darko* on the L-shaped sectional in their family room.

"This movie is way weird," Kinsley declared, covering her mouth with a dramatic yawn. She playfully slapped Rowan's knee. "Come on, Ro. Let's go watch the last episode of *Dawson's Creek* in my room."

Grateful for an excuse to get away, Rowan quickly stood along with her friend. Drake and Kinsley were unaware of her growing paranoias, and she was far too embarrassed to inform Drake the tone of the movie had activated some of her darkest fears.

"Hold up," Drake told them, muting the television. He'd changed even more since Rowan had come to live with her aunt, becoming decently cute and popular with girls his age. Sometimes, like that night, he'd look at her in ways that would make her blush. "Instead of watching that lame soap opera in your room, let's go outside and start making a movie."

With a lift of one eyebrow, Kinsley appeared vaguely interested. "You better not be suggesting anything perverted."

Drake shot to his feet, shaking his head wildly. "What? You're my sister, sicko! Both of you!" Eyes darting around the room, he scratched his shaggy hair. "I'm thinking we could make up some kind of sci-fi drama, just without the special effects. I can work out those details later when I take Introduction to Film next year."

Kinsley twirled a lock of red hair and popped her bubble gum. "You want us to act in your stupid home movie? What's in it for us?"

With the thought of being recorded by a video camera, panic swelled in Rowan's throat. She wasn't nearly as pretty as her best friend, and she remembered her mother's warning that a camera added 10 pounds. "I could try writing something," she blurted, twirling her charm bracelet around her wrist. Her cheeks burned when the siblings shot her matching questionable looks. "I mean...I don't think anyone would want to see me act, but I've spent thousands of hours reading. I'm sure I could come up with an interesting story."

Drake huffed and flashed a sideways grin. "Are you serious, Ro? You're hot—er, I mean...that's what the guys at school say. You were born for this kind of thing."

Rowan mournfully shook her head. "I don't wish to be seen on video."

"She has a valid point," Kinsley decided, slinging her arm around Rowan's neck. "Surely a bookworm like her has developed a knack for storytelling. Drake, you could set the camera up on your fancy new tripod, and play the part of the hero. Maybe we could convince some of our friends to fill in the other parts."

Within a few days, they discovered the time Rowan spent reading had, in fact, provided her with a knack for storytelling. Drake declared her first script to be "the coolest thing ever." She created many more scripts for their movies throughout the following summer—most often silly dramas in which Kinsley was the star and she was a secondary character, like a cashier or doctor. With the camcorder on a tripod, Drake filled the part of the hero as Kinsley suggested. Before long, they'd convinced friends from school to play roles, and Rowan stopped appearing in the films altogether. She enjoyed tapping into her creativity, and unleashing her childish side through fictional characters.

The following school year, Drake convinced the drama teacher to give him access to the school's film editing equipment, and the results of their hobby soon became an elaborate screening event. Taylor and the Lewises would dress up along with them for their movie premieres, and Steph would prepare an elegant meal before they'd watch the film—in the Lewises' backyard when weather permitted. It wasn't long before the screening became a popular event attended by their classmates, too.

Rowan effortlessly melded into the Lewis family. She was there for birthdays and holidays, sometimes with Taylor and sometimes without. They included her on family vacations—to the Hamptons the previous fall, and an upcoming road trip to Orlando after school let out. They'd taken her shopping for school supplies and new clothes in the fall, providing her with the same allowance as Kinsley and Drake. Rowan never wondered who paid for all her needs. It felt so natural that she didn't think to ask.

Following Rowan's 12th birthday dinner in February, after Taylor had returned home and the other kids had retreated to their rooms, Steph and Andy asked Rowan to join them in their living room. Unlike Taylor's eclectic cottage, the Lewis home was grand and modern with a ceiling that stretched two stories high. A wall of glass windows in the living room provided an impressive view of the ocean that still made Rowan's heart skip a beat every time she gazed out upon the lighthouse across the bay. Andy had built the 4-bedroom home the year after Kinsley was born, and Steph's talent for decorating shone in the pairing of white furniture, beige accents, and intricate area rugs.

With a perfect smile, Rowan perched on one of the twin arm-chairs with blue stripes that faced the large sectional where Andy and Steph waited. They'd never asked to speak to her alone, and she was worried they'd somehow overheard her throwing up birthday cake despite the splash of the faucet running at full strength.

"Thank you for the party tonight," she told them. "The lasagna and chocolate cake were delicious, Steph. And the bracelet you both gifted me is beautiful." She fingered the delicate seascape charms hanging from her wrist. "I'll never take it off."

"You're welcome, kiddo," Andy replied, sitting back with one ankle resting on the other knee. He draped his arm behind his wife on the back of the sectional. "Steph and I enjoy seeing you happy."

"You're such a sweet, polite young woman." Steph spoke in a slow, even pace with a toothy grin. "We love having you around, Ro."

"We're always here for you," Andy added, shoving his glasses higher on his nose. "No matter what."

Steph gave an enthusiastic nod. "And we hope you know how much we love you."

"I love you too," Rowan whispered with a lump in her throat. She sensed something was wrong even before Steph gripped Andy's thigh and they each threw her a sympathetic look.

"Your father sent you flowers for your birthday," Steph explained.

"How?" Even though Rowan's stomach was

perfectly empty, it lurched painfully hard as her eyes darted around the house. Fear pinched her chest. "Did they let him out?"

"God, no," Andy insisted, frantically waving his hands through the air. "It's nothing like that. He's still in prison, where he belongs."

"We suspect he has resources on the outside," Steph added in a bitter tone. "But it's okay, sweetheart. You don't have anything to do with the flowers."

Rowan wound her arms around her waist. "Where are they?"

"We threw them away," Andy told her before his lips spread into a hard, unyielding line. "They weren't...appropriate."

Rowan's skin tingled from his dark expression. "I don't understand."

"They were spider lilies," Steph said in a mere whisper.

Rowan's heart gave a little tug when she remembered the time her father had offered her the same flowers as an apology. Was he apologizing for how he'd treated her the night of his arrest? "What's so inappropriate about spider lilies?"

Steph's eyes filled with tears. "You mean you don't know?"

Andy linked his fingers with Steph's. "It's probably time you learn the facts, Rowan, before you find yourself in a situation where they can't be avoided." He let out a shaky breath, steady gaze held with Rowan's. "Your father left spider lilies with each of his victims. That's how the FBI was able to link him to twenty-four murders over the past couple of decades."

A great tremble ripped down Rowan's spine. She'd never been told the exact number of her father's victims, and she couldn't wrap her head around it. Teeth clenched, she told herself not to cry.

"The FBI didn't share that information with the public," Andy continued. "Then, after your father was shot, a witness identified him as the man who'd fled his last victim's home, and they were able to prove he'd used the lilies as his signature. That kind of flower...it holds special meaning. The FBI suspects it was his warped way of wishing his victims farewell. The public...well, once they learned the truth, they dubbed him 'The Spider Lily Strangler' because of it."

With hot tears searing her eyes, Rowan shook her head. "Stop. I don't want to hear any more." She shot up to her feet, praying her legs wouldn't give out. "Can I go to bed now?"

Steph exchanged a concerned look with Andy. "Are you sure you don't want to talk about it some more, sweetie?" she asked.

Rowan gave them a perfect smile. "No thank you. I just want to go to sleep."

That night, and countless nights after, she dreamt of red spider lilies soaked in blood.

7

Blue Bay High School was located inside a massive cement building, constructed ten years after the elementary school down the street. It housed an average of 400 students in grades 9-12, and provided a scenic view of the ocean that made the students wiggle in their seats with the urge to skip class throughout the first month of the fall semester.

The first day of her junior year, Rowan yearned to skip class for a different reason. She was nearly knocked out of her seat when her forensic science teacher mentioned they'd be studying serial killers throughout the semester. Once she realized her pen was trembling in her hand, she dropped it onto her notebook and casually glanced around the classroom to see if anyone had noticed her stranger than usual behavior. Everyone already thought she was weird as her ongoing battle with depression made her especially quiet around anyone she didn't know well.

After Andy and Steph told her the significance of the spider lilies, she'd gone out of her way to avoid learning any more details about her father's killing spree. Despite Taylor's letters to the prison demanding him to stop, her father continued to send Rowan the same flowers every year on her birthday. The mere sight of a floral delivery truck on their road any day of the year pushed her into a blind panic.

When Mr. Armstrong mentioned her father's name in his lecture along with the likes of Bundy, Gacy, and Dahmer, her stomach rose and violently cramped. It would've heaved if she'd had anything left from lunch to expel. One by one, her teacher advanced through multiple pictures of each killer projected on the whiteboard, discussing the methods, arrest, and conviction of each man. Then he advanced to her father's mugshot, and the room began to sway.

Wincing, she was all at once transported back to the night of the arrest. She remembered the blank look her father had given her when she'd called out to him, and how his anger had shaken her to the core. His expression in the image was nearly identical. She gripped the sides of her desk, telling herself she would not pass out in front of her classmates.

Mr. Armstrong pointed at her father's image. "What can someone tell me about Jonathan Rivers, commonly known as the SLS killer?"

Rowan's limbs tingled with cold when Ashley Williams, the most popular girl in Blue Bay high school, immediately shot her hand into the air. "He was a family man, like the BTK killer...had a wife, and kid, and a normal job. He was also a good looking narcissist who charmed his way into getting women to trust him, a lot like Bundy. He lived in Brooklyn, but his spree was super random. He basically killed one victim in every state."

"The confirmed kill count is a bit exaggerated, Ashley," Mr. Armstrong told her with a stern look, "but you're right on with the other points. He shared a lot of characteristics with some of the most infamous killers."

"Yeah, but he wasn't as big of a perv as the others!" Matt Swenson, the football team's prized quarterback, yelled. "He didn't eat his victims, or cut them into pieces. The dude just got his rocks off by strangling women while doing the deed."

Bile seared through Rowan's throat. In recent years she'd begun to suspect, although never confirmed, that sexual assault of her father's victims was involved. Hearing the truth was more than she could handle. Her fingers began to toy with the little charms on the bracelet given to her by Steph and Andy. She would've given anything for an excuse to abruptly leave without causing suspicion.

Ashley rolled her eyes and clicked her tongue. "You mean while he was *raping them*, Matt. And by definition, strangling those women for his pleasure makes him a perv, even if he hadn't killed them. You actually think women are into that kind of thing?"

"Alright, enough," Mr. Armstrong interjected. "We're getting off subject. While your point on his method was crudely stated, it was correct, Mr. Swenson. And next time please raise your hand when you have something to say." He glanced back at the mugshot. "Does anyone know how the SLS killer was caught?"

Ashley lifted her hand. "Didn't his own daughter call the cops after he tried to kill her?"

Stomach violently cramping, Rowan's breath caught in her throat. She had officially become a part of their conversation. How could it possibly get any worse?

The teacher's answer sounded distorted to her ears. "I don't believe it was ever stated on record that he tried to harm his daughter, but you're correct about his arrest. He'd been caught in the act of killing his last victim by her husband, and was injured before he fled to his home. By the time his daughter called the police, they already had a BOLO out on someone matching his description from an eye-witness."

Mr. Armstrong advanced to another image of her father sitting in a courtroom, surrounded by strangers. Rowan swallowed a sharp gasp, nearly choking on her spittle. Her father had gained a significant amount of muscle mass in eight years—or however long since the picture had been taken. He'd become thick-necked, like a professional football player, and his shoulders and chest were twice as broad. She supposed a lack of sunshine was to blame for the waxy white sheen of his complexion, but age was most likely a factor in the creases around his eyes and forehead. His thick hair had been shaved down, military style, and was almost completely white rather than its usual strawberry blond. Much like his mugshot, his gray eyes remained expressionless along with his facial features. She wondered if prison had changed his personality as much as his appearance.

Hit with an overwhelmingly strong rush of

nausea, she realized she wasn't looking at a picture of the man who had raised her. It wasn't the same man who bounced her on his knee while telling her silly stories, or once allowed her to use an entire bottle of bubble bath, or pushed her on the swing at the neighborhood park. The handsome man with an enduring smile she'd cherished was long gone. It was the unfiltered portrait of a cold blooded killer.

"At the time of his arrest, they obtained samples of his DNA," Mr. Armstrong explained. "Project Innocence has recently become involved in his case, claiming those DNA samples were tainted. As it's an ongoing matter, we'll be following his case extensively throughout the semester. Next, we have..."

Rowan closed her eyes as her teacher moved on to another killer. Did her father really have a chance of being set free? She let out a slow, shuddering breath. Somehow she'd survived listening to conversations about him without drawing attention to herself. She doubted she'd be as lucky the next time —especially if it was going to be a common occurrence.

Once the buzzer signaled the end of the period a half hour later, Rowan stalled at her desk, waiting for each of her classmates to file out. She also needed the time to steady her breath. She slowly shuffled toward the front of the classroom, waiting beside Mr. Armstrong's podium as he powered down the projector.

"Mr. Armstrong?"

He turned to face her with a friendly smile that exposed perfect teeth. "Rowan! What can I do for you?" She'd known the middle-aged teacher over the years, mostly because he often supervised the students at events year-round, but this was her first class with him. She was a little sad she'd have to drop it. His smile suddenly faded. "Do you feel alright? You're a little pale."

"I don't think I can continue with this class."

"I can understand if the subject of serial killers makes you a little uneasy, Rowan, but we won't be delving too deep into the gory details. I'll mostly discuss the advancement of DNA testing, and how it has impacted both investigations and convictions."

Her cheeks warmed as she held his crystal blue-eyed stare. He was just as handsome as he was nice, even if he was old enough to be her father. "It's not that...I'm just struggling to get in all my advanced courses for college credits. I want to major in creative writing, and I need to somehow fit in more English classes. No offense, Mr. Armstrong, but I already have all my science credits fulfilled. I must've signed up by mistake."

When he tilted his head, studying her, she was suddenly terrified those blue eyes could see right through her half-assed excuses. She wasn't lying about wanting to major in creative writing, however. That had become a natural course of action considering her love of writing movie scripts, even if half of them were silly. But what if Mr. Armstrong recognized her from his research on the SLS killer? "If you're absolutely sure dropping this class is the right course of action, I'll support your decision. But I've heard you're an excellent student, and one of few who takes school seriously. I'll hate missing out on having you around."

She attempted to flash one of her pageant-worthy smiles, but her lips refused to cooperate. "Thank you, Mr. Armstrong."

After school let out, she immediately visited the principal's office to drop the class. Once home, she fired up the desktop computer her aunt had given her when she'd turned fifteen. Since the basics of her father's crimes had been revealed to her, she decided it was time to fully educate herself before faced with another awkward situation.

With unsteady fingers, she typed out her father's

name, tagging "SLS" on the end. The volume of results that popped up was mind-boggling. The very first article was entitled, *"SLS Killer: A Timeline."*

"Here goes nothing, Scotch," she told the dog curled up at her feet. She clicked on the link, and quickly descended down the rabbit hole of her father's career as a killer. It was gory and disturbing, to say the least. The only way she'd survive all the horrific details was if she treated the facts as if they were research for a paper. Hours later, she'd scribbled her way through half of a new notebook.

Engrossed in her research, she didn't hear her aunt step into the room. "What's up, Ro? Doing home—oh...*my god*. What are you doing?"

"It was time," Rowan told her, spinning the chair around. "They talked about him today in my science class. I thought I was going to pass out in front of everyone—especially when they mentioned his daughter had called the police."

Color trickled from Taylor's round face. "Oh, babe. I'm so sorry you had to experience that." She swiped her knuckle over a fallen tear. "It must've been awful for you. If you want to drop the class—"

"I already did. The office will call tomorrow to get your permission."

"Fair enough." With a firm nod, her aunt plopped

down on the edge of Rowan's bed. Her bright red dress covered with tropical flowers fluttered around her. Within seconds, Scotch leaped into her lap and happily licked her chin. "But, Ro, you need to remember there's no guarantee that someday someone won't put two and two together, and realize you're his daughter. We'd deal with it...together."

"I know." Rowan's shoulders slouched forward. "Did you know they're claiming his DNA samples were tainted?"

"I'd heard about that, yes."

"Why didn't you tell me?"

"First of all, I was respecting your wishes not to be informed on anything regarding your father. Also, I spoke with Detective Novak, and she said the FBI doesn't think there's a chance in hell those convictions will get overturned." Her aunt eyed the notebook. "What's with the notes?"

"At first I believed I should educate myself with all the facts so I'm never caught off-guard that way again." Rowan glanced back at the picture of one victim displayed on the computer screen above the caption, *"Elizabeth Baker, SLS Victim #13."* Looking away, she ran her fingertips over the edge of the notebook, watching the charm bracelet from the

Lewises dance around her wrist. "Then I started reading about each of his victims, and I guess I kind of became obsessed. At first I tried to work out some sort of pattern. Did you know a bunch of them were mothers? Some weren't much older than I am now—college students. There was an exotic dancer in Maine, and a librarian in Iowa. One was a survivor of cancer, for fuck's sake." Her voice thickened with emotion. Irritated with herself, she brushed her forearm over her burning eyes. "From what I've read, it sounds like he hit whatever random city he was in the mood to visit, and didn't have a specific type. He only cared whether or not they were pretty enough to have sex with, which I guess means he found them attractive. It grosses me out just saying that. My father was a disgusting monster who started killing *years* before I was born. He stole these women's lives for nothing more than his own perverted pleasure."

"No argument there."

Tears began to trickle down her cheek. "The thing I can't wrap my head around...the thing that's going to keep me up at night now that I know everything...it's not whether or not he'll get out. It's...I mean...how much of his mental illness could be hereditary?" She broke down with a stuttering sob.

"If—he's a—a—*monster*, w-what does that make m-me?"

"It makes you a survivor, baby girl." Taylor set Scotch down on the bed, and stood to wrap Rowan in her arms. "It makes you a survivor."

8

By the time a light snowfall dusted the quiet streets of Blue Bay, the view of the lighthouse from Taylor's backyard became a utopian scene fit for a snow globe. Taylor's usual broad mix of music was replaced with holiday tunes as she worked overtime on creating Christmas presents for friends and family. As always, the Lewis household appeared as if it had been decorated by Santa's elves. Steph's love of decorating increased with each year she took Rowan and Kinsley to the holiday market in downtown Blue Bay. Choosing locally made ornaments and figurines with the two women was yet another annual tradition that had become a part of Rowan's new life.

Most notably, December marked the third month since she'd resumed sessions with Dr. Walters. She hadn't seen the child psychologist since her fourteenth birthday, and they'd never outright talked about the murders her father had committed. She was reluctant to discuss it with anyone until Dr. Walters expertly coaxed her out of her shell. Rowan was soon pouring her heart out to the no-nonsense therapist with a generic haircut and sensible shoes, and felt a small sense of normalcy once the antidepressants stabilized her mood swings.

One Saturday evening over Christmas break, Kinsley decided it was too cold to keep up with her active social life, and invited Rowan over for a horror movie marathon. With the original *Scream* movie playing in the background, Kinsley thumbed through the school's yearbook from the year prior, rating cute guys on a sliding scale of disgusting to sizzling hot.

Rowan wasn't much into guys, or the concept of dating. Still, she pretended to play along to avoid the gory movie. She wouldn't dream of starting a conversation with Kinsley on why horror flicks made her uncomfortable any more than she'd dream of explaining the countless reasons she wasn't into the idea of dating. Too many of those reasons centered around her father's abuse of women, and her inability to trust after he'd tricked her into believing he was a good man. It was a heavy topic often covered in her recent sessions with Dr. Walters.

While discussing the pros and cons of dating Brad Turner that cold December night, Kinsley twirled a curly lock of fiery red hair around her finger and popped a piece of strawberry bubblegum. In recent years, Rowan's best friend had developed into a large-chested knockout. Creamy white skin, athletic body from years of gymnastics and dance classes, luscious hair grown out to her waistline—she was extremely popular with the senior boys. Rowan was well aware she wasn't as noticeable as her pseudo-sister. She also didn't wear revealing shirts like Kinsley as she preferred to blend into the background everywhere she went.

When the house phone rang, Rowan gave a nervous start. She secretly hoped it was her aunt calling with a minor emergency that would force her to go home for the night. She'd had enough of the actress's bloody screams and Kinsley's starry-eyed analysis of every guy from school.

"Grab it before someone else does," Kinsley ordered, still paging through the album. "It could be Brad, and I'd die if he talked to Steph or Andy. He'll never ask me out on a date if he realizes I'm related to a bunch of weirdos."

Rowan leaped across the bed to retrieve the

chargeable phone on the nightstand. "Lewis residence."

"Hey, Ro," Drake's deep voice rumbled, causing her to shiver. Although she still regarded him as a pseudo-brother, she still hadn't adjusted to his sudden transition into manhood since he'd left for film school in New York. His face and jaw had filled out, and he'd become broad. Muscular. He was utterly unrecognizable as the gangly boy she'd grown up with. "Why are you home on a Saturday night? Shouldn't you be on a date or something?"

"I'm watching movies with Kins."

"Perfect. I was hoping to talk to both of you." His tone was equally friendly and excited in a pitch unfamiliar to Rowan's ears. In high school, he'd been better described as sullen and occasionally mean.

"Hold on, I'll get her on too."

Kinsley's emerald eyes rounded as Rowan held up the phone. "Ooo! Is it Brad?" she squealed, clapping her hands in rapid little bursts.

"It's Drake. He wants to talk with you and me."

"Ew." Kinsley's lips curled into a scowl. Every face she made was extremely dramatic, no matter the situation. Rowan figured it was all those years of acting for her brother's projects. "Why?"

"I don't know. Just listen in." She scooted closer,

and they pressed their heads together near the phone receiver. "Okay, she's on."

"Hey, Kins," Drake sang cheerfully. "I have some exciting news! Wait—is that *Scream* I hear in the background? Did you guys know it took them twenty-one days to film the party scene at the end? There's a joke in the film industry that it was the longest night in horror history."

Rowan glanced at Kinsley and giggled. It was something only Drake would know.

Eyes rolling to the ceiling, Kinsley sighed in a throaty noise. "What's this exciting news, nerd? Please tell me it has something to do with you being transported to another planet."

"Do you guys remember that zombie movie we made for my senior year film project? I uploaded it to YouTube a few days ago."

"What's YouTube?" Rowan asked at the same time as Kinsley demanded, *"Why would you do that?"*

"It's that website where everyone uploads videos for anyone with computer access to see," he explained. "And Kins, I did it for exposure. It already has over *three hundred thousand views*. Almost every single comment left by other viewers is positive. Someone even compared it to *Evil Dead*. And a bunch of people asked if you're a well-known actress, Kins. They said if you're not already, you should be."

"Really?" Kinsley puffed her chest out and beamed with pride. "They said that?"

"I showed it to my cinematography instructor, and he said it's better than average quality. He thinks if the views keep increasing at this rate, there's a good chance I'll get approached by a studio about directing something new."

"Wow, Drake," Rowan said to him. "That's great."

"I just thought you guys should know, since we all created it together and everything. You should both open a YouTube account, and keep an eye on the video. Just make sure you ignore any negative comments. You can find it with a search for 'Drake Productions.' That's the name of the account I set up...hope you guys don't mind. I can give you credit in the comments if you want."

"Um, *duh*," Kinsley answered, snapping her gum. "If this thing goes viral, I obviously want everyone to know my name. This could be a big break for all of us—not just you."

Rowan thought about her name being blasted on the internet, even though she wouldn't be credited with her father's surname, and her heart lurched with fear. "I don't want my name mentioned anywhere."

"Why not?" Drake challenged in a flirty tone. "Too embarrassed?"

"No, I...I just don't want people to know it's me."

Kinsley's eyes darted across the room, and her smile morphed into a scowl. "It doesn't matter why, Drake. She doesn't want her name on there, so don't you dare add it, butt-wad. I mean it."

Drake quickly backpedaled. "Yeah—sorry—you're right. I won't include it, Ro. I promise. You don't have to worry, okay?"

Rowan's cheeks warmed with the stiff tone of their voices. She hated that they knew the reason she'd come to Blue Bay and changed her name even though they'd never asked about her father. Their parents most likely told them her ugly story, and instructed them not to bring it up. She supposed she should be thankful, but most of all, she was embarrassed. Sometimes she worried they'd welcomed her into their family with arms wide-open because they felt obligated. Worse yet, she feared Andy and Steph only brought her into their family because they felt sorry for the girl with a monster for a father.

It was yet another subject to discuss with Dr. Walters.

THE LAST DAY of Rowan's junior year, she decided to approach Taylor with an idea that had formed several months prior during a breakthrough session with Dr. Walters. She realized her timing was perfect when she found her aunt hard at work in her studio in the backyard. It was within those same four walls their bond had strengthened—among countless bottles of craft paint in every type and color under the sun, skeins of yarn in hundreds of shades, ceramic stamps, buckets of clay, soap wafers and oils, draws of craft glue...and that only covered the right side of the shed.

"I want to visit his victims' graves."

The bowl her aunt was working on collapsed in her wet, clay-covered hands, sagging off to one side as it continued to spin around on the pottery wheel. She blinked repeatedly while using the back of her wrists to push wayward strands of her recently dyed, jet black hair away from her face. Finally, she lifted her foot off the wheel's pedal. "Say that again?"

"I feel as if I know these women by now, and I

want to properly pay my respects by visiting their final resting place." Rowan folded her arms over her stomach and leaned back against an empty drying rack. "I'm starting to feel like it's my...I don't know...*duty* as their killer's daughter."

Nodding rhythmically, Taylor switched the power on the wheel. "I can respect that."

"I was thinking it'd take a good month out of my summer. I could be back in time to help you with the market in mid-July. I still have my share of our sales from the last couple of years...it should cover everything I'd need while on the road."

"Baby girl, I appreciate the need to spread your wings *and* the desire to right your dad's wrongs, but I can't let you go driving across the country all alone, and staying in random motels."

"Why not? You've let me drive in New York several times since I turned sixteen."

"It's not that. It's because you're young and beautiful. There are bad people out there."

"Bad people like my father," Rowan clarified with a bitter bite to her words. Her expression darkened. "I'm more aware of the dangers I'd face than the average woman. You've taught me how to defend myself, and I'm smart enough to avoid dangerous situations."

"I know you're brilliant, and I'm confident you'd be careful. It's just..." Wiping the back of one hand across her forehead, Taylor stood. "If you don't want your old aunt tagging along, I'm sure Kinsley would be up for a girls' trip."

"If anyone came along with me, it'd turn into a fun adventure, and that would totally void the entire point of going."

Taylor's chest rose with a deep breath as her gaze ambled back to Rowan's. "What about the nightmares? You don't think you'd be afraid to stay somewhere on your own?"

"I haven't had one in a long time," Rowan lied. She didn't think the nightmares would ever go away, and she wasn't going to let them cripple her for the rest of her life.

"Have you discussed this idea with Dr. Walters?"

"Yeah, I have. She thinks it'll provide me with some level of closure."

"Guess there's no point arguing with the expert." Taylor crossed over to the paint-splattered sink to wash her hands. "After I clean up, we'll go talk to Henry Myers down the street. He's been trying to sell that old sedan of his for the past couple of months. It's a solid car with pretty low miles, and I'm sure I can talk him down to a reasonable price the way he's always hitting on me. You're going to need something more reliable than the old Volvo to take you 'cross country, and we're gonna need to familiarize ourselves with online maps if we're going to plan your route."

Rowan ran to wrap her arms around her aunt from behind. "Thank you for always being on my side." She squeezed her a little tighter. "I don't know why I feel such a strong need to do this, but I do."

"Your path will be unlike anyone else's, baby girl. It's not for you to understand, but to take."

9

The public housing project in downtown Portland, Maine was the kind of neighborhood where break-ins and vandalizing of cars were a common occurrence. After dark, open prostitution and drug use kept young children off the streets. Sheryl Haines, an exotic dancer, had lived there her entire life. Her final resting place just down the road from her home was nearly a four hour drive from Blue Bay. Rowan completed it in one straight shot, without any stops. Knowing she was about to pay her first visit to one of her father's victims put her on edge as she was forever fearful someone would recognize her. She was also eager to begin her journey.

Locating the cemeteries where each of the women were laid to rest had been a process. Detective Novak had contacted one of the FBI agents in charge, and explained the situation. In turn, the agent reached out to each of the victim's families to inquire which of them felt comfortable enough to reveal the burial plots to Rowan. They'd all been surprised when fifteen of the twenty-seven families consented. The process had taken three weeks total, providing Rowan with ample time to properly celebrate Kinsley's graduation before mapping her extensive drive.

Rowan drove past the housing project where Sheryl had lived, and the gentlemen's club downtown where Sheryl had worked for many years. At the time of her death, the 24-year-old was an undeniably attractive young woman with a pixie-like face, alluring dark eyes, and shoulder length chestnut hair that was worn straight in every picture Rowan found. It was believed Rowan's father had followed Sheryl home from the club the year Rowan would've turned 6. He jumped Sheryl outside of her home, and took her into the nearby woods. A hunting dog had found her abandoned corpse the next morning with a spider lily tucked inside her hair.

The cemetery that would be Sheryl's final resting place was peaceful: filled with wildlife, a variety of ancient sculptures and mausoleums, and several rows of vibrant flags to honor the different branches of the military. The air was cooler than in Blue Bay, and the light breeze felt refreshing as it kissed Rowan's face and fluttered through her dark ponytail. Sheryl's grave was marked by a plain stone embedded in the grass, hardly bigger than a brick, and too small to fit any words beyond:

SHERYL ANN HAINES
BELOVED DAUGHTER

ON THE DRIVE UP, she had carefully considered what she wanted to say when visiting Sheryl's grave. Dr. Walters suggested it might not be Rowan's place to apologize for her father's actions, but Rowan was overwhelmed with guilt when she thought of the beautiful brunette's life being taken so soon, and the grieving mother she'd left behind.

With the single white rose she'd purchased from a nearby florist in hand, Rowan collapsed to her knees in front of the marker and gulped in shaky breaths. She feared she'd made a mistake in deciding to visit her father's victims. Seeing Sheryl's name eternally engraved in stone with her own eyes made it too real, too heartbreaking. The crippling pressure in her chest was too much to bear. Bitter tears filled her mouth as she placed the rose on the marker, whispering, "I'm so sorry he did this to you, Sheryl."

She quietly sat beside the marker for a while, allowing her tears to flow freely until she spotted an elderly couple off in the distance. Once back inside her car, she checked in with Taylor, sending her a simple text: *Made it 2 Portland. Headed to Boston now.*

The experience had drained her, so she stopped at the first gas station she passed on the interstate to fill her car's tank and grab an energy drink. One of Taylor's concerns had involved the families who may have consented only because they harbored a hidden agenda, and the idea had stuck with Rowan. Paranoia prevented her from making eye contact or speaking with anyone to cross her path, even when the cashier asked if she was having a good day.

It was a short drive to Boston, and she was quickly able to find the next victim's gravestone in the third row from the back left side of the massive cemetery as described. The temperature was several degrees warmer than in Maine, even with a chance of rain. Once she noticed the cemetery was filled with an abundance of early afternoon visitors, she pulled the hood of her spring coat over her head.

Not much was known about Melanie Harrison

aside from the fact that she was a mother of two young boys, and a dental hygienist. The only picture Rowan found online was a grainy black and white portrait taken from an old yearbook picture in which Melanie's features were unclear. She'd been 28 when Rowan's father took her life behind a convenience store where she'd stopped on her way home from work to get pull-up diapers for her youngest son.

Rowan struggled not to break down as she knelt beside the pretty granite headstone, adorned with angels and hearts. Melanie's husband's name, Richard, was etched beside hers, his date of death left blank. Beneath their names, they'd added:

PROUD PARENTS *of Seth and Michael*

AS SHE TRACED the names with a fingertip, hot tears rushed down her face. She curled her icy cold fingers into fists, wondering how anyone—let alone the man who'd loved her and raised her for 11 years—could be heartless enough to end a mother's life. If one of the boys had been young enough for diapers, he'd likely grow up without remembering a single thing about his mother. She shed extra tears for

Melanie's two sons, praying their father had been strong enough to raise them on his own, and the death of their mother hadn't destroyed their lives in the way her father's actions had ruined hers.

When it felt as if she had no more tears to shed, she dried her face and set the white rose at the base of the headstone before shuffling back to her car. On her way, she passed two young men leaning against a simple white Subaru. One had been crying, and the other offered a brusque nod with a rather haunted expression. Her stomach tightened as she quickly did the math in her head. They could easily be the age of Melanie's sons.

While she wasn't sure she was strong enough to continue, she knew she had to honor those she'd been able to locate. They deserved so much more.

That night, she drove five plus hours to Allentown, Pennsylvania, the nearest location of the next victim. The sun had already set by the time she arrived, and she wasn't excited by the idea of visiting a cemetery in the dark. Taylor had sent extra money along on the condition that Rowan stay away from motels directly off the interstates or in sketchy areas, so she checked into a motel in the heart of a clean neighborhood.

She called Taylor to let her know she was settled

in, and answered each of her aunt's questions to her satisfaction. No, it hadn't been too much to handle when she visited the first two graves (a lie), yes, she had been eating well (she'd only grabbed a bag of carrots for lunch and was too distraught to eat dinner after stopping by Melanie's grave), and yes, the drive went smoothly (if you discounted the truck driver who almost veered into her outside of Boston). Regardless of her answers, Taylor must've sensed the trip had been harrowing as she volunteered to fly out to meet Rowan for the remainder of the trip.

"I can do this on my own, Aunt T. I promise…I'll be fine."

"If at *any* point you change your mind, give me a call and I'll be on the first flight out." Taylor sighed heavily into the phone. "What you're doing is noble, Ro, and I'm incredibly proud of you. You know I love you madly, right?"

"I know." Rowan located the remote control for the television, and mindlessly clicked through channels. "Have you seen Kinsley around since I left?"

"As a matter of fact, she stopped over earlier to see if I'd heard from you. Lord, that girl is a drama queen! Although I can understand. It's because she's worried about you. Steph and Andy are too. None of them understand why you feel the need to do this on your own. But it's not for them to understand. As long as you're safe and satisfied with your journey, nothing else matters."

"I'm being careful." She eyed the chain and deadbolt locks she'd engaged after checking into the small room. "You don't have to worry."

After ending the call, it took several hours for her to fall asleep. There were too many noises surrounding the motel with thin walls, and she couldn't stop thinking about Melanie's sons. The haunted look in the eyes of the older man would stay with her for years. She hoped he found the help he needed before knowledge of his mother's death ate him alive.

The next several days were similar to the first as she visited graves in Washington, Pittsburg, Toledo, Chicago, and Des Moines. Each stop felt more draining than the last, forcing her to consume more and more energy drinks until she was buzzing with caffeine. Without anyone around, there wasn't a need to eat like everyone else and purge. She simply refrained from eating anything other than cold veggies.

She drove late into the nights, and stuck to motels in nice areas of the cities. While on the road, she found herself wondering how her father had picked each location. Was he merely checking cities off of a bucket list? Were they places he had visited at one point in his life, and wanted to return? According to Detective Novak, the FBI had found records of each of his flights, and confirmed there weren't auctions or conventions for salesmen on those particular dates. One of the agent's theories was that her father had purchased flights based on times and prices. Another theory was that her father had thrown a dart at a map. Jonathan Rivers was the only one who knew the real reason, and he wasn't giving up any information as he still claimed innocence.

She also couldn't help wondering what her parents would think if they knew of her mission. Taylor promised not to tell Vanessa, and Rowan knew she wouldn't cave, especially as they almost never communicated anymore. Rowan hadn't spoken to her mother in several years, and that was fine with her. A part of her feared her father would experience some kind of sick thrill if he were to learn his daughter was acknowledging his work.

As she finished paying her respects at Sara Newman's grave in Des Moines, she rose to her feet and came face-to-face with an attractive, gray-haired woman in a simple black dress. In her bare arms, she cradled a massive bouquet of several dozen red roses.

"Can I help you?" the woman asked, pressing her thin lips into a tight line. Her dark, sad eyes flickered from Rowan to the white rose she'd left at the foot of the grave. Then, slowly, her mouth dropped open. "My God. You're her, aren't you? You're the daughter of the man who took my sweet Sara from us."

Shame and grief blanketed Rowan as she held the disbelieving stare of the grieving mother. Her legs wobbled beneath her. "I'm—"

"Agent Stone said you'd be stopping by at some point." The woman's lips twisted into a mournful smile. "I just never imagined it'd be *today* of all days." She bent to dust cut grass off the top of the headstone. "This would've been Sara's forty-fifth birthday. Her former students still send a rose every year in memory of their favorite teacher."

Rowan was all at once angry with herself. Why hadn't she thought to check the dates to ensure she wouldn't be visiting on dates of importance to the families? It was a stupid mistake—one she wouldn't make twice.

"Mom!" a man called from off in the distance, charging toward them. "I told you not to come here today! Get away from her!" He was as tall and solid as an oak tree, and his eyes burned with anger when he addressed Rowan. "My mom may have consented to this visit, but I certainly did not! Get the hell outta here before I call the police!"

Rowan's empty stomach violently cramped as she whirled around and ran for her life. Sara's brother continued to yell, but his voice was quickly drowned out by the sound of Rowan's anguished cries as she blindly sprinted toward her car.

With hot tears rolling down her cheeks and snot dripping from her nose, she drove away until she could no longer see. She pulled off into an isolated rest stop somewhere south of Kansas City. It was a major violation of her aunt's rules, but she couldn't stand to face anyone after what had happened.

After she parked the car and checked twice to ensure the doors were locked, her mind went to dark places. She was starting to understand why her mother had turned to drugs and alcohol. She would give anything to numb the pain.

She continued to cry until she passed out.

10

Interstate 35 stretched from Duluth, Minnesota, all the way down to Laredo, Texas, and covered a lot of uninteresting prairie ground in-between. Even with the warm temperatures June had to offer, there was no guarantee for clear roads when driving through the heart of the Midwest. Tornados, flash floods, hail storms...bad weather was anything but a guarantee. Once the swelling from her crying jag went down enough to see, she was lucky to find I-35 dry and clear. She continued South toward Dallas and Austin before veering West toward Phoenix.

With every destination, her fear of the unknown grew a little more. What if the victims' families knew each other, and Sara's brother had notified them of Rowan's last location? She trembled as the California sign came into view, slightly relieved. The state where her father's murderous killing spree began marked the final leg of her trip. Over the next few days, she visited graves in four cities—Los Angeles, Monterey, San Jose, and finally San Francisco where she'd been given the location of her father's 4th victim. He'd killed Dawn Fredrick shortly before he'd met her mother, and two years before Rowan was born.

As she knelt beside the small granite marker with Dawn's name and years of her time on earth, she recalled the woman's story with crippling clarity. Dawn had been murdered inside her own apartment, left for her 8-year-old son to discover her naked, badly battered body. Rowan winced with an onset of tears. She hadn't been much older than Dawn's son when she had unintentionally put an end to her father's reign of terror with a call to the police.

Her tears fell hot and fast. She felt a kinship with the boy when she tried to imagine how his life had changed with his mother's death. She gripped the cool blades of grass surrounding the marker in her fingers, silently cursing her father for betraying her and her mother, and ruining countless other lives.

She was ready to curl up beside the grave, cursing her father for bringing her into the world when she felt a prickling sensation along the backside of her neck. She was being watched. She subtly turned her head, catching the glint of a pair of binoculars from the nearby hillside. Her entire body shook as she wiped her face dry with her sweater sleeve and calmly made her way back to her car.

THE MAN WAITED until it was quiet before he approached the isolated grave. The simple granite marker had been provided by the state and was easy to miss.

"Hi Mom…" he cleared his throat and started up again. "I've come to—"

Visit. Talk to you. Cry. Scream?

He never knew what to say. He finally just stood shuffling from foot to foot as clouds moved in off the Pacific and the light faded. It reminded him of all the dark nights he'd spent in the abandoned house as a teenager after she'd died and left him all alone.

He was undoubtedly a different person than that scared little punk. But her death had left him with so many unanswered questions that could never be answered, and his life would never be the same.

Squaring his shoulders, he promised himself that he would move on, and wouldn't set foot in the cemetery ever again. It was too depressing to see her name in plain block letters. It conjured up too many painful memories.

He *had* to move on.

SINCE THE DAY Rowan had learned the details of the murders, the question of whether or not she'd develop the same malevolent tendencies over time weighed heavy on her conscience. Since then, she'd explored the subject of genetics in great detail with Dr. Walters. For years, she'd begun to suspect that her parents were estranged from her grandparents for a good reason. And she wondered why her father's parents had also been absent in her life, as well as how they were dealing with the aftermath of their son's unthinkable deeds. She was ready for the answers that no one was willing or able to provide, starting with her mother's parents.

After a few hours of pulling herself back together, she doubled back to a neighborhood southwest of San Jose where her maternal grandparents lived in a gated mansion on a winding hill. It'd been easy enough to obtain their address as they had sent Rowan elegant Christmas and birthday cards every year since her father's arrest, each envelope bearing the same return address in Los Gatos. When she pulled up outside the sophisticated monstrosity with a low-tiled roof pitch, stucco siding, and half-round arched windows and doorways, she almost understood her mother's need for perfection and elegance a little better. With her already sore stomach clenching and sick but managing to hang on, she pressed the button on the intercom.

"Yes?" a slow and rather dry female voice answered.

"Do Kitty and Kelly Miller live here?"

"May I ask who's inquiring?"

"Rowan Brooks—uh, I mean *Sienna Rivers*. Their granddaughter."

A full minute passed without any reply. Rowan's nerves were ready to snap when a buzzer sounded, and the intricate wrought iron fences slowly parted toward the house. She drove forward without really touching the accelerator, afraid her tires would mark up the immaculate stone driveway leading up to the house.

The curved front door opened as she parked. A slender, white-haired woman with a narrow nose, thin eyebrows, and the same hazel eyes as her mother's held her gaze on the doorstep, appearing hesitant. In a trendy cream colored pantsuit and excessive jewelry that caught like periscopes in the California sunlight, Rowan briefly considered her grandmother could be a celebrity. She wasn't sure whether or not she should exit the car until the woman gave a half-smile and motioned for her to enter. Nonetheless, Rowan was still reluctant to advance.

"Sienna?" the woman asked.

Rowan nodded. "Only I changed my name to Rowan."

"I can't believe it," Kitty whispered, eyes filled with moisture. Her gaze swept over Rowan's jeans and sweater before again settling on her face. "You're absolutely stunning, my child." She opened her thin arms wide. "If you don't mind, I have waited far too long to hug my only grandchild."

Rowan rushed forward and sunk into the woman's embrace. She was surprised to feel an intense swell of emotions blossoming inside her chest. Exhausted from her journey, she broke into tears. Kitty's grip tightened until the emotion passed, and Rowan pulled away with her shoulders squared.

Kitty dabbed at the corners of her eyes with a crooked finger. "You're more beautiful than I ever could've imagined, sweet child. Perhaps even more beautiful than your momma."

Rowan wiped her face, frowning. "Why didn't you ever come to visit?"

"That's a long, complicated story." With a stiff smile, Kitty rested a hand on Rowan's shoulder. "Perhaps one better told in the comfort of the backyard with a cool drink." She eyed Rowan's car. "You drove all the way from Connecticut? Did you make the journey all on your own?"

"That's also a long story," Rowan answered with a sniffle and a sad smile.

"Well, then, you best grab your things and come along inside. You can stay the night...or longer, depending on your plans." Kitty's smile warmed, but a tired sadness lingered in her hazel eyes. "Let's find you a tissue and a warm cup of tea."

She led Rowan to a spacious room decorated in soft pinks with a four-poster walnut bed in the center, and a stone fireplace flanked by half-empty walnut bookshelves. "Feel free to settle in and freshen up, dear. I will be waiting in the backyard."

Rowan deposited her small suitcase on the down bedding before using the attached bathroom and splashing water on her face. All at once, she appreciated how confused Alice must've been when falling down that rabbit hole.

The lofty interior, expertly decorated in neutral hues, was even more elegant than its facade. The house seemed never ending, filled with bonus rooms that looked as if they'd either never been used, or were awaiting a photoshoot for a magazine. Rowan was certain her aunt's cottage and the Lewises' home could've each fit twice inside the main level.

As instructed, she found her way to the well-manicured backyard where her grandmother paced near a set of intricate patio furniture. Topiaries of all shapes and sizes and vibrant rose bushes dominated the landscaping, and Rowan spotted a flag marking a putting green over a slope on the far end. She eyed a smaller version of the main house stretching along the length of a swimming pool and hot tub. "Does someone else live here?"

Kitty responded with a graceful laugh. "No, it's just the two of us. I keep telling Kelly—ah, I should say, *your grandfather*, that it's past time to downsize, but we have put enough time and money into this home that he doesn't have the heart to put it on the market." She motioned to the lounging chairs facing the pool. "Have a seat, darling. The chef will be out shortly with refreshments, and you can let him know what you wish for him to prepare for dinner."

The lush green grass wavered before Rowan's eyes. Her grandparents lived in the biggest house she'd ever seen, they had a personal chef, and her grandmother spoke like someone out of another century. She saw a glimpse of her mother's childhood, and wondered if that's why she'd raised Rowan with the expectations of perfection. The need to call Dr. Walters itched against her brain. "How do you expect me to process this?" she blurted, refusing to move. "Why are you talking to me as if we've known each other forever? Do you expect me to act like all of this is normal?"

Shoulders squared, Kitty's stern gaze met Rowan's as she lifted her chin. "I have never found myself in a predicament quite this uncomfortable. I am doing the best I can to make you feel at ease."

"It would make me feel more *at ease* if you'd stop pretending, and tell me the truth I've been searching for my entire life. Why didn't my mother speak to you? Why didn't my parents bring me out here to visit?"

"You remind me of myself at that age. Determined...strong." Kitty proceeded to perch on one of the chairs, and smiled warmly when Rowan plopped down into another at her side. "Your grandfather and I graduated high school together, and married the week after. We were young and extremely poor when he accepted a position on the ground floor of Silicon Valley. We waited nearly a decade for him to climb the corporate ladder, and started a family once we could afford the best of everything. As the saying goes, your mother was 'born with a silver spoon in her mouth.' I don't suppose she ever mentioned the trips we took to India and Greece when she was a young girl, or the month she spent in Monaco as a teenager."

Rowan mutely shook her head. She had no idea her mother had come from a wealthy family. She couldn't recall seeing any evidence of her mother's childhood.

Kitty's mouth tightened with irritation, and a storm stirred in her eyes. "Your father, on the other hand, came from Poco Way. Back when your mother first began dating him, it was a rather undesirable area in San Jose. We were afraid your father was only after your mother's inheritance. She thought we were being unfair and cruel when we insisted she stopped seeing him. Considering what we know about your father now, that he had already murdered several women before he had courted your mother, I stand firmly behind our skepticism."

"So you stopped talking to her because she wouldn't break up with her boyfriend?" Rowan hadn't intended for the question to come out sounding so harsh, but the situation left a bitter taste in the back of her throat.

Kitty let out a soft laugh. "That's not exactly how it played out. Your mother was blinded by love. Jonathan was a real charmer…made her believe they were destined for each other. Vanessa was angry that we wouldn't accept him, and therefore *she* cut *us* out of her life. We were unaware they had eloped and relocated to New York until we decided it was time to become concerned for your mother's wellbeing." Her gaze became distant. Forlorn. "By the time we'd located them, your mother was pregnant with you. Your father threatened to never let us see our grandchild if we didn't back off and let them initiate contact on their terms, when they were ready. Of course, his answer was always the same. There were always threats, and it was never a good time." Wincing, she lifted a wrinkled hand to her temple. "Oh, how I wish we wouldn't have listened to that vile man. I regret not hopping on an airplane and calling his bluff."

A bolt of rage rippled up Rowan's spine. It sounded as if they'd given into her father's threats without a fight. "Why didn't you come for me after he was arrested...after my mother was committed and I was sent away?"

"Your mother was adamant that we not get involved. I can't say why, but perhaps she was embarrassed. By the time we heard of her commitment, you were already living with Taylor. Because you didn't know us at the time, we were afraid it only would have caused you more trauma than you had already endured."

"I understand families sometimes become divided over disagreements, but I don't get how a mother could turn a blind eye to a daughter in desperate need of saving. Why haven't you at least come to visit?"

"Taylor didn't feel comfortable allowing it without your mother's blessing." In the warmth of the sunlight, Kitty's eyes sparkled with unshed tears. "But she's been kind enough to keep us updated on your life."

Guilt punched Rowan's gut. "Taylor didn't know I was coming to see you."

"I figured as much." Kitty reached for Rowan's hand. Her touch was cool, and her bones felt frail.

"We're so proud of the young woman you've become, Rowan. Through it all, you've maintained excellent grades, and seem to be thriving. Not everyone would be strong enough to survive your hardships."

Rowan wasn't sure how to take the compliment. She didn't think anyone had ever given her that level of praise. Although she wouldn't know how to describe her life so far, the idea that she was "thriving" felt ridiculous. It was impossible to conclude she was doing well when she was still afraid of her own shadow. With a stiff smile, she withdrew her hand from Kitty's to hug herself. "Do you know where I can find my other grandparents?"

Kitty's eyes turned cold as she lifted her narrow chin. "The last I'd heard of them, they'd moved away from Poco Way after your father was found guilty."

"I need to meet them. It's important to me."

"Then we'll hire a private investigator to locate them. In the meantime, you are welcome to stay here with us as long as you would like." Kitty patted Rowan's knee before standing. "I would enjoy the opportunity to get to know you better."

11

Silicon Valley housed nearly the same amount of golf courses as cutting edge tech companies. Some promised a challenging course with reasonable fees, while others had a reputation for excellent food and quiet driving ranges. Kelly Miller had played 18 holes nearly every week throughout his career, sometimes as a leisurely sport, but most often as a business tool with some of the world's wealthiest CEOs and their board members. After a day of entertaining half a dozen Japanese businessmen, he joined his wife and long-lost granddaughter for dinner prepared by the live-in chef.

Rowan's grandfather was broad and distinguished with sharp features and dark hair worn cropped on the sides and longer on top. While he projected more warmth than his wife, he was soft-spoken and let

Kitty do a majority of the talking. They didn't have much to say after Rowan explained her mission to them, although Kitty did squeeze her hand and flash a teary-eyed smile. By the end of the evening, Rowan felt enough of a connection with her estranged grandparents that she was confident the trip wouldn't be the last time they'd see each other.

She slept hard beneath the heavenly soft comforter in the guest bedroom, and didn't wake until after noon the next day. The bed was so comfortable and the room was so pretty that she took her time getting up and dressed. Kitty had left her a note on the kitchen island, written in perfect cursive—something Rowan struggled with, but was able to read with a little patience. She informed Rowan that their private investigator had already begun searching for her grandparents, and the chef would cook her whatever her heart desired at any time. Kitty had gone to her weekly bridge club, and Kelly was consulting for his previous employer, but they would both return in time for dinner. The letter was accompanied by an envelope of cash and their driver's phone number. Kitty suggested Rowan spend the afternoon enjoying the beach. The note concluded with, "we're so pleased you've come to us."

Although the past ten days had been grueling, she felt a bit lighter after honoring her father's victims the way she'd wanted. She was by no means happy and carefree, but the ball of dread that she'd felt since hearing about her father in Mr. Armstrong's class had loosened. She decided it would be okay to allow herself a little fun. She would move forward with memories of her father's victims safely tucked away in her heart, without forgetting their stories.

A handful of minutes after she called for a ride, her grandparents' driver, Emmett, arrived in khakis and a pale yellow polo shirt. He was a doughy man close to her grandparents' age with a baby face and a great sense of humor. Rowan sat in the front seat of the sparkly clean black SUV on the forty minute ride to Del Mar Beach, enjoying Emmett's stories involving her grandparents. He often took them to charity events, and was paid by the Millers to provide transportation to veterans whenever Kitty and Kelly didn't require his services. He mentioned neither of them were big drinkers, but Kitty occasionally indulged in a glass of champagne and would become giggly.

Emmett parked outside a large surf shop a mere block away from the public beach. Rowan used the cash from her grandparents to purchase a pink bikini with modest coverage, a small bottle of sunscreen, and a jug of water. She changed inside a nearby public bathroom and stuffed her belongings and a towel she'd brought from her grandparents' house into the free cloth bag they'd given her at the store. As she started for the beach, Emmett assured her he'd stay in the neighborhood to await her call.

The West Coast projected a more laid back vibe than Blue Bay, and the warm air felt dryer than out East. Amongst jagged cliffs and modern beach homes with oodles of windows, Rowan spread the towel in the rough sand away from other beachgoers, and applied sunscreen while keeping an eye on the hordes of surfers riding the intense waves. Although a layer of guilt remained prevalent as she let the sun soak into her already tanned skin, her stomach fluttered with excitement. She never dreamed she'd get to experience a local hangout while in California. She wondered if her parents had spent time either apart or together on that same beach. Had her father been a typical teenage boy, or had there always been a darkness within that prevented him from experiencing a normal life?

Hours later, she'd fallen asleep while people-watching, and woke when something nudged her arm. "Hey...Sleeping Beauty."

She brought her sunglasses up to rest on the top of her head, wincing as her eyes adjusted to the harsh sunlight before focusing on the figure towering over her. He was tall—six feet or more—with lean muscles, and his skin was deeply bronzed from endless hours in the sun. His pupils were lost in a set of round and widely-set, beautiful dark eyes beneath disheveled eyebrows. The wet, shaggy auburn hair framing his square face dripped down onto his wide shoulders, and his strong jaw sported at least a day's worth of stubble.

Based on his board shorts the same shade of blue as the clear sky and the white surfboard tucked beneath one arm, she realized she'd seen him riding the waves earlier, and thought he was cute. Although she'd still never dated or possessed any real interest in the opposite sex, her belly fluttered.

"You're gonna be the envy of all the lobsters," he told her in a rich, scratchy voice. He motioned to her body with his chin, then his beautiful eyes darted away as he shifted his stance. "Not that I was checking you or anything...I mean I'm not a pervert or...whatever. I was just walking past, and noticed..."

He possessed a chill, quiet ease about him that Rowan was instantly drawn to, and the favorable reaction took her by surprise. Aside from Drake and Andy, she tended not to trust men. But unlike the guys from her school in Blue Bay, this one wasn't overly cocky or sure of himself. She decided he was several years older—most likely in college.

Cheeks warm from both the sun and the sudden rush of affection, she straightened her spine to sit properly and snagged her shirt from her bag, draping it over her shoulders. "I didn't intend to fall asleep."

Charming dimples slid into his cheeks when he grinned. "That tends to happen a lot here."

She peered up at him through heavy eyelashes, fairly confident there wasn't anything unsavory he could do to her on a public beach. Still, she felt sheepish around anyone who wasn't her aunt or a member of the Lewis family. "Are you a local?" she guessed by his slight accent.

"I'm a San Diegonian, San Diegite, if you will, but I've recently relocated to a hotel just a little ways down the beach from here." He jammed the wide end of his surfboard into the sand and leaned back to shake more water from his hair. "I'm gonna take a wild guess and say you're not 'san' anything."

Detecting humor in his voice, she timidly shook

her head. "I'm from the East Coast. I'm here visiting my grandparents."

"I thought maybe you were going to say England, or—" He let out a quiet chuckle. "Never mind. They sent you here alone?"

All at once feeling awkward, she flashed a rehearsed smile and lifted one shoulder. She wasn't interested in delving into her personal details with a cute boy, and she worried he was beginning to mock her.

His eyes scanned the crowd as he asked, "I was just headed up to get some grub. How do you feel about fish tacos?"

"They put fish in tacos?" She wrinkled her nose, trying to imagine their taste. "I've never heard of such a thing."

His dimpled grin returned. "Then you're in for a treat." He extended a hand to her. "Come on, East Coast. I'm buying."

Scraping her bottom lip through her teeth, she eyed the lighthouse charm on her bracelet, hesitating to accept the offer. He seemed nice enough. Then again, everyone could've said the same about her father before he was caught. Unease swelled in her belly. What had she been thinking when she made the decision to visit the beach on her own? Did it make her brave, or downright foolish?

He pointed to a cluster of food trucks parked in the nearby road with lines 20 patrons deep. "The tacos are right over there. We can eat on one of their picnic tables, or come back here." He turned back to her with the palms of his hands exposed, and a sweet smile on his lips. "I promise I won't try anything weird. I can eat with one hand behind my back if it'll make you feel better. I just thought you'd maybe like some company since you're here by yourself."

Was it a pity invite? Maybe he thought she was too young to be there alone. But he was cute, and made her laugh. Deciding his company *would* be nice, as long as they remained around large groups of people, she finally nodded and tossed her belongings into her bag. Once she was on her feet, he scooped her bag up and threw it over his shoulder before retrieving his surfboard.

"How do you like it here?" he asked as they strolled side-by-side. "Other than the boring weather."

"It's…busy. The size of the crowd here is a little overwhelming. But I enjoyed watching the surfers. It looks like they're having a great time."

He turned to her, one thick eyebrow lifted. "You say that like you've never surfed."

"The waves in Blue Bay aren't this big."

"We have to remedy that, East Coast. *Immediately*. You can't come to visit California without giving surfing a try."

"*Me? Surf?*" Panic slithered through her guts, creating a greasy knot. "I—I don't think I'd be very good at it. I'm not a very good swimmer."

"You're in luck because I happen to be an excellent swimmer. Not quite triathlon worthy, but close. I wouldn't let you drown." He flashed her a natural, easy-going smile. His eyes caught the sunlight, sparkling with the brilliance of a thousand diamonds. Up close, their nut brown color melted beneath the sun into a liquid honey at the edges, and his angled nose hooked a little to one side. He was far more than just "cute" as she had first concluded from afar. "You should've seen me the first time I tried surfing. I was like a baby giraffe learning to ice skate." Then he nudged his arm against hers, causing a burst of tingles to travel down to her core. "You won't know if you're any good unless you give it a shot, right?"

"I'm not sure." Holding his dark stare, she attempted to mirror his smile, wondering why it suddenly felt so effortless. "Let's see how I do with these fish tacos of yours first, then I'll decide."

He nudged her again. "Why do I get the feeling you don't get out much, East Coast?"

The tacos ended up being delicious, and later her stomach and cheeks ached from hours of laughter. He'd tried his best to help her surf no matter how miserably she'd failed. She wasn't quite strong enough to pull herself up, and her coordination was off kilter. He eventually gave up and had her sit on the back of the board while he got down on his stomach to steer them ashore. She'd enjoyed the view, marveling at how the sinewy muscles in his back and arms worked with every stroke of his arms.

While she wrapped herself inside the towel from her grandparents' place, both the surfer and his board plopped down next to her in the sand.

"I think my stomach got the biggest workout of all," he admitted with one of his charming little grins. "You can probably rule out surfing as a hobby, but getting you out there was totally worth the entertainment."

With a rush of embarrassment, she dipped her chin down. "Was I worse than a baby giraffe on ice skates?"

"I plead the fifth on that one," he teased, holding

one hand up. "But you earned serious points for trying—especially when I didn't think you'd really let your hair down like that. Besides, just think how boring life would be if everything came easy. Sometimes it takes a good fall to remind us we're not infallible."

She wondered what obstacles he'd faced in his life—if they'd been anything close to what she'd experienced as a serial killer's daughter. Sometimes he spoke as if he'd lived a thousand lives, and sometimes he was as playful as a little kid.

The pad of his thumb brushed over one of her biceps, making her skin buzz delightfully warm. "You better get yourself some aloe before you go back to your grandparents' place. Hopefully they don't mistake you for dinner and toss you into a pot of boiling water."

Although she had slathered more lotion on a good twenty minutes before they'd gone out in the water, her skin was admittedly hot and sore. "I don't think I've ever burned before." Her mother never would've allowed it. She glanced back at the ocean, surprised to see the brilliant sun was sinking into the deep blue horizon. "Oh no! What time is it? I need to leave!"

Disappointment shone bright in his beautiful eyes. "You can't stay a little longer?"

The idea of watching the sunset with him sent a thrill through her. Hanging out with him had been as effortless as being around the Lewis family. She hadn't thought about her father and his victims, or anything about her messed up life the entire time they'd spent in the water. She'd merely existed and lived in the moment. She'd been unaware of how badly she needed to laugh and just *be* after carrying the weight of her father's heinous deeds on her shoulders.

"I'm sorry." She scrambled to collect her things. "My grandparents are expecting me back for dinner."

"And I'm guessing someone like you has never broken the rules before." With a chuckle, he stood and helped her fold her towel. "How'd you get here?"

"They dropped me off." She was too embarrassed to admit the truth. She didn't want him to think she was rich and spoiled when he was living in a hotel.

"Want a lift back? I could also *drive* with one arm behind my back."

Out of nowhere, a thought came to her, tensing her muscles with a fine tremor. Was that how her father had lured in some of his victims? Many of them had been ambushed, but with some it was believed he had charmed his way into earning their trust so they'd go elsewhere with him. The tacos sloshed in her stomach as a chilling shiver started at the base of her spine. This guy could be no different than her father had been at that age. Her father could've met one of his earlier victims from California on that very same beach.

All at once feeling horribly uneasy, she swooped down to gather her things and clutched them against her wet body. She avoided making eye contact as she started to walk away, knowing it would only take one of his cute little grins to change her mind. "I'm sorry, but I have to go," she called over her shoulder.

"Wait!" he called back. "Will you be back here tomorrow? You didn't even tell me your name!"

As she hurried her steps, she realized with a stab of disappointment that she didn't know his name either. They'd been so relaxed around each other introductions hadn't felt necessary.

12

Kitty Miller wasn't capable of cooking much beyond a simple pot of spaghetti, and her severe arthritis prevented her from doing basic household chores. But she found joy in growing different varieties of roses, and could often be found simply taking in their beauty from a chaise lounge in the backyard. She was most fond of her Rowan Rose Austin shrubs, and strived to grow perfect petals of the cupped, mid pink rosettes. The second morning of her granddaughter's stay, she cut enough stems to fill a delicate bowl, and set them on Rowan's nightstand. As she woke Rowan with the news that the investigator had located her paternal grandparents, the roses' delicate, fruity fragrance wafted around them.

"Iona and Sean Rivers relocated to a rural

community in South Dakota around the time of your father's conviction," she explained.

Feeling more awake, Rowan shoved the blanket aside and sat upright. "Do you have their address?"

"I do." Kitty threw her a shamelessly pleading look. "But won't you please stay here with us just one more day? At least let us fly you to South Dakota and back to Connecticut. We could arrange to have your car returned."

The fish tacos squirmed about in her stomach like they hadn't digested all the way. She was actually going to meet her father's parents. "I'm sorry, Grandma Kitty. As much as I loved getting to know you, I really need to go."

She stayed for lunch and exchanged teary-eyed goodbyes as Kitty promised they'd fly her back out over Christmas break for a visit. It wasn't until she checked into a hotel in Wyoming that she learned her grandparents had slipped a five thousand dollar check into her suitcase. It was accompanied by another note written in perfect cursive, stating they realized money couldn't make up for all the years they'd lost, but they hoped it was a start. They'd each signed their names under the salutation, "with our eternal love." As strange as it felt to receive that generous of a gift from someone she had just met,

Rowan burst into tears. She'd spent years wondering if any of her blood relatives cared whether she lived or died. The relationship she'd formed with Kitty and Kelly could've been the start of something significant.

While staring up at the motel's grungy ceiling, she put much thought into whether she should rip the check into pieces, or place the money toward her college education. Most of the universities she had her eye on were expensive—probably out of her league as she wanted to pay the tuition on her own. It would be too much of a burden for Taylor, and Rowan didn't want a cent of her parents' money if anything remained. Once Taylor got over Rowan's decision to visit her grandparents behind her back, she would give her unbiased advice. As far as she knew, Rowan had spent the past several days resting up in California before she started the trip home. She'd never intentionally lied to Taylor about anything too major, and only considered it a white lie. After all, she *had* spent much of the time recharging her spirits.

After passing countless fields growing leafy green crops Rowan couldn't identify, she rolled into her paternal grandparents' acreage in southern South Dakota just before sunset. At the end of a long gravel driveway, a small, mossy green house in dire need of painting was surrounded by wide, green pastures in which four horses frolicked and lazily munched on grass. A tabby cat slept on the hood of a rusted 2-door car parked in the driveway, barely lifting its head to assess the commotion with the sound of Rowan's engine.

Even though her adventures in the prior two weeks had given her a new sense of confidence, she was terrified to meet the people who had raised her father. The unannounced visit felt like an invasion of the worst kind. Her fears were validated when a short, elderly man came bursting from the house, brandishing a shotgun in the crook of his arm. "You a reporter?"

Rowan's lips parted. The man was a shorter and much older version of her father, with snowy white hair instead of strawberry blond. The angles of their features and broad shape of their faces were quite similar, only this man's face was marked with sharp wrinkles. He was at least a decade older than her maternal grandparents, and moved in a gingerly gait with a slightly hunched back.

"N-no, sir," she stuttered.

The man gripped the shotgun firmly in his hands.

"Then who the hell are you, and what the hell do you want?"

The screen door behind him creaked. An even older woman in a long padded coat with gray hair fixed into a neat bun on top of her head slipped out of the house behind him. Sadness shone in her eyes, as well as in the way she carried herself.

The woman poked the man with her elbow. "Put that away, you fool. Don't you see it?"

The man scowled back at her. "See what?"

"She's a mirror image of her daddy...only with her momma's tiny nose and beauty. God willing she inherited Vanessa's humanity too."

Rowan's locked her gaze with the woman's, and they shared a tentative smile as Rowan stepped closer. "So you *are* my grandparents?"

Iona responded with a slow nod.

Although Sean repositioned the shotgun with the barrel aimed at the ground, he still didn't appear too friendly. "Sienna?"

"I go by Rowan now," she told him.

"How on earth did you find us?" Iona asked a moment later.

"I drove to California to meet my grandma and grandpa Miller. When I told them I wanted to meet you too, they hired a private investigator."

"At least they put all that money to good use for a change." Iona rolled her eyes to the darkening sky. "Although it's discouraging to learn a P.I. was able to track us down when we thought we'd been so careful."

"I know all the horrible details of what my father did to those women," Rowan blurted. "I want to know what he was like before—as a kid. I want someone to tell me the gentle man I knew as a little girl wasn't a total lie. I need to know a part of the father I loved was human."

Iona's chest rose with a tired, heavy sigh. She exchanged an unsure glance with her husband before wrapping the long coat tightly around her frail body. "Since you came all this way, you better come in and settle in for the night. We'll talk in the morning."

Neither of her grandparents offered any physical contact once she retrieved her suitcase from her car and joined them on the narrow front steps. They stood aside as she entered their small home ripe with the stench of cigarette smoke. A little living room featuring an ancient couch and tattered recliner facing a small television blended into a kitchen hardly big enough for the basic appliances and a table for two. Down a small hallway, she noted there were only two doors. With nothing hanging on the dark paneled walls and a heavily worn carpet, the house projected a bleak vibe. Rowan wondered if her grandparents were truly poverty-stricken, or if they lived simple as a way to punish themselves for raising a diabolical man.

"I'm afraid we don't have anything to offer you other than the sofa," Iona said while lighting a fresh cigarette clamped between her teeth. "Bathroom's first door in the hallway. While you do your business, I'll grab you a blanket."

By the time Rowan finished relieving herself of her last energy drink in the outdated bathroom, the lights were out and the house was quiet. With the guidance of the pale moonlight shining through the only window in the living room, she found her way back to the couch. Discovering it stunk of something unbearable, she curled into a ball on the chair and silently cried herself to sleep.

THE AROMA of bacon and the clanging of pans pulled Rowan from a light sleep. She rubbed the sleep from her eyes and saw her grandmother standing at the stove.

"Hope you slept all right," Iona called out over her shoulder. "You didn't look too comfortable."

"I'm sorry to have imposed on you like this. If I had known of any way to contact you ahead of time—"

"Don't matter. You're kin." Iona waved a fork through the air. "Breakfast will be a while—a good hour at the very least. Your grandpa ran into town to get flour and milk for pancakes. I made some bacon to tide you over."

"You didn't have to go to so much trouble."

"Nonsense. You need to eat. Today was grocery day anyhow. It's always a production to run to the store when we're so far removed from civilization. Besides, I wanted to send your grandpa away so we could engage in real talk. He still doesn't believe Jonathan could've hurt those women, even after sitting through all the wretched testimony at his trial, proving he'd done it all."

Rowan fingered the edge of her frayed jean shorts. "It must've been hard for both of you...especially after they found him guilty. Is that why you moved here?"

"We had no other choice. Jonathan's legal defense bled us dry, and your grandpa inherited this shack from his aunt."

Rowan's heart surged. "You paid for his attorney?"

Iona leaned away from the stove to grab a pack of cigarettes, and slipped one between her lips. "I prayed for his innocence, but it was all done in vain. Sorry if the smoke bothers you. I picked up the filthy habit during the trial. I needed something to calm my nerves. Now I can't seem to quit." She slid the full pan of bacon onto a plate before holding a lighter up to her cigarette. "Come have a seat. Would you like some apple juice?"

"That'd be great." Rowan's stomach rumbled as she made her way over to one of the chairs at the small table. She'd dropped a good ten pounds since leaving Blue Bay, and would never hear the end of it from Taylor. "Thank you."

Iona set the bacon on a plate between them, grinning through a haze of smoke as Rowan eagerly snagged a piece to nibble on. "You have good manners. Your momma did a good job of raising you."

"I've been living with my mom's best friend since the night my father was arrested," Rowan replied in a matter-of-fact tone. "I don't really remember whether or not my mother taught me to be polite.

The memories I have of my parents fade a little more with every year."

"Anything before that night feels like a lifetime ago," Iona mused, tapping her cigarette into an ashtray. "Can't tell you how many times I've wished it had all been a bad dream. For the longest time I even wished the good Lord would take me so I wouldn't have to live with the truth any longer."

The bacon stuck inside Rowan's throat. "Did you know? I mean…when he was little, or a teenager, did you get a sense that something might be wrong with him?"

"Your daddy started out in life as a sweet baby and a curious toddler. As he got older, I sensed he had a dark side. He had a horrible temper that would appear out of nowhere, and it was always directed at women—never his father or brother." Iona's eyes glossed over as she paused to suck on her cigarette. "One time…when he was around nine or ten, I caught him torturing the neighbor's cocker spaniel. I won't go into the horrific details of what he was doing to that poor dog, but believe me, it wasn't good. I promised him I wouldn't tell his daddy if he promised to never harm another animal. I figured the good in him would override the bad. My Jonathan liked to help me garden and was always doing his chores without being nagged. He'd cuddle up with me while I read him stories, and begged me to take him on day trips to visit the ocean." With a pained look, she inhaled more of the cigarette. "Makes me ill to think I'm the one who introduced him to Spider Lilies…used to be my favorite. Now I can't even look at them without losing my lunch."

"I know what you mean," Rowan muttered, finally able to swallow the bacon.

"Up until the thing with the neighbor's dog, if someone had told me my sweet boy would be capable of murder, I wouldn't have believed them. He had me fooled. His daddy, too. As he got older, I secretly started to fear him. He grew increasingly cruel when we were alone. No one knew I felt that way, although I sometimes think Jonathan sensed it. There was an incident his junior year after I'd grounded him for failing a class, and he had a date to the spring dance with your momma. He wrapped his hands around my throat and squeezed so tight that I truly believed I was going to die. For whatever reason, he finally released me right before I passed out, and went to the dance anyway. After that, he stopped coming around…I figured he'd found a place to stay with older friends. I didn't ask. I was glad I didn't have to fear him anymore. We discovered your momma had been sneaking him into their pool house at night. Once your grandparents found out, your daddy talked your momma into running away with him."

"Had you seen him since?"

"Not until the trial. The man I saw…the one I've visited several times in prison…that isn't my Jonathan. I truly believe the darkness in him has taken over any part of him that was still good." Iona reached across the table to take Rowan's hand. "It's time you mourn the loss of your daddy, kiddo. I truly believe the man you loved as a little girl isn't ever coming back."

The candid conversation with her grandma Iona would be Rowan's last. Two weeks after Rowan returned to Blue Bay, Taylor received a call from a funeral director in South Dakota. Iona had died of a massive heart attack due to untreated heart disease, and her husband died of unspecified causes two days later.

13

During the two weeks in which the kids from Blue Bay's high school and elementary were on Christmas break, the town nearly became as lively as in the summertime. Snowshoeing, hiking, skating, cross-country skiing, ice fishing, snow tubing—the young children and teens never seemed to sit still, and filled the city streets like ants on a log. Rowan's senior year, she was somewhat disappointed she'd be missing out on her last year of partaking in the annual activities as she packed for her grandparents' in California.

She'd kept in close contact with her mother's parents since her first visit. Kitty called several times every week, sometimes with Kelly on speakerphone. Once every month Rowan would receive a letter—always written in her grandmother's elegant cursive, and always accompanied by a generous check. At first Rowan planned to reject the money, feeling as if she didn't deserve it. Then Taylor sat her down to explain the extent of Kitty and Kelly's wealth, and encouraged her to politely accept their charity. She also disclosed the fact that they'd been sending Taylor money to cover the expenses of raising Rowan since shortly after her father was sent to prison.

By the time she was settled back inside her grandparents' guest room with the fluffy comforter and big walnut bed, she no longer cared that she was missing out on Blue Bay's activities. Some days, she'd lounge beside the pool and read while her grandmother tended to her flowers. On others, Kitty took her shopping and spoiled her with new clothes and jewelry. On the three days her grandparents were busy, she returned to the beach and watched the surfers for hours, hoping to be reunited with the honey-eyed cutie.

Her last night in Los Gatos, she nibbled on swordfish and roasted vegetables beneath a star-filled sky in her grandparents' backyard. A few minutes into the meal, Kitty said to her, "Your grandfather and I would like to pay for your college education."

Rowan dropped her fork onto her plate and stared back at her grandmother, dumbfounded. By that time, she had applied to several community colleges within driving distance from Taylor's, and planned to balance the first two years with several jobs so she could afford the final two years of a creative writing degree at NYC.

"The gift of your tuition comes with one condition," Kitty explained as Rowan stayed mute. "You must choose a university within reasonable driving distance from our home. The choice lies with you whether you want to live here with us or on campus, but we'd like you to come by for dinner every Sunday either way. Lord knows you could stand to gain a few pounds, and we've missed out on so much of our only grandchild's life already. If you'd be so kind as to accept our offer, we would cherish your company...immensely."

Kelly gently nudged her side with his elbow. "We'd love to have you, kiddo! How can you say no to living in the sunshine year-round?"

Rowan glanced back and forth between her grandparents, wondering how they could appear so normal when they sounded so insane. Kitty sat ramrod straight in her chair, every single white hair in place and pale pink pantsuit neatly pressed. Kelly wore his usual golf attire, and the creases around his eyes deepened with his dazzling white smile. In the ten days she'd stayed with them, she had started to see beyond Kitty's cool demeanor and Kelly's quiet nature. They were both kind hearted, and seemed equally pleased to have her around.

She shook her head as tears burned behind her eyes. "I couldn't possibly—"

"It was either that or a second vacation home in Maui," Kelly teased, throwing her a wink. "We both chose your education."

With tears glistening in her eyes, Kitty set her hand over Rowan's. "You've had enough hardships in this lifetime, dear child. It would be our honor to help you achieve your dream of becoming a published author."

She considered the offer for an entire week after she'd returned to Blue Bay before she gracefully accepted. Early into the New Year, Taylor took her to dinner in Manhattan to celebrate when she received an acceptance letter to California Bay University. It was her first choice as the tuition was more affordable, and their creative writing program received great praise. Within a month, she was registered for classes in the fall.

Rowan and Taylor followed her father's appeal through updates from Detective Novak. She assured them nothing would happen anytime soon as the process could take years. Rowan threw her frustration into writing, and continued to write every free moment of her senior year. With Kinsley off at drama school in New York, and Drake directing his first B-movie in Hollywood, her social life had been reduced to dinner only a few times each month with Steph and Andy, and trips into the city to visit Kinsley. The desire to release the stories going through her head kept her planted behind the laptop purchased with one of her grandparents' checks.

Taylor was moved to tears whenever she'd read one of the stories, and proclaimed Rowan to be the best author since Hemingway. Even though she knew her aunt's praise was a gross exaggeration, the positive feedback from her composition teacher had also been favorable.

Dr. Walters was the only one who knew the heartwarming stories Rowan wrote of were fictionalized versions of what her father's victims may have lived on to become...a stripper who works her way through nursing school and meets the love of her life in the ER...a teacher who starts an after-school program for less fortunate kids and receives national awards for her efforts...a dental hygienist who battles with the highs and lows of empty-nesting after both of her sons enlist in the military. Each story held a special meaning. Each one was carefully crafted to honor the women who had been taken too soon. She poured her heart into giving them the happily ever after that had been stolen from them.

Several weeks after a small graduation party held in Taylor's backyard, Rowan packed her belongings into the back of a used Jeep she'd also purchased with her grandparents' checks. Many tears were shed as she wished the neighbors and her aunt farewell before hitting the road with Kinsley at her side. The friends-turned-sisters took their time on the country-wide adventure, tenting in national parks and exploring the different sites each state had to offer.

It was a much different trip than the one Rowan had embarked on the previous year, and memorable for only good reasons—her favorite being the cute farm boy from Iowa who finally gave Rowan her first kiss one late night beside a group campfire. Although she found it to be a little slimy and a lot awkward, she was relieved she could finally stop lying to Kinsley about the imaginary kisses she'd shared over the years, including one with the honey-eyed surfer in California. Kinsley had lost her virginity at fifteen and was constantly after Rowan to lose hers. Rowan swore to herself she'd never allow sex to be casual, and would wait until she met someone she felt she could fully trust. It was her greatest fear that a man like that didn't exist.

They arrived at Rowan's grandparents' in time for the 4th of July celebrations, ending the holiday with an impressive fireworks show put on by the city. Over the next several afternoons before Kinsley flew back to New York, they visited Del Mar Beach where Rowan kept a close eye—bordering on obsessive—on the surfers. She put all of her energy into willing the honey-eyed surfer to find her again. Several times she convinced herself she'd spotted him, only to be disappointed when it turned out to be someone else. At one point, she decided his gig living and working in the nearby hotel must've been a temporary stop on the way to something bigger. It was probably for the best anyway since she'd put on a handful of pounds since their last encounter.

Living with her grandparents after Kinsley left required some serious adjustments. It was more challenging to purge her calories in private without someone noticing, and her nightmares returned. Once again, she'd become paralyzed with shadows creeping across her bedroom walls. During the first semester, a round of homesickness became so crippling that she struggled to pass four out of five of her classes. Then her grandparents flew her back to Blue

Bay for a week during Christmas break, and the time spent with Taylor and the Lewis family refueled her spirits enough to excel in the remainder of her freshman year.

As her relationship with her grandparents began to grow, so did her love for writing. She divided the following summer between crafting new stories with the advanced elements of writing she'd learned in college, waitressing at her grandparents' favorite fine-dining restaurant, and volunteering at a local shelter for abused women and their children. She was most content when consoling the victims, and even contemplated changing her major to something in social services.

She quickly befriended Harlow Thomas, another volunteer from Los Angeles who had also just finished her freshman year at California Bay University. Harlow's boundless energy and openness reminded Rowan a little of Kinsley, although the two women's physical characteristics couldn't have been any different. Harlow was biracial, inheriting a degree of her father's mocha skin and thick dark hair along with her mother's graceful cheekbones and almond-shaped, deep blue eyes. A small part of Rowan was jealous of her new friend's stunning looks. A bigger part of her was paranoid as Harlow tended to draw extra attention from men of all ages when they were together.

On the rare days she didn't have any commitments, Rowan would either visit Harlow's apartment in Redwood City, or they'd meet up on Del Mar Beach. Rowan's hope of seeing the honey-eyed surfer from two years prior waned that summer—especially after a group of local surfers swarmed Harlow one afternoon, and a dark-haired one with intense eyes had caught Rowan's eye. By the time he approached her that same night when they crashed a bonfire on the beach, the honey-eyed cutie became a distant memory.

"Rowan, right?" he asked, lifting both his plastic cup and his thick brows. The deep rumble of his voice made her toes curl. Mossy green eyes and dazzling white teeth shone in the fire's intense light when he grinned. "I'm Koby."

Behind her own plastic cup, she threw him a curt smile. "I remember." She took a small sip of the malty drink Harlow had handed her, wondering how anyone could possibly enjoy the taste of whiskey. It burned down to her stomach with the appeal of gasoline. "Do you and your friends have these parties often?"

He shrugged. "I just met this crew." He stopped

to chug down the rest of his drink, then pinned her in place with a stare. "Harlow mentioned you moved here last year from the East Coast. Guess that explains why I hadn't seen anyone so beautiful until you started coming around."

The pickup line made her inwardly cringe, but his wide smile chipped at a little of the ice around her cautious heart. Still, she wasn't totally sure how to engage in conversation with someone she found mildly attractive. She secretly willed Harlow to stop flirting with one of the other surfers across the fire pit long enough to save her from the awkward encounter. "Have you always lived in California?"

"Since birth." His grin momentarily waned. "My parents brought me to this beach almost every day when I was a kid." He gazed past her to the dark ocean lit by the tiniest sliver of moonlight, then his eyes once again locked with hers. With the return of his enduring grin, her heart sped. "Wanna go for a swim?"

Eyes wide, her breath caught. "Now?"

"Why not?" His fingertips brushed over her forearm when he leaned in closer. "I'd like a little alone time to get to know you better."

Blushing, she studied the broad contouring of his jaw and his chiseled cheekbones, deciding he was several years older than the other surfers he hung around. There was something especially sexy about the way he carried himself like an older man rather than the mindless partiers she'd met on campus. Yet it made the fact that she wasn't comfortable with her body that much worse. She didn't have large breasts like the women she'd seen him flirting with on the beach earlier, and her waist was several inches too wide. "I don't have a suit on."

"It's dark enough that no one will see...I won't even try to sneak a look." He leaned in a little more, brushing his warm lips over her earlobe as he spoke. "Come on, Rowan. I promise to show you a good time."

She wasn't sure if it was the buzz from the whiskey, or the flutter of attraction in her gut that made her agree to strip down to her underwear. It felt as if she was deeply immersed inside a dream when she walked hand-in-hand into the water with the attractive stranger, continuing on until the roar of the ocean overpowered the music and laughter of their friends. Despite her squeals when the icy cold water reached her belly, he continued to pull her even deeper. Trepidation spread through her chest when she glanced at the fierce set of waves ahead. "Koby...I'm not the best swimmer."

"You're safe with me."

She continued deeper until the frigid water felt like an iron fist around her lungs. Lip caught between her teeth, she hesitated. Glancing over her shoulder, she tried to find Harlow among those gathered around the orange flames licking at the jet-black sky. What was she doing?

Right when she was going to turn back around, a wave came crashing down on them. The connection of their hands was broken. The current sucked her under. Blind panic closing her throat made it impossible to think. She waved her arms and legs, refusing to slip quietly into her death—not without a fight. She hadn't survived her father's infamy to die young, before her life had any real sort of meaning.

Next thing she knew, she was yanked through the water until her head surfaced. She coughed and sputtered into the freezing cold air as a set of hands clamped down on her biceps. "Rowan! Holy shit! Are you okay?"

Her eyes flipped open to meet the look of concern spreading over Koby's broad face. She nodded amidst another cough, and he pulled her close against his muscled chest, folding his arms around her back. "I'm so sorry. That wave came out of nowhere."

She flung her arms around his neck, gripping him like a koala to a tree. The warm embrace quickly calmed her severed nerves, and stilled her chattering teeth. They stayed wrapped in each other for several moments before he tilted his head back, holding her gaze in the waning light. He leaned in, wet lips capturing hers. His breath was hot, and the taste of booze and weed was strong on his tongue. Fire blazed through her belly. She wanted more. From the bulge in his boxers that brushed against her thigh, she was certain he wanted more too.

He leaned away, beautiful lips spread with a wide smile. "Let's get you back by the fire. You're freezing."

After that night, Rowan convinced Harlow to meet up with Koby and the other surfers more often. Although Rowan wasn't ready to spend time alone with him on dates as he kept requesting, their kisses grew more frantic with every beach encounter. There were days she considered herself lucky to have found someone who could see past her insecurities and odd behaviors. Other days, she couldn't believe she was allowing herself to fall for him.

14

Once fall weather in San Francisco began to sneak in, the average temperature between day and night sometimes varied around a 20 degree difference. Although the visits with Koby and his friends on the beach became less frequent because of the colder temps, Rowan finally agreed to meet with Koby alone. Over burgers and chocolate shakes two blocks from the beach, the sparks between them only intensified. Still, after things got hot and heavy outside of the restaurant, she insisted he walk her to her car, and they call it a night.

With only ten days before fall semester would begin, Harlow's roommate announced she was moving back to Nevada, leaving Harlow alone to cover the apartment's steep rent. At the next Sunday dinner, Rowan threw out feelers to her grandparents before confessing her desire to move in with her friend. As long as she promised to continue the Sunday tradition, they promised not to hold any ill-will when she moved out of their home.

After Rowan was settled in the new apartment, Harlow decided they needed to celebrate. Koby and the others brought alcohol, and they partied late into the night. Koby kept Rowan close, often holding her in his lap. Later, when some of their friends began passing out, he led her out onto the small balcony where they kissed and groped each other for nearly an hour. Rowan was already warm and fuzzy all over from countless vodka lemonades by the time he made her achy with desire. Getting close to him had felt reckless at first. By that night, she was beginning to think he might actually be one of the good guys.

Her breath caught when his fingers slipped beneath the wire on her bra, stroking the underside of her bare breast. "Let's take this party into your bedroom," he panted into her ear.

She felt as if she was moving underwater when she followed him through the living room and into her new bedroom. Once the door was closed behind them, he pulled her in close for a deep kiss. She tangled her fingers in his thick dark hair, and let herself get lost in the moment. She cherished the way he kissed her with urgent passion and desire—as if he couldn't get enough. As if he wanted to devour her.

"You look good enough to eat," he confirmed, tugging his t-shirt over his head and tossing it on the hardwood floor. "I really wanna be with you, babe... in the worst way." He coaxed her down to her brand-new mattress, pressing his gloriously tanned chest against her as they rolled around, continuing with passion-fueled kisses. Her toes curled and her belly glowed with want. He eased her little beaded top over her head, gently untangling her dark curls from the silky material. Her stomach twisted with unease. No one had seen her completely naked since she'd been little and couldn't bathe herself. All at once, she heard her mother's voice scolding her on how much she'd let herself go. When she covered her bare stomach, he nudged her arms away and his mossy green eyes dusted over her chest. "I hadn't expected you to be this hot."

"Wait," she pleaded as he began to undo the hook on her bra. She carefully nudged him down to his back and straddled him, holding her bra in place with one hand. The room was spinning, and vodka burned her throat. She knew next to nothing about the good looking surfer with intense eyes. She had avoided asking him personal questions, knowing he'd likely want answers about her in return. The extent of her knowledge ended with the fact that he lived close enough to Del Mar Beach to walk, and he fixed cars at his dad's auto shop. His actual age and his home life remained a mystery. With a start, she realized she had only learned his last name was Snyder a few hours ago. "We're moving too fast...I barely know you."

"We're not gonna get any better acquainted with you way up there." Winking, he reached for her hand and drew her over him. "Come back down here, beautiful, and give me those sweet lips."

Protest died in her throat as the kissing and undressing continued. He was so handsome with his shirt off and hair askew, and she was drunk enough to forget she'd only known him a handful of weeks, or that she'd vowed to only to sleep with someone she loved.

The remainder of her first night in the new apartment with Koby became a hazy blur of lost memories. She would only remember wondering if any of her father's earlier victims had gone to bed with him willingly.

THE SECOND MONDAY IN OCTOBER, Detective Novak called Rowan with the news that her father's attorney had filed an appeal with the New York State appellate court. "It doesn't mean he'll actually be released any time soon. They're simply saying there were errors in the trial that require reversal. It's a long, drawn-out process."

Anxiety and paranoia began to plague Rowan on a new level. She slept with every light in her bedroom on, and refused to venture outside after dark. She found any and every excuse not to get together with Koby. Both her social life and her focus on school went by the wayside.

A few days after the detective's call, all four of Rowan's Jeep's tires were slashed, and a rock was thrown through her apartment several days after that. She began to fear that maybe her father actually *had* been released, despite Detective Novak's assurance that he was still in prison. The building super hired a security guard to monitor the property, and her streak of "bad luck" quickly concluded. Harlow was convinced the two incidents were random acts performed by different thugs.

After several phone sessions with Dr. Walters in Blue Bay, it was decided Rowan should meet in person with a psychiatrist in San Francisco. Her medication was adjusted, and she soon resumed a quasi-normal life. Her grandparents had persuaded her to give up the waitressing job when they sensed she was struggling, but she continued to volunteer several hours each week at the shelter. She returned to Blue Bay for a week over Christmas break to learn Taylor's beloved Westie had gone blind and wasn't doing well. Once Rowan convinced her aunt it was time to let Scotch go, she accompanied her to the vet the next day. They sobbed in each other's arms as the sweet dog took his last breath.

Early into the spring semester, Rowan was in charge of intake at the shelter when a wounded mother and her two teenage children came seeking asylum. The mother had narrowly escaped death at the hands of the father, and was too afraid to report the incident to the police. The mom was taken to the hospital for treatment of her serious stab wounds, and Rowan was left in charge of the traumatized children.

She felt an instant kinship with Wren and Stormy, the knobby-kneed brother and sister who shared the same date of birth, only a year apart. When two police detectives came to question the siblings about their father, details of the night the detective had questioned Rowan after her father's arrest returned with blinding clarity.

You called the cops on your own father?

You little bitch!

After all I've done for you, this is how you repay me?

She wiped her damp palms on her thighs, focusing on the present instead of slipping further into the past. These kids needed her. After the detectives left, she fed them pizza and soda. It was unnerving how normal the pair seemed. She didn't have to be an expert to understand their lives were full of violence.

"Our in-house counselor will be here tomorrow if you want to talk about what happened with someone who can help," Rowan told them between sips of her soda. "You're welcome to talk to me about it, but I'm not a professional or anything."

Wren, an acne-plagued fifteen-year-old with a sharp nose and greasy brown hair that hung in his eyes, looked down at the slice of pepperoni in his hand when he shrugged. "It's nothing we hadn't been through before."

"We'll be fine," Stormy agreed, reaching for another slice of pizza. Despite hollowed cheeks and a protruding collarbone, she was a cute fourteen-year-old with dainty facial features and warm brown eyes that deemed her pretty in a haunting way. The way they wolfed the pie down, Rowan wondered when they'd last eaten. "Every time Daddy threatens to kill her, they make up the next day."

"Only this time mom won't be around the next day, and neither will dad," Wren scolded, throwing his sister a scowl. "Those detectives were on their way to throw him in jail, dummy."

"Calling your sister names isn't helping anything," Rowan told him, suddenly jealous she didn't have a big brother or *any* siblings. It might've made losing her parents a little more tolerable. "You're lucky you have each other. Your mom could be in the hospital for awhile, and your dad could be in jail for even longer. Nothing about this will be easy for you."

Wren snorted and rolled his chocolate eyes. "I'm sure they tell you to say that kind of stuff to kids like us, but what do you know, lady?"

She held the surly teen's gaze. "You'd be surprised."

He tossed the rest of his pizza slice onto his plate. "Try me."

"My dad is serving several life sentences in prison, and my mom basically abandoned me when I was eleven."

Both kids stared at her, slacked jawed. "For real?" Stormy asked after a minute, tucking her stick-straight brown hair behind both ears.

"For real," Rowan confirmed. "So if you ever want to talk to someone who understands, whether I'm here or not, you can call me. I'll give you my personal number before my shift is over."

Wren's scraggly eyebrows shot upward. "What did your dad do?"

Rowan flashed a sad smile. She didn't feel comfortable revealing her secret with them, but she didn't want to lie to them either. "He hurt a lot of people."

In the middle of the night, Wren and Stormy's mom died. Her husband had pierced several of her internal organs, and the surgeon was unable to stop the bleeding. Stormy called Rowan the next morning, sobbing. Rowan skipped her classes to be with the siblings as they grieved. It broke her heart to learn no one would be coming for them as arrangements for emergency foster care were made.

Rowan vowed to stay in touch with the Martin kids, and it was a promise she kept. She visited them every week at their different placements, bearing little gifts each time. Stormy was a budding artist who burned through painting supplies once Rowan had taught her the basics. She even took an interest in running alongside Rowan to strengthen her body. Wren developed a passion for music, and spent hours lifting weights while listening to the songs Rowan burned onto CDs for the portable player she'd given him.

As Harlow dated guy after guy, determined to find The One, Rowan formed a bond with Wren and Stormy that she knew would last for years to come. They'd begun to think of her as a big sister, and were always calling her for advice. After their father was sentenced to twenty years in prison for their mother's death, their calls became more frequent.

Once spring semester was over and the days became longer, Rowan resumed her job at the restaurant, and spent a good portion of her free time with Wren and Stormy. They'd been placed with a wealthy couple in downtown San Francisco whose own adult children had left home, and seemed content. They appeared healthier and happier in their new surroundings. They'd made new friends in the neighborhood, and Wren had begun to date a girl from his new school. They'd each found jobs for the summer to keep them busy, and thrived on their hobbies. A few times Stormy came to volunteer at the shelter alongside Rowan.

One especially warm weekday in July, Rowan picked them up from their foster home in her Jeep, and they headed to the beach for the afternoon. While Stormy and Wren took turns jumping the waves on a bodyboard, Rowan kicked back in the sand and lost herself in a thick novel about the French Revolution. She was so engrossed in the story that she nearly peed herself with fright when a deep voice said, "I didn't think I'd ever see you again."

The frantic beats of her heart slowed somewhat as Koby jammed a surfboard into the sand between them. Until that moment, she didn't realize how much she'd missed seeing him in his element with board shorts and bare feet. The way his dark, wet hair hung in his eyes—several inches longer than the last time she'd seen him—and his fit chest glistened with water droplets, she was reminded of how turned on she'd been the night he'd suggested they go into her bedroom. Wetting her lips, she set the book facedown in her lap. "Koby, hello. I—"

"I don't understand what happened, Rowan." Wet arms crossed over his large pectorals, he cast her a look that seemed more hurt than angry. "Why'd you blow me off after we slept together?"

Fighting against the slight tremor in her stomach,

her eyes flickered beyond him to where Wren and Stormy playfully splashed in the water. She didn't know how to end a relationship any more than she'd known how to get it started. "I had a great time with you, Koby. It's just...I guess I wasn't in a place in my life where I could get involved with someone. I'm sorry if I led you on."

"I'm sorry too." His mossy green eyes briefly closed before he plopped down at her side. "I thought we were pretty great together. I mean, it was hot." His voice deepened when he whispered, "All that kissing and fooling around..."

Dipping her chin to hid her burning cheeks, she nodded timidly. Why did her body have to betray her mind? She was dead set against being with him, yet she couldn't deny she still felt a pull toward his hard body. With a line of sweat forming along her forehead, she silently willed him to go away.

"We could give it another try...keep it casual," he said. "I'll go at whatever pace you want."

"With school and work, I don't have any time to spare." Her tone was firm despite the trembling of her body. "I'm truly sorry."

"I miss you, beautiful. I miss your dreamy lips... that sweet body..." Leaning against her, he slowly dragged his fingertips along her bare thigh, leaving a trail of fire on her skin. "Give me another chance. Ten minutes somewhere private, and I'll remind you of how good we had it. My car is parked just down the street."

Pain spread through her chest as the beach swayed before her. Visions of her father luring his victims in a similar way made it impossible to breathe. Frantic for help, her eyes sought out Wren and Stormy. She discovered Wren watching in the distance, eyebrows knit with concern. When he started marching toward them, Koby sat taller at her side and leaned away, chuckling. "A little young for you, isn't he?"

"He's a kid from the shelter. I can't go anywhere with you because I'm on the clock," she lied. "And anyway, it's over between us. You're a handsome and charming guy, Koby. I can't imagine you'll have any problem moving on with someone else."

"If that's how you really feel, I guess I don't have any other choice." He climbed back to his feet and grabbed his surfboard. "It was nice knowing you." Before he left her alone, his intense green eyes held hers for so long that she felt forced to look away.

Moments later, Wren wrapped one of the towels from Rowan's beach bag over his dripping shoulders. "Who was that dude?"

Rowan flashed him one of her pageant-friendly smiles. "Someone I used to date."

"You sure didn't look too happy to see him. There's no color left in your face."

"The sun's starting to get to me is all." She motioned to Stormy in the distance. "Go grab your sister. There's enough time to stop for ice cream before we head back to the city."

As soon as Wren turned his back on her, she gulped in shallow breaths of air. She told herself to be rational, that Koby wasn't her father. After she returned to her apartment early that evening, it took several weeks before Harlow was able to convince her to go outside again.

15

Shortly after Rowan had met the Martin siblings, she'd begun to journal her experience as a serial killer's daughter—something Dr. Stacy, her new psychiatrist, had suggested. The story quickly took on a life of its own, becoming dozens of pages in length. That fall, at the start of her junior year, she accidentally turned the manuscript into an English professor in place of their assigned essay. It wasn't until she was summoned into his office the next day that she'd realized her mistake.

Professor Robinson was a willowy black man in his 50s with graying temples and a wry sense of humor. Rowan took an instant liking to his slow, Louisiana drawl and the way he spoke about writing like it was the most noble and exciting career a person could embark on. From behind a masculine oak desk, he greeted her with an easy smile when she entered his office. She wasn't surprised to find him surrounded by shelves stuffed with books.

"Have a seat, Miss Brooks. I wanted to speak to you about the manuscript you emailed for this week's assignment." He motioned to a large stack of papers in front of him. "I didn't grasp the scope of what I was reading until I was several pages in. At that point, I was far too invested to stop." Behind his wire-rimmed glasses, his dark eyes studied her as she sat. "I must say you have a natural gift for prose. I'm assuming, however, the story about your father being the SLS killer was submitted unintentionally."

Horror burned Rowan's face as she shot back up onto her feet. "I'm sorry, Professor! It was an accident! I was exhausted, and—"

"No need to apologize. I called you in here because even though I believe you sent it in error, it's undeniably phenomenal work. I have a friend who would froth at the mouth to get his hands on your story. He's a senior editor for a reputable publishing house in New York."

Sickness swept through her stomach. There wasn't any possible way she'd let his friend see what she'd written. She didn't want another soul to know her story. "I only wrote it for myself...as a part of therapy. I didn't intend for anyone else to read it." Eyes wet, she sunk back into the chair across from him. "Like I said, I sent it by accident."

"In that case, I'm the one who should apologize. Still—"

"*No one* knows I'm his daughter, Professor Robinson. Just my family and a couple of friends back home." She hadn't even told Harlow the truth.

The professor rubbed at his wrinkled brow. "I understand, although it's a shame. I'm sure you don't need anyone telling you that your story is rather unique. I'm willing to bet my friend would offer you a substantial advance once he'd read this."

"Please, you can't tell anyone. I changed my name to stay hidden. If the media found me—"

"You don't have to explain yourself, Miss Brooks. This conversation and the manuscript will remain strictly between the two of us. But there's something I'd like you to consider." He steepled his fingers and set his elbows on the stack of papers. "There's a wealth of emotion in this story...something even the most experienced writer strives to accomplish in their work. Would you consider altering the facts, and rewriting it as a work of fiction?"

Her lips parted with an answer, then promptly snapped back shut. She'd dreamed of becoming a published author ever since she'd begun writing stories for Kinsley and Drake. But there had to be a better way to accomplish her goal.

"I'll tell you what," he said to her. "If you're at all interested, you can work on rewriting in the first ten pages. I'd submit them to my friend as something submitted by one of my students. If he likes what he sees, you can decide if you want to proceed any further." His lips spread wide with a kind smile that she instinctively trusted. "No matter what you decide, your secret is safe with me."

SUMMERTIME IN NEW YORK was often brutal. Triple digit temperatures mixed with noxious exhaust from buses and cars lingered inside the city's unforgiving grid of concrete skyscrapers, resulting in the kind of stench that upends a person's stomach, and an oppressive heat that seeps beneath the skin. Two months before Rowan's final year of studies was to begin, she flew to New York and braved an unusual spike of heat to sign a contract for a book deal with one of the city's top publishing houses. Although they'd been in contact with Rowan for months, and the grueling process of editing the revised manuscript was already underway, it would be another year before the fictionalized story of her life as the daughter of a serial killer would be released. That evening, Taylor and the Lewises drove into the city to meet Rowan, Drake, and Kinsley for a celebratory dinner.

At the time, the Lewis kids were living ten blocks apart in lower Manhattan. Kinsley was the understudy for the star of an off-Broadway comedy, and Drake had begun directing his first big-budget film. Kinsley had made reservations at the trendy restaurant inside an old warehouse in Chelsea. They served everything from soul food to Japanese, and the waiters dressed in black from head to toe were incredibly attentive to Kinsley's demands. Rowan had never felt so grown-up knowing they'd all gathered to celebrate her accomplishments.

While waiting for their dessert, Kinsley held her champagne flute up in the air. "I'd like to toast our dear, sweet Rowan!"

Drake quickly topped off Rowan's champagne before everyone around the table lifted their glasses. The way he'd been doting on her all night, Rowan was starting to worry his feelings for her had gone beyond neighborly.

Wide smile aimed at Rowan, Kinsley continued

with tears in her beautiful emerald colored eyes. With her hair in a complicated updo and makeup expertly applied, she could've been mistaken as a thirty-year-old movie star rather than a mere twenty-two. "Fate made you our sister all those years ago, and we're insanely proud of what you've become. I know your journey hasn't been an easy one, but you've taken it with courage and grace. May you have a long, successful writing career! Love you, sis!"

"Love you too," Rowan mouthed back as everyone clinked glasses.

While everyone in attendance was aware of how Rowan's book deal had come about, Rowan's grandparents and friends in California were blissfully unaware of the book's subject matter. She figured she'd eventually have to tell them, but in the meantime, she was simply grateful to have a strong support system in her aunt and childhood friends. The decision to go forward with the book hadn't been an easy one, and she'd leaned on everyone in attendance to assure her she wasn't making a mistake.

Outside of the restaurant, Taylor gave Rowan the biggest hug of her life, holding her tight for more than just a brief moment. "I'm wicked proud of you, Rowan. You're doing so well in college, and you took in those poor kids from the shelter and gave them hope. Now this...becoming a published author while you're still so young. You continue to amaze me, kiddo. You're so strong, so beautiful—inside and out. You took the shitty situation you were dealt with, and decided to live your life with purpose."

Rowan squeezed her back. "I'm not sure I can say with confidence that I'm living with purpose, but I am happy. And couldn't have done any of it without you, Aunt T."

"You would've found your way out of the darkness eventually." Taylor drew back with a sadness sweeping over her expression. "When are you going to tell your mom about the book?"

"Never, if I can help it."

"She wants to see you, Ro. She said she has something she wants to give you." She gripped Rowan's forearms and smiled. "Remember she was hurt by what he did, too. You're not the only one dealing with PTSD and seeing monsters among the shadows. The man she loved betrayed her in the worst way imaginable. Discovering how he'd hurt all those women...watching the testimonies and seeing the evidence at trial...it was too much. I can't say I'd do any better if I'd been in her situation. None of us probably could've."

It wasn't anything Rowan hadn't heard before. Both her therapist from Blue Bay and the therapist she'd begun seeing in California had each told her something very similar in their sessions, asking her to consider forgiving her mother. She hoped there would come a day when she could let her mother back into her life, but she wasn't quite there yet.

After they'd walked the Lewises and Taylor to their nearby hotel, Drake and Kinsley took Rowan to their favorite club on the lower East Side. Despite having turned 21 in February, it was Rowan's first experience drinking in a bar. She continued to order champagne, and it didn't take long for the bubbly liquid to mess with her senses. With plans to crash on Kinsley's couch for the night, and stay in Blue Bay for a few days before heading back to California, she let go of all inhibitions. The pseudo siblings danced late into the night, generating far too much attention from single men looking to hook up, and triggering Drake's protective side. The sparkly, light blue cocktail dress Harlow had loaned to Rowan for the occasion hadn't helped. By the end of the night, she was eager to change into a t-shirt and pajama bottoms.

Prepared to exit the packed dance floor, she tugged on a short sleeve of Kinsley's sexy little emerald dress the same shade as her captivating eyes. "I'm gonna step outside. I need some air."

"Not alone, you're not." Kinsley set her hands on Rowan's shoulders and steered her toward the exit. "There are a ton of psychos and pervs in this city, and you're wicked drunk."

Drake was soon in step with them, exiting out a side door. Even at the late hour the heat was still unbearable. The street outside the club swarmed with sweaty partygoers and an excessive amount of traffic. Rowan was more than happy to be reunited with her old neighbors, but she felt oddly out of place among seasoned New Yorkers. Kinsley's strict diet and workout regimen had given her ample curves suited for a cover model, and her face had taken on a more graceful angle. Drake resembled his handsome father more every day, only with a thicker head of sandy brown hair, a well-groomed beard, an impressive six-pack, and dreamy eyes. They both emitted an air of sophistication that made Rowan feel like a foolish juvenile.

"This weather is shit," Drake grumbled, inhaling a cigarette. Although he'd begun smoking years ago while still in college, he never did it around his parents. Through a cloud of smoke, he grinned at

Rowan. "I still can't believe our Rowan is going to become a bestselling author."

Her cheeks warmed. "You're getting ahead of yourself."

"Bullshit. You're just being polite...as always." His perfectly white teeth flashed beneath a crooked grin. "Once you've hit number one, I'll produce the film adaptation, and Kinsley can play the lead."

"O. M. G. Can you *imagine?*" Kinsley squealed, bouncing on her Gucci heels. "Our childhood dreams would become a reality for all three of us!"

The dark neighborhood swayed as Rowan chewed on her lip, envisioning her friend acting out the modified version of Rowan's life on a big screen. She still wasn't convinced she was doing the right thing by fictionalizing her story. "What if someone puts two and two together, and exposes the truth about who I am?"

With a shake of his head, Drake's fingers expertly kneaded one of her shoulders. "No one is going to link 'R. Brooks' to the SLS killer, Ro. The public hasn't seen pictures of you since you were little with blond hair and covered in makeup. They won't link your gorgeous face to the scraggly little kid you were back then."

Rowan blushed a little with the compliment.

Drake was handsome, but she still regarded him as a brother. "I didn't realize I'd been 'scraggly'."

"You still need to add a few pounds," he grumbled, sucking on more nicotine.

"Besides, you've changed enough facts to throw people off," Kinsley added. She'd read one of the earliest drafts of the fictionalized version, and had bombarded Rowan with questions afterward, wanting to separate facts from fiction. It was the first time Rowan had discussed the details with anyone other than her aunt and therapists. "No way anyone will figure it out."

"I hope you guys are right." Snatching Drake's cigarette, Rowan took a long drag. She hadn't smoked since she'd been with Koby, and liked the calming buzz that rushed to her head when she inhaled.

With a scowl, Drake plucked the cigarette from her fingers. "Since when do you smoke?"

"It's a filthy habit," Kinsley agreed, stealing it from her brother. She inhaled, then let out a dreamy sigh with a cloud of smoke. "Except when *Bill's* doing it. Then it's downright sexy."

Rowan lifted her eyebrows. "Who's Bill?"

"William Halsrud, my producer." With a wolfish grin, Kinsley leaned in closer to her old friend. "He's tall and handsome...super dreamy. You'd love him, Ro. He's the *best* writer in the industry."

"He's old and washed-out," Drake interjected. "Don't even think about hooking up with him, Kins. He's known in the industry for seducing second-rate stars. He could single handedly ruin your career."

"You don't know what you're talking about," Kinsley snapped, tossing the cigarette onto the pavement. "Just because you're Mr. Big-time now doesn't mean you have a say in who I sleep with!"

"So you *are* sleeping with him?" Drake moved close to his sister, gripping her wrist. His beautiful face twisted with an ugly scowl. "What in the hell are you thinking, Kins? That guy's a sleazeball! Don't be stupid!"

The anger in his voice all at once reminded Rowan of the night her father was arrested, and the way he'd yelled at her mother.

"Stop asking questions, you stupid bitch, and get me another towel before I ruin the goddamn floor!"

Rowan's stomach surged, and the heat on her skin was suddenly too much to handle. "I think I'm gonna be sick," she announced, darting away from them. She made it around the corner of the building in time to throw up in private. Tears streamed down her cheeks as dark memories from that night continued to unfold.

The blank look her father gave her…

The detective holding her hand in the SUV…

The look of disgust from her mother at the police station…

Kinsley was soon behind Rowan, holding her curled hair back behind her head as she continued to empty her stomach. "Let's get you back to my place, party girl."

Drake hailed a taxi, and they all piled in. Rowan rode with her forehead pressed against the back door's cool glass as the Lewis siblings carried on about an upcoming Broadway show. She was grateful when the taxi finally quit swerving and making jerky stops.

While Drake paid the driver, Rowan watched a handsome man embrace a washed-out blonde in front of an elegant hotel adjacent to Kinsley's apartment building. The man was tall and muscular, looking divine in a dark gray chambray shirt and khaki shorts. His thick brown hair was worn long on the top, cut shorter on the sides. Rowan's belly warmed as she watched the couple's PG-13 kiss. It reminded her how badly she longed to find a man she could trust—one who cherished her and made her feel special. She hadn't been with anyone since Koby, and yearned for more passionate touches and stolen kisses.

Eyes wet, she turned away from the couple and ran her fingers over the sterling silver charms on the bracelet from Steph and Andy. She had a dozen reasons to be happy. But if she was being honest with herself, she was incredibly lonely. She could only live with Harlow for so long before her friend found the man of her dreams and settled down. Would Rowan ever be able to let a man in that way, or would the trauma of her past always prevent her from enjoying a peaceful future? Did she even deserve a happily ever after, or was she doomed to pay a lifetime of penance on her father's behalf?

"After you, beautiful," she heard the man say.

There was something in the man's dialect and the way his beautiful eyes drank in the leggy blonde when Rowan turned back to them that stirred something deeply buried in her memories.

"Oh, Riggs," the woman sang, seductively kneading the man's firm backside. "Always the gentleman."

Riggs, Rowan thought. Even his name was dreamy.

Drake hooked his arm through Rowan's and

inclined his head toward Kinsley's building. "Come on, Ro. I'm not leaving until I know you two are safely tucked in for the night."

Before turning away, Rowan caught the man's gaze as he escorted the woman into the hotel. She was all at once reminded of the cute surfer she'd hung out with California, and had obsessed over for years after. Leaning on Drake's shoulder, she allowed him to lead her away. The champagne had done a number on her head.

16

Part of the excitement of New York City was never knowing who would be seen walking the streets. Celebrities felt more at ease when surrounded by millions of locals, and took a casual approach to running the smallest of errands. While Riggs Forrester didn't think he'd seen someone famous, he was certain he recognized the stunning brunette in the sparkling blue dress. He glanced back one last time to where she'd been standing. Something about her felt…familiar. He shook his head, figuring the unusual vibe was only because she'd been incredibly attractive.

He dragged his feet as he took Chelsea through the grand glass doors of the hotel, reluctant to take her up to the penthouse. Women often pursued him for different reasons once they realized he was wealthy. It wasn't obvious at first because he wasn't the type to drive flashy cars or wear expensive clothes. He'd worn the same knock-off watch since he was a teenager. He didn't even own a suit, even though Victor recommended he wear one whenever he met with the board of directors. His standard uniform in California consisted of a casual button down and khaki shorts, although he preferred to be barefoot on the beach with a longboard—one of his only luxuries—under his arm. Guests at his hotels often assumed he was an employee, and he preferred it that way.

Riggs had a way with people, easily charming them with his laid back personality—it was how he'd gotten where he was in life. He'd started out as a bellboy for one of Victor's hotels in San Diego shortly after he'd quit bouncing between youth shelters and foster homes. The billionaire saw something in Riggs and soon promoted him to the front desk...then management...then Victor gifted him with the sole ownership of the Del Mar Beach property back when Riggs was only 21. Although Riggs was a hard worker and took his job seriously, he also recognized luck had played the biggest role in his fate. If Victor hadn't seen something in the homeless teen, Riggs wouldn't be traveling via private jets and wouldn't have substantially-sized bank accounts that would allow him the option to retire before the age of thirty. Rather than living the high life with his good fortune, however, he'd invested in new properties, including the new hotel in which he crossed over the threshold with Chelsea at his side.

The visit to New York was only supposed to last a handful of days. Victor had fallen ill with pneumonia a few months after moving into the new hotel, and Riggs was his sole family member just as Victor was his. Riggs had planned to check in with Victor and hire a private nurse before he returned to California. Then Victor was hospitalized for a week, and returned to his penthouse in a weakened state. Riggs didn't feel comfortable leaving his beloved friend and mentor alone on the other side of the country.

He'd met Chelsea at the hotel's stylish and trendy bar a few days after he arrived in the city, and they'd been seeing each other on a regular basis throughout the three months since. He suspected she was onto his financial situation simply by the way he'd been treated by his employees while seated at the bar. What he felt for the sexy socialite couldn't be defined as love, but he enjoyed her company and the great sex. Although he was known as being a ladies' man, the truth was he often went out with women merely because he had a problem saying no when they'd ask him for a date. He'd be equally content enjoying his free time either surfing or working out in his private gym.

Inside the penthouse's private elevator, Chelsea began to unbutton Riggs's shirt while sliding her collagen-injected lips up and down his thick neck. The silky material of her tiny dress over her full breasts felt sinful against his bare skin. She fulfilled every guy's wildest fantasy, from her tight body with long smooth legs and her DDs to her thick hair the color of sunshine and her inviting lips. Riggs suspected she'd undergone plastic surgery the way every facial feature was perfectly aligned and sized just right. Once she'd accidentally swiped to an old picture of herself on her phone, and he noticed she'd had a bulbous nose, thin lips, and a much flatter chest. Although his attraction to her couldn't be denied, he often asked himself why he continued to spend time with her. She was a spoiled daddy's girl and led a mostly uninteresting life that primarily consisted of premieres and club openings. Those things weren't his scene. Never would be.

"I can't believe you're finally taking me to see your place."

"I told you, it's Victor's," he replied, omitting the truth. "I'm only crashing there while I'm in the city."

She didn't know it was Riggs's hotel, and he intended to keep it that way for the time being. Once she started trailing kisses down his chest, he grabbed onto her hips before she sunk to her knees. "And he's home, resting, so we have to be quiet."

"Don't worry, baby. I can be super *duper* quiet," she whispered, catching one of his earlobes between her teeth. "Your grandpa won't even know we're there." She pressed her curvaceous body against his, pale blue eyes alive with desire as she ran a manicured fingertip over his lips. "God, you're too beautiful to be real. Are you really going to leave me on the East Coast all alone? There are more than enough hotels in New York. I'm sure you could find one to manage. Or Daddy could hook you up with something at one of the bank's branches."

"I have too much going on in California to stay here." He was in the process of acquiring another property in Hawaii, and needed to be in San Francisco early the following week to meet with his lawyers and the board of directors.

She watched her finger draw mindless patterns over his hard chest. "What if I came with you? I'd give anything to watch you catch a wave, surfer boy."

Even though the visual of her in a bikini dried his throat, he couldn't imagine her enjoying the laidback lifestyle he lived in California. He doubted she'd consider giving surfing a try, even with his help. She was self-absorbed and took her perfect image far too seriously.

"I work long hours at the hotel...not a lot of time left for surfing. What would you do with yourself? Your social calendar would remain pretty empty, and there isn't much for shopping in the area." At least nothing high-end enough to meet her standards.

As the elevator doors slid open, he gently nudged her back and took her hand to lead her inside the penthouse. The hotel's remodel had taken over a year after he'd acquired the property. One of New York's most top-rated designers had assisted him in turning it into a coveted destination. Every detail from the luxurious mahogany hardwood floors and floor-to-ceiling windows to the marble countertops and sleek white sofas had been hand-picked by Riggs. The resulting look was a blend of New York chic and California casual.

Chelsea released his hand to spin around on the polished floors. "This place is even more lit than the rumors!" She raced over to the windows to gaze at the sparkling city lights stretched as far as the eye could see. "And check out this view of the Empire State!"

Inside the sleek kitchen, Riggs chose one of Victor's hundred dollar bottles of champagne from the temperature controlled beverage refrigerator and poured it into a crystal flute. "I'm going to check on Victor." He handed the flute of champagne to Chelsea and placed a sultry kiss against her lips. "Go enjoy the view on the terrace. I'll only be a minute."

On the furthest end of the penthouse, the soft glow of light shone from beneath the master bedroom's door. Riggs held his breath and gave the slightest knock.

"I'm awake," Victor called out.

Riggs wasn't surprised to find his mentor sitting upright in the tufted king headboard, snuggled beneath the white down comforter, thick hardcover book in hand. The 79-year-old had brought his extensive collection of books when he'd relocated to New York, and Riggs had hired a contractor to install custom bookshelves around the perimeter of the master suite. Riggs had read many of those books since Victor had taken him under his wing, and knew the old man was into everything from fluffy romances and women's fiction to gory horror and true crime. Although Riggs had never set foot inside a secondary school, over the years Victor had provided him with enough books on running a business that he would've been confident enough to teach a course on the subject. Victor suspected Riggs's IQ was near genius level by the time he'd graduated high school, and had offered dozens of times to send him to the university of his choice at no cost. Riggs wanted no part of institutional-style learning, and preferred to educate himself at his own speed.

Victor's illness had aged him another 10 years, but in recent days the color had begun to return to his thin cheeks and wide, narrow lips. He'd stopped dyeing his thick hair its usual coal black a few years after Riggs had met him, and it had turned a noble shade of gray that matched his distinguished profile. He removed his reading glasses, hazel eyes lighting with happiness when he looked Riggs's way. "There's my boy!"

"You're looking better, Victor. How was your day?"

"Fine, except for my bath with Damien. Can't you find me a hot female nurse?"

Crossing over to sit on the edge of the bed, Riggs chuckled. "Wouldn't want you harassing the help."

"Well, an old man can dream. Speaking of hot women...you're not staying with that beautiful young lady tonight?"

"I brought her here for the night."

Victor set the book face down in his lap and threw him a blank stare. "That's...unexpected."

Huffing out a long breath, Riggs ran a hand through his short hair. He missed his younger days when he wore it down to his chin. "I hope you don't mind."

"You've put me up in the penthouse of your lovely hotel, and you're worried about hurting my feelings?" Victor patted Riggs's knee and chuckled. "I'm pleased you've finally formed an attachment to someone, son. Perhaps you won't live the lonely life of a bachelor after all."

One of Riggs's eyebrows lifted. "I thought you liked that lifestyle."

"It may have been right for me, but I don't think it suits you. You're too kind-hearted to be alone, Riggs. Besides, I came back to New York so I could relive my younger days before I check out. Every street in this city brings back memories of the time I spent with my dear Elsa."

Riggs felt a rush of empathy with the mention of Victor's only wife. She'd been struck by a taxi while crossing the street, and died a mere ten days after their honeymoon—before they were able to start the large family they'd dreamed of creating. Victor had been younger than Riggs when she'd died, and never loved another woman after Elsa. Riggs glanced over to their wedding portrait mounted in a square space amongst the bookshelves. Victor was 22 and Elsa was 19 when they were married in a small ceremony in the heart of Central Park. The Sweden native had been graceful and petite, barely breaching the center of Victor's broad chest. They'd made a striking couple—both with dark hair and piercing eyes—and would've made attractive children.

Turning back to Victor, Riggs smiled. "I wish I could've met her."

Victor nodded. "Me too. Except you would've charmed her into leaving me with those dimples of yours." They both grinned and shared a laugh. Then Victor set a darkly veined hand on Riggs's knee. "In all seriousness, what are your intentions with this young woman?"

"Her father's rich, so once she learns I'm worth more than I've been letting on, she might not go wild." Or at least he hoped. Recently, he'd begun to wonder if Chelsea would make a good wife, or if she'd blow his fortune on shoes and purses. While he was certain there was someone out there better suited for him, he wasn't sure he wanted to spend the rest of his life searching. He was young enough at 26 and not in any real kind of hurry, but his patience had worn thin after a string of bad relationships, and he was tired of being alone. "I'm considering keeping her around."

Victor responded with a grave shake of his head. "I wouldn't be so hasty. You'll know when you've found your other half. From what you've told me, I think we both know this woman isn't the one. I'm sure there's someone out there who's exactly right for you. Someone just waiting for you to crash into her life." Victor patted Riggs's knee. "Don't be impatient, son. It's important to listen to your heart."

Riggs inwardly sighed. Although he didn't love Chelsea, he was beginning to think companionship was more important than a four letter word that held empty promises.

17

Commencement at California Bay University was traditionally a casual affair. Proud parents from all over the country attended in CBU gear, some even waving little pendants or flags with the university's mascot, and the students typically wore shorts and sleeveless shirts beneath their robes to survive the long ceremony beneath the full strength of the sun. The afternoon Rowan graduated magna cum laude, it was pleasantly warm. Steph and Andy flew out the night before with Taylor, and they all stayed with Kitty and Kelly. Unable to skip rehearsals, Kinsley promised to join them in time for dinner at the Millers' mansion the night of the ceremony. Drake couldn't get away as he was deep into editing his film, but he sent a $300 bottle of champagne accompanied by a long note in which he gushed with pride.

When Rowan marched onto the football field as "Pomp and Circumstance" blasted from the speakers, she nearly fell flat on her face. Vanessa, her mother, was almost unrecognizable among the other parents as a platinum blonde. Rowan was sure she'd undergone the dramatic change for that very reason. When she'd sent a formal invitation to her mother, she didn't dream Vanessa would actually fly all the way to California.

After the ceremony, Rowan's friends and family headed south from the university to Los Gatos. The weather was perfect for an outdoor party—sunny and not too warm without a single cloud in sight. A light breeze surrounded them with the fragrant scent of Kitty Miller's prized roses. While the other guests mingled around the sophisticated backyard of her grandparents' home, drinking hundred dollar champagne and munching on elegant hors d'oeuvres, Stormy sat with Rowan and Harlow on a cluster of patio furniture overlooking the pool.

"I'm happy for you, but you look super old in that robe and hat," Stormy told her.

Laughing, Rowan nudged the slender teenager. "Be careful, kid. You'll be wearing something very similar in a couple of years."

"I wish I could go on your book tour with you,"

Stormy pouted, playing with the hem of the simple dress Rowan had helped her pick out earlier in the week. Her foster mother had braided her long brown hair and applied a slight dusting of makeup on her eyes and cheeks, making her appear several years older than usual. Puberty was morphing her into a knock-out. "What am I supposed to do all summer while you're gone?"

"Go to the beach and meet cute boys," Harlow answered, nudging the teenager's ribs. "I'll even take you and show you how it's done."

Rowan threw her roommate a sharp look. "Better yet, you can hang out with your friends."

Harlow giggled. "What am *I* going to do while you're gone?"

"Go to the beach and meet cute boys," Rowan said, making Stormy giggle.

Harlow's eyes widened. "Speaking of, I ran into your old boyfriend the other day on the beach! He was surfing by himself."

"Koby?"

"He was asking all kinds of questions about you...what you've been up to, where you're going, if you're seeing anyone...I'd say he still has a thing for you." With a broad smile, Harlow nudged Rowan's shoulder. "I must say that man is looking *fine*."

Memories of the night Rowan slept with him hardened her stomach. "If you think he's so fine, maybe *you* should date him."

"I'm over California boys," Harlow decided, scrunching her nose. "I'm not dating again until I'm settled in Boston."

It was Rowan's turn to pout. Harlow had accepted an event planner position with a non-profit organization in the heart of Boston, and she'd be moving in two months. "What am *I* going to do without *you*?"

Harlow leaned in close, eyebrows raised and a small smirk dancing on her lips. "You know, since you still aren't sure where you want to go after your book tour, you…could…always come be my roommate again! You should think about it, Ro! I'm sure Boston is filled with handsome, charming bachelors searching for beautiful, intelligent authors to marry!"

"I'm not sure about Boston, but it's likely I'll return to my aunt's until I figure out where I want to live. It's a short train ride from Boston to Blue Bay."

"Sounds perfect." Glancing across the yard, Harlow stretched her arms high into the air, exposing the silver charm on her dark navel. Rowan had always been jealous of her roommate's keen sense of fashion, including the mustard-colored two-piece dress she'd worn beneath her graduation gown. "I better go rescue my parents from your grandma. My dad looks bored to tears."

"Later," Stormy called after her. She snuggled up against Rowan's side. "I don't want you to leave," she muttered, winding her arms around Rowan. Her voice shook a little when she asked, "What if I don't ever see you again?"

"I'll be back around Christmas to visit my grandparents, and I'll make sure to schedule time to hang out with you and Wren while I'm here." She playfully tugged on the tail of Stormy's braid. "I promise I won't disappear from your life, Stormy." They both knew it was a heartfelt promise as they had each lost their parents in different ways. Rowan tensed when she spotted her mother headed their way with a tentative look. "You should grab your brother and head down to the game room in the basement. I think he might actually be asleep."

Stormy sat upright to glance over at her brother slumped in a chair beneath the covered patio, and giggled. "Okay. He loves your grandpa's old-school arcade games."

Rowan kissed the girl's temple before she skipped

away. Vanessa gave her a warm smile as they passed. Her smile grew when she stood before her daughter and set her large leather hand bag down by their feet. Rather than the usual designer labels she'd donned throughout Rowan's childhood, Vanessa wore a tasteful white sundress adorned with little pink and yellow flowers. The sides of her straight, shoulder-length hair were pulled back with bobby pins, and her hazel eyes watered. Rowan told herself she must've been face-to-face with a stranger when Vanessa's mouth, stained pink with lipstick, trembled with a smile. "She seems like a nice young lady."

"She and her brother are a brave pair." Rowan squirmed in the chair. Every last one of her insecurities flared under her mother's gaze. She was aware of the extra pounds she'd put on with all the celebrations she'd attended that week, and her hair wasn't as beautiful as it had been when she spent hours caring for it as a child. She couldn't imagine what her mother must've thought of her visible freckles and discount store sandals. "They've been through a lot."

"Your aunt told me their story. I'm glad you're there for them. I'm sorry I wasn't there for *you*, Sienna." In the warm California sunlight, her eyes sparkled with moisture. "I sometimes forget that isn't your name anymore."

Rowan looked away. "You weren't there, but I had Taylor and the Lewises."

Vanessa sat in the spot where Stormy had been, and took her daughter's hand, waiting for Rowan to meet her gaze. "Nothing about what happened to both you *and me* was okay. I couldn't deal with the reality of what your father had done. It broke me in ways I didn't know the human spirit could break. I just wanted to numb the pain and guilt for not knowing I was married to a monster. The anti-anxiety meds they prescribed after your father's arrest did the job—I spent the next three years chasing that high." Tears spilled down her cheeks as she continued. "I failed as your mother. It was my *job* to protect you, and I let you spend all those years in the same house as a sick, vile man. There were times I left him alone with you, and—"

"You couldn't have possibly have known he was capable of murder. I know deep down in my heart that if you had any idea of the kinds of things he was doing, you would've taken me away long before that night." Rowan placed her other hand over her mother's. "I forgive you, Vanessa. It's taken me a lot of years and a lot of hours of therapy to understand what it must've been like for you. What Jonathan did isn't your fault—not in the slightest. He ruined your life, *and* mine. The man we loved is gone, but we still have each other, and I'd really like to get to know you again. You seem...different. In a good way."

Vanessa hiccuped with a little sob. "You want to see me again?"

Rowan's stomach churned as she answered with a slight nod. "But first I have to tell you something that might be really upsetting, and hard for you to understand. I, um, wrote a book. About what it's like to be a serial killer's daughter. And it's going to be released next week."

"Oh, Sienna," her mother whispered, pulling her hands away. Color rushed away from her face as she heaved a quivering breath. "How could you—"

"I fictionalized it. The facts, names, places... everything is different. And the killer's story ends when he's stabbed to death by one of his would-be victims. I'm writing as R. Brooks, so no one other than my inner circle will know my secret." Rowan wiped her damp hands on her knees. Maybe telling her had been a bad idea. Her mom looked ready to faint. "It started out as a therapeutic thing. I'd already been writing stories about his victims for years, pretending they'd lived, and giving them the happily ever after he stole from them. It helped—my nightmares and anxiety weren't as bad for a while. Then one day I found myself writing about my experience as Jonathan's daughter, and I turned it into a professor by mistake."

Her mother shot up to her sandaled feet, eyes closed, body trembling. "How could you do this to me when I'm trying to heal?" Her eyes flipped open again, wet with tears. "I cannot *believe* you're trying to make a profit off what he did!"

"That's not at all what this is about!" Anger at herself simmered in her gut, threatening to burst with the force of a geyser. Had she been foolish enough to believe her mother would've given her praise? Nothing she'd done had ever been good enough for Vanessa. Every time she'd won a contest, it was because the other girls were having an off day, or she'd been lucky the judges hadn't seen the weight she'd put on after eating the night before. "Believe me, it wasn't an easy decision to go ahead with the idea at first. But it just so happened that my best work came out in the process of sorting through my feelings. All the reviewers that were given advanced copies say it's a well-written book with an engaging story. But no one will know who I really am

—not even my editor or my publicist—and I plan to keep it that way."

"I cannot *believe* you'd be this selfish!" With her face covered in blotches of red, Vanessa bent down to dig inside her large handbag. A moment later, she produced a stack of envelopes tied with twine. "These are letters your father has written to you since his incarceration. I didn't want to give them to you until I thought you were mature enough to handle whatever it is he has to say. I thought that day would come when you became a college graduate, but I guess I was wrong!" Sneering, she tossed the stack at Rowan.

Rowan recoiled as the letters slapped against her legs and fell to the ground in a cascade of dirty white envelopes. As her mother began to storm away, Rowan shot to her feet with sickness and disbelief rocking her to her core. "Mother, wait—"

"Sell them to the media," Vanessa spat over her shoulder. "You can buy yourself a flashy car!"

18

The nationwide tour for *The Devil's Daughter* lasted three months and spanned across seventeen different states. While many cities drew in crowds that lined up around the buildings, in others there had only been a few diehard true-crime and horror fans. The summer was consistently hot, although some stops offered thick humidity—namely Jacksonville and—while others—like Vegas and Phoenix—singed against skin.

The lowest points for Rowan centered around her association with the cities in which her father had taken victims. The letters from him lingered in the back of her mind like a festering canker sore, spewing poison into what should be a victory lap for her writing. She hadn't touched the stack since her mother had tossed them her way. When Kitty had offered to burn them, Rowan asked her to merely store them away somewhere safe. Rowan didn't know whether or not she'd ever want to read them, but she wanted the option to remain.

Rowan's editor had sent an escort named Ann Kester along to pay the bills and manage appointments for press junkets and interviews before the book events. At first, Rowan wasn't sure about the older woman who wore pantsuits, expensive pumps, and a string of pearls around her neck every single day. They had a lot of disagreements over the small things in the beginning. Not only that, but Rowan realized her mood swings came from a flare up of her old friend, PTSD.

After a few phone sessions with Dr. Walters, she was able to keep things under control until she saw a video clip online comparing her book to the SLS killer's story. Ann found her sobbing on the floor of her hotel room. Once Rowan caught her breath, she confessed to being the Spider Lily Strangler's daughter, and told her about the unread letters. From that moment on, the two women forged a bond, and Ann became incredibly protective. She ensured no one took pictures of Rowan, and arranged for security to escort them to and from their cars. If anyone asked questions too close to home she'd end the interview, saying they'd run out of time.

The most tolerable parts of the tour involved locations that allowed her to visit her grandparents in California, Harlow in Boston, and Taylor and the Lewises in New York. Slowly, but surely, she put the letters behind her and sealed them up with her juvenile hopes of a relationship with her mother. By the time she returned to Blue Bay, feeling both exhausted and accomplished, her book had hit number one on the New York Times Best Seller list. She still couldn't believe she had officially become a bestselling author, even after Steph and Andy threw her a surprise party the night she returned home.

Drake was the last one to remain seated on his family's plush white patio furniture alongside Rowan after their elders had tapped out for the night around midnight. With soft blues music playing from the speakers, bulb lights strung overhead, and the gentle lull of the ocean waves, Rowan briefly wondered if the others had ulterior motives when they'd left her alone with Drake.

"I told you this would happen," he said while cozying up to her on the gliding loveseat. He filled her flute with more champagne, then clinked his glass against hers. "Just wait until offers for foreign rights and movies come trickling in. One day we'll be walking the red carpet together in Cannes. Maybe with Kins, too."

"I'm still a little overwhelmed by the idea," she admitted, taking a long sip of the bubbly liquid before resting her head on his shoulder. Since the tour, she'd become relatively comfortable having released the book under her new name, but there were still nerves quivering just beneath the surface. A fear that she'd be called out. "If they approach me with a movie deal, I'll do my best to see that you and Kins are part of the package."

"It's sweet of you to offer, but that thing I said about the three of us being involved in your project was said in vain. It doesn't always work that way." He slipped an arm over her shoulders. "Tell me more about this tour. Did you meet anyone that might come around and try to sweep you off your feet?"

With a hearty sigh, her eyes tracked the lighthouse beam as it flickered over the dark water. "I don't know that I'll ever be ready for a relationship. Some of that stuff I wrote in the book…about not being able to trust men because of what my father did…that part wasn't fiction."

"Do you trust me?"

The question felt so raw and vulnerable that she

tilted her head up to meet his gaze. "Of course. But that's—"

Before she could utter, "different," his mouth was covering hers. The soft bristles of his facial hair tickled her chin and upper lip when she kissed him back. With a deep inhale, she was filled with the heady scent of his cologne. If she was being honest with herself, she had never felt a sexual attraction to him. That didn't change with the gentle brush of his tongue, or the caress of his fingers against her cheek. The kiss was soft and pleasant, only lasting long enough to make his intentions known.

He bid her goodnight after, brushing his lips over her cheek. She lay awake in bed for hours, fingering her charm bracelet while struggling to understand what the kiss had meant, and how it made her feel.

THE NEXT MORNING, her editor called to let her know they were publishing *The Devil's Daughter* overseas. He also wanted to meet with her in New York the following week to pitch a deal for a second book. However, it would have to wait until she was finished with her next job: standing in as Kinsley's maid of honor.

Her best friend was marrying William Halsrud, "the sleaze-ball producer" Drake had warned his sister to stay away from. Kinsley had announced their engagement the night she'd flown out for Rowan's graduation party. Although Rowan was glad her friend had found someone she described as "out-of-this-world handsome" and "delightfully charming," the fact that Kinsley was marrying someone fifteen years her senior didn't sit well with Andy or Drake.

Less than a full week after Rowan had returned to Blue Bay, she was packing for the wedding and boarding a plane to Maui. Taylor, Steph, and Rowan were unable to curb their excitement for embarking on their first trip to the Hawaiian islands, but Andy and Drake continued brooding throughout the entire thirteen plus hour of flight time. Rowan hadn't talked to Drake since their kiss. She was grateful he didn't try to speak to her until after they arrived in Kahului.

The resort had sent two town cars to collect them from the airport. When Drake announced he and Rowan would ride together in one, no one voiced their protest, including Rowan. A conversation with him was unavoidable. Besides, she was eager to get it out of the way so she could enjoy the vacation without drama.

The moment the driver closed the back door behind them, Drake snaked an arm around her waist and kissed her once again. It was a slower, deeper kiss that involved a hungrier sweep of his tongue and urgent press of his body. "I've been dying to get another taste of you," he whispered, burying one hand in her hair and touching his forehead to hers. "Damn, Ro, you have the softest lips *and* hair." His lips brushed over hers once more. "Forget sightseeing on this trip. I'd rather spend every day getting lost in you."

She'd been stunned into silence by the unexpected kiss, and didn't dare move in fear of giving him the wrong impression. "I…uh…don't know about this," she said, slowly sliding away as the car pulled forward. The rejection reflected in his chocolate-colored eyes broke her heart a little, so she took one of his hands and kissed the backside. "I love you, Drake. You've been good to me ever since the day I moved into my aunt's—except maybe for the time you smeared Nutella on my pants before that movie we made about aliens, aaaannnd, a few other incidents." She laced their fingers together, disappointed when she still didn't feel anything for him beyond kinship. She knew he would be good to her and treat her well. "But I'm not willing to ruin what we have by throwing romance into our relationship. And if we started something, your family and my aunt would cheer us on, wanting us to work as a couple. What happens if we decide it *doesn't* work? Who would be there to pick up the pieces if you broke my heart or I broke yours?"

"I would never break your heart, Ro." Eyes clouding over, he released her hand and flexed his jaw. "You've already been through enough bullshit. I want to kick your old man's ass whenever I think about what he did to you."

"Your protective side is one of the many things I adore about you." Smiling, she placed her hands on either side of his bearded jaw. "You're a good man with a really big heart. And I don't have to tell you that you're maddeningly attractive, because we both know you're well aware."

His lips tilted with a playful smirk. "Then what's the problem?" He gathered her hands in his before she could return them to her lap. "I love you too, Rowan. Always have, always will. I think we could have a beautiful life together."

"I wasn't being facetious when I told you I'm not ready for a relationship with anyone, Drake. I still have a lot of healing to do—especially with my mother. I don't have the energy to deal with anything else."

He brought their tangled hands up to his chest. "There you go, already breaking my heart."

"I would never." Trying to lighten the mood, she rolled her eyes to the car's ceiling. "Besides, I'm sure there are plenty of women out there who would *love* the chance to nurse you back to health."

His expression remained stoic. "Is there any way I can aid you in this healing process? It kills me to think you're still suffering."

"You can continue to be there when I need you... as one of my oldest and dearest friends."

"Always." He leaned in and pressed his lips against her forehead. "Be honest, it's my mouthwash, isn't it?"

Laughing, she nestled in against him and rested her head on his shoulder.

KINSLEY MET them in the marble and bamboo clad lobby of the grand resort with an armful of pink orchid leis. In a flowy belted maxi dress with a bright palm leaf print, red hair pinned back on one side with a bright pink hibiscus flower, cheeks stained a soft pink, she perfectly fulfilled the blushing bride stereotype. She'd never looked so happy as she greeted each of her family members with a kiss on both cheeks before placing a lei over their heads. When she reached Rowan, the old friends linked fingers on both hands and Kinsley squealed. Laughing, the rest of their family members approached the front desk.

"I can't believe you're getting *married* in a week!"

"I know!"

"When do I get to meet Will?"

"He's playing golf with his dad and brothers on the resort's course. They'll be back in time for tonight's luau." She released Rowan's hands and gestured to the panoramic view of the ocean beyond the lobby. "Isn't this resort fabulous, Ro? Wait until you see the set up for the ceremony! There was already a waiting list *five years long* before it even opened its doors, but Will got us bumped up to the top. We're going to be the first couple to get married here! Isn't it fabulous?"

"It's pretty fabulous," Rowan agreed, glancing at the modern glass chandelier sparkling over their heads. "I can't wait to see the rest of it."

Kinsley peered around Rowan to watch her

parents direct the small team of bellhops steering their luggage on wheeled carts, then snagged Rowan's hand. "Let's go. I wanna give you a super quick tour before you check into your room."

Rowan glanced at her aunt. She'd stepped outside to cough into the crook of her arm. "I should help Taylor with the luggage."

"Taylor's fine. They're super accommodating here. Your aunt will probably be given the assistance of a hot young stud…you know…to help her unpack…and *whatever else* she may need."

"She would never," Rowan decided, allowing Kinsley to lead her away. Her aunt was still devoted to the memory of her late husband, and hadn't so much as flirted with another man.

"Hey, she's a woman with needs just like the rest of us. How long do you think it's been before that poor woman got laid?" Kinsley turned to her and winked. "That's why I booked you each your own room while you're here…in case one or both of you wants to get a little chick-a-bow-wow." She dramatically waved over her head as they rushed past their family. "We'll meet up with you guys later!"

"Where are you two going?" Steph called back.

Giggling much like they did as little girls, the two women dashed out of the building into the warm, tropical paradise that awaited. Rowan had never seen anything as beautiful as the rich green grass accompanied by swaying palm trees, a labyrinth of tiki torches, and cheerfully bright flower gardens. The sun had already disappeared behind another island looming in the distance, staining the sky with an impressive blend of lavender, orange, and pink that partially reflected in the ocean. Couples and families strolled along the shore, frequently stopping to capture the moment with their phone's cameras.

"There it is," Kinsley told her, pointing to the edge of the property. "That's where they're going to set up the chairs and the arch—just wait until you see it! We're exchanging vows right as the sun's setting." She wrapped one arm around her friend's waist and released a satisfied sigh. "Isn't it fabulous, Ro?"

A rope of anxiety twisted through Rowan's chest. Why was Kinsley in such a hurry to get married? It didn't feel right when Rowan had yet to meet Will. How could she picture her friend living a happy life when she didn't know anything about him? What if he really was a dirtbag like Drake had claimed? "Are you sure you love this guy enough to spend the rest of your life with him, Kins?"

Kinsley leaned her head on Rowan's shoulder. "I've never been more sure of anything, sister."

The same old questions plagued Rowan's thoughts as she breathed in the balmy air. Would she ever trust a man enough to fall in love? There was no denying she was lonely for the kind of companionship she witnessed with married couples, like the Lewises. And she had needs, even though she hadn't slept with anyone since Koby. But would she ever be willing to commit the rest of her life to one person?

The idea of putting her happiness in a man's hands and hoping he wouldn't break her spirit was terrifying.

Tingles erupted down her spine as a tall, muscular man wearing a white button down and khaki shorts sauntered barefoot in their direction, moving with the kind of confidence all attractive men possessed. All at once, she was unable to draw in a breath as lost memories flooded her consciousness. There was no mistaking the nut brown eyes that melted into a liquid honey color at the edges, the angled nose hooked a little to one side, or the dimpled smile.

Her pulse whooshed through her ears, louder than the waves crashing behind him. It was the cute surfer she'd met on Del Mar Beach.

19

Kinsley Lewis waved Riggs down, and he opened his arms to hug the breathtaking actress. The sun trailing beneath the island of Molokai cast a warm glow over her brilliant red hair. She looked like the A-lister she'd one day become, and he was happy she'd convinced her fiancé to hold their wedding at Riggs's newest property. It was arguably a literal piece of heaven on earth, and his best investment to date.

"Is this Will?" asked a voice.

Kinsley drew away with a bubbling giggle, hand bearing her large diamond engagement ring held against her mouth. "Oh my god, no!" Then she flashed Riggs a playful smile. "I mean, no offense, because I certainly wouldn't complain if you were my fiancé."

"None taken," Riggs responded. He turned to

meet the other woman's stunned expression and gripped the back of his neck, eyes widening. "No way. It's…you."

His lips spread with a grin he felt in his gut. He was standing face-to-face with *her*—the girl who'd been the highlight of his dreams for a time. The one he'd fantasized about for an entire summer after he'd taken her surfing on Del Mar Beach. The one who'd been formal and awkward at first, but later made him laugh so hard his stomach and face muscles ached for hours afterward. The one he immediately thought of whenever the harmonic opening of The Beach Boys's song *"God Only Knows"* appeared on his favorite playlist.

She had grown into womanhood…and then some. She was no longer stick thin, and carried herself with confidence. The light cluster of freckles dusting the bridge of her little nose and the apples of her cheeks remained, and weren't concealed with a heavy application of makeup like most women he'd dated. Her dark mane the color of rich hot chocolate was just as full and naturally curly as he remembered, and suited the graceful angles of her face. Most notably, he didn't detect the haunted look that had lay dormant in her gray eyes the first time they'd met.

Although she was still considerably slender, the addition of small curves and soft angles on her hips and breasts added to her attractiveness on another level. The white jumper she wore was modest, highlighting what appeared to be the legs of a loyal runner, deeply tanned. He found the outfit more attractive than Chelsea's skimpiest of dresses. As far as he was concerned, this woman was more alluring than a sea goddess.

He swallowed the lump lodged in his throat. "Did you come all this way for more surf lessons, East Coast?"

"That really *was* you," the freckled brunette answered. Graceful eyelashes thickened with mascara fluttered rapidly over her deep, colorless eyes. "In New York…with that blonde. Last summer. Oh…my god. I thought it was just the champagne messing with my head."

"I *thought* you looked familiar!" Riggs exclaimed with a rush of excitement, stabbing his pointer finger through the air. "I saw you too!"

"Hold on." The bride-to-be's bright green eyes flipped between them before settling on her stunned friend. "You two know each other?"

"Not officially," Riggs told her. With a quick,

soulful laugh, he held his hand out to the stunning brunette. "Riggs Forrester."

Her petite hand was delightfully soft and delicate. "Rowan Brooks."

His heart gave a little squeeze. *He finally knew her name!* He lifted one eyebrow. "Miss Lewis's maid of honor."

Hands set on her hips, Kinsley frowned. "I'm *super* confused."

Rowan turned to touch her friend's arm. "Kins, this is the surfer I told you about—the one who gave me a lesson the summer I met my grandparents."

"*Shut...up!*" Kinsley yelled, gawking Riggs's way. "No freaking way! What's this about New York last summer?"

Rowan glanced at him out of the corner of her eye. "I saw him the night we celebrated my book deal in the city." Color spread across her cheeks. "He was...uh...standing outside of the hotel next to your old apartment."

Riggs's heart knocked against his ribs. He wished he would've said something that night—called out to her, asked if they'd met. Chances are good he wouldn't have kept Chelsea around if he'd thought he had even the slightest chance with Rowan. "I was in the city visiting an old friend who lives in that hotel." He felt his lips stretch with a bigger smile. "You're an author?"

"*Bestselling* author," Kinsley corrected him with a proud smile. "Her book, The Devil's Daughter, made the New York Times list just last week!"

"Wow. That's impressive." Riggs wanted to ask her age, but knew it wasn't socially acceptable to ask a woman. Victor had taught him better. Still, she seemed incredibly young to have accomplished said feat. When they first met, he was convinced she was jailbait. Maybe it would've been safe to make a move on her after all. He couldn't wait to return to his place and look her up on the internet. Wikipedia would likely know her age. "I wish I had a pen so I could ask for your autograph...maybe get a tattoo of it later."

A flattering sweep of color entered Rowan's cheeks as she waved a hand through the air. "Don't be silly." Then, with her gaze suddenly clouded in confusion, she glanced back at Kinsley. "Wait. How do *you two* know each other?" She pointed at Riggs. "What are *you* doing here?"

"He's the resort manager," Kinsley told her. "He's been my contact since we booked the wedding."

"Really?" Rowan's sensual lips spread with a toothy, girlish smile. It wasn't anything like the painfully plastic smile she'd first thrown him in California. The beauty of it cast warmth through his belly. "That's wonderful. I just arrived here, but from what I've seen and heard from Kinsley, this place is fabulous."

Riggs passed her a playful wink. "Maybe I can take you out for another round of surf lessons while you're here."

Her perfect lips rounded into an 'O' shape when she took a step back. "Oh, I don't know about that."

Sensing she was withdrawing, he decided to bring Kinsley into the conversation. "You should've seen her. Did she tell you the details of her wipeouts last time?"

Kinsley threw her friend a wolfish smile. "Oh yeah. I heard *all* the details."

Rowan daintily poked her friend's ribs with an elbow. "Okay, that's enough. We should get back to our families."

"Oh no you don't," Riggs said, hooking her arm. When she let out a wide-eyed gasp, he quickly released it. "Sorry. I just meant I'm not letting you slip away from me this time. Not until I get your room number." He rubbed his fingers together at his side, basking in the brief contact with her skin. It had been just as soft as he'd remembered from their day on the beach.

Rowan blinked slowly, as if still trying to get over the way he'd manhandled her. *Christ.* He needed to get a grip before she ran off for good.

"You certainly don't waste any time, Mr. Forrester," Kinsley sang with a wiggle of her arched eyebrows.

Riggs longed to kick his own ass. Both women were going to think he was a pervert. "I just want to ensure the staff gives you everything you need...I... uh...mean in addition to the rest of the wedding party, of course. I can just look your number up in the system." *Now he was offering to stalk her.* He scratched his head and gazed back at the resort, wishing he could start the encounter over. "Anyway, if you decide you want another lesson, call the front desk and ask for me by name. I can't promise you'll be competing against Bethany Hamilton any time soon, but I'll give you your money's worth." He leaned in to kiss her cheek, willing himself not to mess up and kiss her lips instead the way he wanted, or inhale her mystical scent like a freak. She smelled of fragrant flowers and sunshine. "It was good to see you again, *Rowan.*"

Her voice trembled when she touched his forearm and whispered, "You too, *Riggs*."

He was pleased to sense their reunion had seemed to affect her nearly as much as she had with him. "Let me know if there's anything you need," he told Kinsley, pecking her cheek. "I'll see you later at the luau."

He tossed one last smile in Rowan's direction, committing the soft details of her face to memory. As he walked away, reality hit him harder than her unexpected slap. Although he wasn't a free agent, he desperately *wanted* to be now that he'd found her. What would he do about Chelsea?

WHEN HE RETURNED to one of the six $10,000/night oceanside villas he'd claimed as his residence during the first stage of renovations, Chelsea was stretched out on a chaise lounge chair overlooking their private infinity pool. Riggs resisted the nagging urge to throw a towel over her naked body. He'd become increasingly annoyed with her lack of modesty—even more so than ever after running into Rowan, who'd left plenty for his active imagination. It was bad enough Chelsea refused to cover herself whenever someone under his employ needed to stop by for maintenance or an emergency that required Riggs's attention. He was even more irritated by the fact that Chelsea never did *anything* other than shop at upscale boutiques and hop around to the other islands on his private jet with her new, equally spoiled girlfriends.

He quietly padded across the bamboo floor, beyond the wall permanently open to the elements, and veered through the industrial kitchen. He nudged the bedroom's koa wood door closed behind him, hoping the click hadn't echoed through the high ceilings. Groaning, he flopped down onto the simplistic king bed without acknowledging the bedding with 22 carat gold woven directly into merino wool, the Tahitian sideboards with Tiffany's lamps, or the jaw-dropping panoramic view of the ocean through the thirty foot wall of windows. He draped an arm over his eyes, willing the world to disappear.

It was becoming clearer with every passing second that he had a major problem. It was difficult to fight the draw to the beautiful girl from the East Coast, but there were too many complications, and he wasn't some two-timing asshole. He'd met more than his share of guys with those types of dishonorable intentions, and stayed far the hell away from them. He still didn't love Chelsea the way he probably should after all the time they'd been together, yet he was obligated to give her more than a quick wave and a shove out the door. She'd uprooted her life in New York to be with him. Of course she'd only agreed to the move once she discovered he was, in fact, the owner of several hotels, and could take care of her the way her father had. Riggs always suspected her father was supplying the money used to fuel her expensive shopping habits, but he had no idea she'd never held a real job in her lifetime until recently.

Instead of Chelsea, he had overwhelmingly strong feelings for a woman he virtually knew nothing about. He wasn't even certain she was available. What he *did* know is Kinsley Lewis had specifically requested a single room for a Miss Rowan Brooks, and she'd be lodging at his resort for exactly two weeks.

While it wasn't enough time to convince Chelsea they were finished, and move her off the island before properly exploring his attraction to Rowan, he was certain he could use the time to get to know Rowan better—via the only option available. *As a friend.*

20

The Blue Heaven resort bustled with jovial guests as they gathered for the inaugural luau later that night on the beach behind the main lodge. Hundreds of twinkling lights were strung across the palm trees overhead, and the aroma of pork combined with fragrant flowers wafted through the air. Wait staff donning traditional Polynesian clothing maneuvered through rows of long tables, serving hollowed pineapples containing Mai Tais and adorning flowers, while a local musician strummed a small ukulele and sang of finding love in paradise from a bamboo stage.

It was certainly the perfect setting for love and romance, Rowan thought. Hours after running into Riggs on the beach, her heart was still soaring. He had flirted and flustered around her exactly the way she'd remembered that blissful afternoon they'd spent together in California. She hated saying it, even if it was only in her head, but she was sure fate had something to do with their reunion. She absentmindedly fingered the bracelet from the Lewises. Was the universe sending her a sign? When she'd flinched from his touch, she was sure she'd die from embarrassment. Still, she'd been so relieved to officially meet him that she was surprised she hadn't broken down in tears.

Kinsley's wedding party sat in their assigned seats at two different tables, sipping their Mai Tais while Rowan's gaze tracked Riggs like a magnet. Macadamia nut lei strung around his neck, he moved from guest to guest, greeting them with his most charming dimpled smile. He'd changed into a black button-down that hugged his muscular arms and chest, paired with tan dress shorts and leather sandals. She assumed he'd showered as his brown hair was neatly combed back instead of wind-blown like it had been earlier. His honeyed eyes held a greater level of intensity than she'd remembered—to the point she feared they'd possess the power to sever her every last nerve with one look.

Kinsley had insisted Rowan borrow one of the dozens of dresses she'd packed, knowing everything Rowan packed would've been modest. The shorter than average length of the dress alone made it something she never would've picked for herself. The black little number with a white floral print and a plunging neckline made her as uncomfortable as the dresses she'd worn for pageants. After Drake had eyeballed her when their group met in the lobby, she'd barely resisted the urge to return to her suite to change. She adjusted the elaborate lei with fragrant orchids and tuberose they'd given her at the entrance of the luau, hoping to camouflage some of her cleavage.

"You're gonna marry that beautiful man and have his beautiful babies," Kinsley sang in her ear. "There were so many sparks flying between you two on the beach, I'm surprised I didn't literally get burned. And I do mean *literally*."

Rowan's cheeks burned as she checked over her shoulder to make sure Drake hadn't been listening from the table behind them. "Keep your voice down," she warned. "He could have a wife or girlfriend here somewhere."

"Pshhh. If he does, you could take 'er."

"What on earth are you two conspiring about?" William inquired from Kinsley's other side. He leaned in, dark green eyes ablaze with mischief in the light of the tiki torches. "If you're thinking of running off with a different bloke, my darling wife-to-be, might I remind you I can play chopsticks on the piano with my bare toes."

Rowan secretly swooned a little with his British accent. Kinsley had played down her fiancé's looks—Rowan felt he was more than attractive enough to be an actor instead of a director with wild ash blond hair, narrow features, and a shortly trimmed goatee. She'd only met him twenty minutes prior, but she already enjoyed his wit. She hoped the rumors Drake heard about him seducing Broadway actresses were untrue, because he acted as if the world revolved around Kinsley.

As handsome and charming as Rowan found William to be, he was still second-rate to the hotel manager who'd suddenly caught her leering. Flashing what was sure to be a cringeworthy smile in the pageant world, Rowan raised the pineapple containing her drink as if to toast him. "He caught me staring!" she snarled at Kinsley behind the drink. "What do I do?" All at once she realized just how badly she was lacking in the art of flirtation.

"Start by ending the ventriloquist bit. Put the pineapple *down*, and act normal."

Rowan's breath caught as Riggs veered around a table and moseyed their way. The chances she could carry on another conversation with him without embarrassing herself were slim to none. Stomach fluttering with nerves, she clutched Kinsley's leg beneath the table, lightening her grip when her friend let out a little squeak.

He approached on Rowan's side, sliding his arm behind her chair, and cloaking her in his warm, masculine scent. "Aloha, ladies! You both look positively *stunning* this evening." His eyes lingered on her a beat longer than on Kinsley, messily balling her nerves inside her throat. "It's a real pleasure to see you again."

"Well, if it isn't the dashing bachelor who made our nuptials possible!" William stood and shook Riggs's hand. "Good evening, mate!"

"How was your golf swing today?"

"Below par. Isn't that a saying in the States?"

"Beats me. I only know surf lingo." With a funny little smile, Riggs winked at Rowan. "How are the Mai Tais?"

"Strong," she decided, "but good. *Really* good."

"The Kalua Pua'a will be ready soon—that should soak up a little of the booze so you'll be ready for another."

"Everything is positively fabulous," Kinsley told him, motioning to the elaborate set up. "I've never seen a buffet offer so many delectable options! And your staff—everyone is so perceptive of our needs. This is one classy resort, Riggs. I'm assuming as the manager, a lot of that is your doing."

"I'll accept the compliment." His eyes narrowed on Rowan. "Can I borrow you for a minute?"

Her Mai Tai sloshed inside her stomach. She was far too frazzled to be alone with him. When Kinsley pinched her thigh beneath the table, she blurted, "Yes! Of course!"

Riggs offered his hand like a true gentleman, and she slipped her fingers inside it as she stood. Holding his warm grip felt as natural as everything else felt with him—enough that she didn't realize she was still doing it until he began to lead her away. "I'll return your maid of honor in plenty of time for the main course," Riggs told Kinsley.

"Don't hurry anything along on my account," she teased, flashing him another one of her wolfish grins. "She's all yours for as long as you need."

With her friend's suggestive undertone, Rowan lost her step and wobbled on her wedged heels. Riggs held their intertwined hands up to keep her ankle from twisting. "Still lacking in coordination, I see. Maybe another surfing lesson isn't such a good idea."

She tugged her hand out from his, determined not to let his charm get under her skin. "And I see you're still a comedian."

She walked a step behind him in the opposite direction of the beach and partygoers, away from the resort. Guilt slithered through her as she took the opportunity to check him out from behind. His hair was several shades lighter than her mocha brown—more of a caramel—and was buzzed short on the sides. She imagined the longer locks on top, slightly wavy, would feel thick and coarse inside her fingers. He possessed just enough muscle definition to make her believe he either surfed or ran often in addition to lifting weights. The corded sculpt of his neck and biceps were as big of a turn on in her eyes as the perfect lift of his rear-end.

Her heart stilled as he breached a stone path illuminated by tiki torches, leading into a cluster of eucalyptus trees. It was too dark. Too quiet. The kind of place where shadows played too many tricks. Her throat closed and her vision spotted with black as absolute, sheer terror stopped her dead in her tracks. "Where are you taking me?" she demanded. "Why did you lead me away from my friends?"

"I was just hoping for a little privacy." Turning to her, he casted a glance back at the luau behind them.

The accidental brush of his fingertips over her arm nearly had her jumping out of her skin. "I promise I wasn't planning anything sinister."

Calm down, she told herself. *You're overreacting.* She let out a shaking breath and patted the complicated bun Kinsley had bobby pinned to the back of her head. With her composure restored, she flashed him a well-crafted smile. "Sorry I snapped at you. I just..." *Didn't want to end up dead,* she said to herself.

"No, I get it. We're still strangers. But I want to change that." He shifted his weight and jammed his hands in the pockets of his shorts. "Since you're only here for two weeks, I wanted to lay everything on you up front. You and I made some kind of connection in California. It's something I can't shake—don't know what it is, but I haven't been able to shake it...shake *you*...ever since that day we went surfing together."

She released a nervous laugh unbecoming of her usual demeanor. "I'm not sure what to say, except that's a lot of shaking."

"I hated myself for not asking your name sooner. I hated that I didn't get a chance to see you again."

Tingling warmth spread through her belly, increasing the pull of attraction that begged her to stand on her toes and kiss him. "You wanted to see me again?"

"Yes I do...er...I mean I *did*. Back then." He stepped closer and dusted his fingertips over her forearms. "Damn it....I *still* do."

Lips parting with surprise, she held his beautiful gaze. Without the warmth of the sun shining on them, his brown eyes appeared as black and mysterious as the ocean without moonlight. Their shimmering intensity made her wonder what he'd been through. Did he have a dark past too? Her heartbeat rattled her entire body. She didn't know whether to be elated or uncomfortable with his confession. Although she'd once dreamed of seeing him again, she hadn't been lying when she told Drake she wasn't in a good place for a relationship.

"Riggs, I—"

"Suppose you could cover yourself with something?" Frowning, he sidestepped around her and ruffled his perfectly combed hair, letting out an annoyed grunt. "That damn dress...it's incredibly distracting."

She huffed and tugged on the plunging neckline. There wasn't any way to make it less revealing. "It's Kinsley's." She stared at his strong backside, wondering when he'd face her again. Wondering when he'd stop sending mixed signals. "It's not my normal style."

"It's not helping my cause."

"Your cause?"

He spun back around, eyes still averted away. "I want to give you more surfing lessons...or take you hiking...whatever you want, whatever you're interested in...whenever you have free time away from your family. I don't care, I just want to spend time with you."

"You're confusing."

"We'll spend time as *friends*. You and me. Friendly. We can be friends, right?"

"Of course," she confirmed. When disappointment settled over her shoulders she quickly reminded herself she didn't have room for a man in her emotionally complicated life. And it wasn't like she was going to move to Hawaii in order to date Riggs. Being his friend would be safe. And she could do safe. "But if we're going to be *friends*, you'll have to eventually look at me again."

"Only if you promise you'll never wear that dress again, or anything equally sexy."

Flattered he'd seen past her imperfections, she decided she'd attempt to flirt the way Kinsley had before becoming engaged. "Okay, but what will I wear for our surf lessons? I only packed bikinis."

"I'll buy you a wetsuit. One that covers everything and goes up to your chin."

An unexpected laugh bubbled from her throat. "Should I wear one of those hideous swimming caps, too?"

"That might not hurt." The ferocity in his eyes stole her breath. "I'm not in a position to start anything at the moment, so we're going to start our story off as friends, and see where life takes us." His tongue swept over his lips when he glanced down at her mouth. "You might be a bestseller author, but based on the way I caught you looking at me earlier, I have a really good feeling I know how this particular story will end."

21

Whenever Rowan wasn't involved in pre-nuptial activities in the week leading up to Kinsley and William's wedding, Riggs took her to remote locations for several more failed attempts at surfing lessons, daily jogs on the beach, and little tours around the island. As far as Rowan was concerned, it didn't leave them anywhere near enough time alone. They fell into a comfortable friendship, one without premise or expectations, although sexual tension remained high—just as it'd been that fateful day in California.

But their fourth morning together, while their bare feet pounded the golden sand in perfect unison and the gentle breeze from the ocean fluttered through their hair, Rowan considered ending it all with the utterance of one question.

"How'd a sweet girl like you decide to write about the life of a serial killer's daughter?"

His words struck her with the force of a lightning bolt. She stopped suddenly, bending in half. Belatedly, she braced a hand on her running shorts over her hips, as if warding off a runner's cramp. The question wasn't anything she hadn't been asked before, mostly while on tour. She'd usually smile gracefully, and say the idea had come to her during a conversation with a friend about true crime. But hearing it from Riggs, knowing she had no choice but to lie to him, swamped her with remorse.

"You alright?" he asked, circling back to her side.

She willed herself not to look up at him, knowing the sight of his beautifully muscled chest pricked with sweat from their run, and the tension of muscle in his thick thighs beneath sweat-wicking shorts would make her insides dance with joy. It wasn't a sensation she could allow to mix with the jarring impact of his sudden question. Just being around him made her light-headed enough already. Her ponytail danced when she shook her head. "I didn't drink enough water this morning."

From the corner of her eye, she saw him glance toward the thicket of palm trees on the edge of the resort's property. "We can walk the rest of the way."

She sucked in a lungful of salty air and stood, swiping her fingertips between the dip of her breasts beneath her sports bra. "That would probably be best."

They cut toward the lawn and passed through the resort's flourishing garden. He gave her an animated tour of the different species of flowers, explaining how he'd worked closely with the landscaping company to breathe new life into the outdated resort. Her chest lifted and her pulse steadied when she was certain the subject of her book had been forgotten. Then he said, "The book is really good, Rowan. I've been reading a few chapters every night, whenever I can't sleep. I can see why it made a best-seller list, although it makes me wonder how *you* sleep at night."

"I don't," she replied, her words clipped.

"Sorry, I didn't mean to—"

She stopped and turned to him, well-practiced smile stretched over her lips. "It's alright."

His eyes darkened. "No, it's not. I upset you."

"I'm the one who should be apologizing. I shouldn't have snapped at you. It's just...there are things from my past that keep me up at night. Things I don't like to talk about." She didn't want to taint their easy-going relationship by telling him about her father. She didn't want to wonder if he'd pitied her, or wondered if whatever sickness her father had could be hereditary.

The heat of his hand covered her trembling fingers and gave a little squeeze. "I know the feeling. If that ever changes, if you decide you want to clear your head and dump everything on someone else, I'm here for it. Maybe not always physically, but at least a phone call away."

Her smile melted along with her heart. "That's kind of you."

Irrefutably charming dimples slipped onto his cheeks with a grin. "Screw kindness. It's the kind of thing friends do."

TWO DAYS BEFORE THE WEDDING, Riggs arranged to take Rowan, Kinsley, Taylor, and Steph on a hike through Pipiwai Trail on the northeast side of the island. He flew them to the location in a private helicopter on which the women sipped on champagne and reminisced over Kinsley's past relationships. Rowan drank more champagne than planned when she needed an excuse to stop grinning at Riggs the entire time he sat directly across from her on the ride. Not only was he handsome and funny, but he'd been overly kind and generous to her and her family. She had to remind her heart several times to calm down, because she knew it would be far too easy to love him.

Taylor had to sit out on the hike to the Seven Sacred Pools after she broke into a coughing fit during a laughing spell. Although Rowan worried she was coming down with something, Taylor claimed it had been brought on by all the champagne. The experience was otherwise quite lovely, Rowan decided. She wondered if the others noticed how quickly Riggs gravitated toward her all afternoon, no matter their proximity.

Following the hike, Riggs then treated the four women to the highest spa package the resort had available. When they returned to Kinsley and William's penthouse, feeling reenergized, he surprised them with an intimate steak and lobster dinner by candlelight on the lanai. Since Kinsley deemed bachelorette parties to be tacky, the women continued to drink champagne on the lanai for several hours after watching the jaw-dropping sunset. Steph and Taylor were unable to stop gushing about the "prince" who'd treated them to the most magical day they could remember.

Rowan couldn't help but agree, and that scared her.

THE NIGHT BEFORE THE WEDDING, Riggs was nearly finished with Rowan's book when he heard the padding of bare feet against hardwood. The door swung open and Chelsea waltzed in, bare hips and enhanced tits swaying as she waved her designer sunglasses through the air. "Alissa said she saw you with Kinsley Lewis and her sad little gang earlier this afternoon. I can't believe you agreed to let that second-rate producer and his child bride get married here."

Riggs wanted to roar at the skies in anger—something he hadn't done since he was a surly teenager without a real home. Chelsea had finally shown her true colors *after* he'd invited her to live with him in Maui. Had he known she was prone to so much ugliness, he would've left her in New York without having to think twice.

"Will and Kinsley are actually really chill people, Chels. You should come down from your high pedestal for a change. Make an effort to get to know them."

She lowered to her knees on the mattress, straddling him with the kind of beckoning look that long ago would've revved his motor. He'd wised up, however, and knew it was the kind of expression she made when she was ready to declare something, and wouldn't allow her mind to be changed under any circumstances. "You realize we can't get married here now, right? No way I'll follow in the footsteps of some second-rate producer and a skanky understudy. We'll have to go to Greece, or the Maldives."

Riggs's gaze followed the manicured fingers stroking over his chest, wincing with the sight of the 4 carat diamond ring he'd proposed with on Valentine's Day—the same day he'd asked her to move to Maui. If time travel was a real thing, he'd pay whatever it took to go back and kick his own ass.

Sucking air through his tightening jaw, he peeled her hand off his chest. "About that...I think we should slow down. Think this through a little longer. Are we really ready to settle down?"

After causing five figures' worth of damage to the villa, Chelsea took off with a friend for a week on Kauai, likely cozying up to men more wealthy than Riggs and Victor combined. If he hadn't made her sign a prenup, the process of ending their relationship would've been simple and painless. And with the terms her attorney had added, he stood to lose everything. The more he got to know Rowan, he started to believe it might be worth the cost.

Later that night, after the rehearsal dinner, Kinsley and William's friends and family indulged in tropical drinks while dancing beneath a sky filled with brilliant stars. Although it wasn't intended to be as elegant of an affair as their upcoming reception, Riggs had gone out of his way to make the first occasion of its kind at his resort an Instagram-worthy event. He'd personally selected the 3-man, college-aged band after watching clips of them paying tribute to such greats as The Beach Boys, Jack Johnson, and Billy Joel. Rope lights wound around every palm tree in sight, and larger globe lights had been strung between them. Freshly cut tropical flowers in crystal vases among floating votive candles adorned every round table covered in soft pink linens. It was as romantic as it was beautiful to behold, especially as his eyes continuously gravitated to the most attractive woman in attendance.

Whenever he caught Rowan looking his way, he struggled to contain his excitement. Every time she flashed him one of her carefree, youthful smiles—instead of the bullshit ones she threw whenever she felt uneasy—he wanted to gather her into his arms and steal a taste of her sultry lips. Better yet, he wanted to crawl into one of the resort's hammocks by the ocean with her cocooned inside his arms, and pretend the rest of the world didn't exist. Their time together had been cut in half, and he couldn't stand to think about it ending.

AS THE CELEBRATION was winding down, William approached Rowan just moments after she'd thrown Riggs another genuine grin. "What's with you and that handsome bloke running this resort?" he asked, eyes animated with the lights strewn overhead. "He certainly appears to fancy you."

"We're just friends," Rowan answered with an air of confidence.

One of his eyebrows crooked into an inverted V. "Is he aware of that?"

Deciding it was best to ignore his interrogation, she stirred her piña colada and motioned to Kinsley with a lift of her chin. "You two seem happy."

When she braved another look in his direction, she caught his dark eyes leering over the curves beneath her modest sundress. "I could never be *unhappy* with an exquisite piece of arse."

Fingering the charm bracelet around her wrist, She carefully swallowed the lump building in her throat. Surely she'd drank too much, and was misreading the signals he was sending. "In that case, you're lucky to have Kins. She's the definition of exquisite."

"I'm not so sure about that, love." Unmistakable lust spread through his gaze when it connected with hers. "I can think of one arse even more exquisite."

The harsh burn of alcohol seared through her throat. Hitting on his fiancée's best friend the night before their wedding was beyond despicable. How could he do that to Kinsley? In one breath, he'd confirmed her fear that no men could be trusted.

Bracing herself against the surge of her stomach, she gritted her teeth through an elegant smile. "I won't presume to know what's going through your head right now, *William*, but I'd suggest you return to your future bride before I decide to make a scene."

He bent down to her ear, the stench of hard alcohol on his hot breath. "And I'd like to suggest you keep your ridiculous accusations to yourself. Imagine Kinsley's misfortune once she learns her 'bestie' tried to bed her future husband the night before their nuptials."

She stood perfectly straight and eased back to

look him in the eye. "You really think she'd believe your bogus story over the word of a friend she spent half her life protecting from creeps like you?"

Unease gripped Rowan's insides as he spoke. "To be perfectly clear, love, you're referring to the word of a *serial killer's daughter.*" A swirl of amusement spread through his gaze as he bent in once again, lips curled with a Cheshire Cat grin. "Who would *you* believe?"

22

Riggs stepped in behind Rowan with a firm hand pressed to the small of her back. "Everything alright over here?"

With a silent gasp, Rowan stumbled backwards. Heart racing, she desperately tried to pull in a breath. Kinsley had shared her well-protected secret with William, a disgusting excuse of a man. Now that he'd shown her how truly ruthless he could be, who knew what he'd do with that information? He had the power to reveal her identity…to ruin her career. The need to flee assaulted her insides with an urgent tug.

"I need some air," Rowan wheezed, staggering away with her drink still in hand. The hot burn of piña colada and her building tears made it hard to think. She dropped the cup and wound her arms around her stomach as she stumbled away.

Catching the shadow of someone close behind casting over the sand, her heart galloped and the icy fingers of fear dug against her brain.

"What'd that guy say to you?" Riggs demanded from right behind her.

She startled with the sound of his voice. As hard as she tried to steady her breathing, it continued to fall in harsh, shallow gasps. Her best friend was marrying a womanizer, just as Drake had suspected, and there wasn't anything she could do without his counter-accusation threatening to destroy nearly a decade's worth of friendship. Not only that, but he was armed with critical information that could transform her life into a neverending circus.

Coaxing her farther away from the party, Riggs rubbed circles against her back. "Nice and easy. I think it's a good idea for you to sit down, and put your head between your knees until you can breathe properly. Don't worry, I won't let anyone bother you."

When his hand moved from her back to her shoulder, she gave into the gentle pressure and squatted down to the ground, sucking the damp tropical air into her lungs. The deep lull of Riggs's voice soothed over her nerves. "That's right. In through your nose, out through your mouth. Atta girl. You've got it."

Once her breathing steadied, humiliation weighed heavy on her bones. "You must think I'm mentally unstable." With a shake of her head, she covered her burning face with her hands. "Riggs—"

"No need to explain yourself."

"There's a lot going on in my life…things I wish I could tell you, but I can't." She removed her hands to meet his kind expression. "At least not yet."

He offered a kind smile. "There's no rule saying we have to bear our souls to each other in order to remain friends."

She jerked her gaze back to the party. "I can't go back there. I can't let William see me like this after what just happened." She clutched his muscular bicep with a sudden bout of nausea gripping her belly. "How am I going to face Kinsley tomorrow?"

"One step at a time. I'll help you figure this all out after I take you to your suite."

Gazing into his honeyed eyes, lit with a level of compassion she'd only witnessed in her aunt, she nodded with a surge of enthusiasm. He lodged his arm beneath hers, helping her rise back onto her feet. With a rush of appreciation filling her chest, she tightly wound her arm around his waist, holding him close for a single heartbeat before allowing him to lead her away.

RIGGS PATIENTLY WAITED in the hallway outside Rowan's suite as she dug for her key-card inside the small handbag he'd retrieved from her table. If any of his less-than-loyal staff members witnessed him entering a room with a beautiful female guest, Chelsea would have his balls. Hell, her attorneys would make sure she had *his fortune*. He was already lucky Chelsea had been too busy to catch on to his activities while she'd been around.

Still, he wasn't going to abandon Rowan after she'd suffered a significant panic attack. And he had faith the majority of his well-paid employees would remain tight-lipped.

It had been alarming to witness a woman as strong as Rowan in a fragile state. Whatever that English prick said to her had been damaging enough to strip her of her usual in-control attitude. He'd be damned if he let the incident completely slide before the newlyweds left his resort. The fact that Rowan couldn't weigh more than a buck and a quarter made him seethe with even more anger. What kind of jackass threatened a woman less than half his size?

He heaved a silent sigh of relief once they were safely inside the suite. He made a bee-line toward the kitchen and pointed at the white sofa. "Have a seat. I'll get you some ice water and a wet washcloth."

Behind him, he heard her drop down onto the linen furniture. "I wouldn't have guessed you could be so bossy."

Who would've guessed she could become so rattled, he thought to himself. She remained quiet as he gathered the promised items and crouched down on the hardwood floor beside her legs. "Hold the cloth against the back of your neck, and drink as much of the water as you can stomach without getting sick."

"Yes, sir." From the slight slur of her words, he suspected she was decently intoxicated. As he watched her empty the glass, his hands balled into fists at his sides. Why hadn't her friends and family kept a better eye on her when it was obvious something had forced her into a delicate state of mind? He had picked up on little things throughout the week, like the extreme way she reacted to being surprised, and the way she slightly recoiled around other men.

Plus there were those damn artificial smiles that she tossed out like candy at a parade. He could almost picture her delivering a matching wave while perched high on a float, sparkling crown on her head. He didn't understand how someone could both project the vibes of an elegant beauty queen, yet be so soft and gentle on the inside. He only hoped her hot-and-cold demeanor wasn't because some bastard had broken her.

"Better?" he asked, taking the glass from her petite fingers.

Head inclined, she studied him through narrowed eyes. "Why're you so good at this? How'd you know exactly what to do when I...you know?"

He pushed off from the floor and sat on the sofa a cushion's distance away. "I helped a friend get through panic attacks many years after he'd lost his wife."

Her expression softened. "How tragic."

"It was, but he's better now thanks to years of faithful therapy and meditation." His brow furrowed when he glanced at the perfectly made bed through the bedroom's doors, adorned with chocolates and a sprinkling of plumeria petals. Why did the cleaning staff's usual turn-down treatment suddenly allude to a heightened degree of romance?

"You should get some sleep. Tomorrow's going to be a big day."

"Would it be rude to ask you to stay a little longer? Maybe just watch a sitcom or something silly until I fall asleep?" Yawning, she brought her knees up to her chin and wrapped her arms around her legs. "At least until the demons go away," she muttered sleepily.

Discontent seized his spine with the force of a giant's fist. What kind of "demons" plagued her, and why? His mind began to wander with horrifying possibilities.

"No problem," he replied. The long, brightly colored dress she wore was a significant improvement from the skimpy number she'd worn to the luau, yet it still filled his head with provocative thoughts. Resisting the natural instinct to draw her into the safety of his arms, he grabbed the remote instead, flipping through until he came across a rerun of *Will and Grace*.

With another yawn, she rested her head on the back of the cushion separating them. "I seriously adore this show. Jack and Karen are the best."

"Let me know if you want something from room service…on me. I could order haupia, or guava chiffon cakes—"

He stopped with the sound of her soft snores to study her at her most vulnerable. The way her dark lashes fanned across the apples of her cheek stirred something in his chest. She must've known she was a natural beauty the way she wore very little makeup. But why did it seem as if she was always on guard the way she threw out insincere smiles, and so often sat rigid, as if ready to run? She looked younger when sleeping—softer. At peace.

He covered her with the lightweight blanket strewn over the back of the sofa. By the time his eyelids became too heavy to keep open, her head had shifted down onto his shoulder. As a reward for behaving around her, he allowed himself the pleasure of getting a proper inhale of her scent. She wore perfume that smelled of lilacs and something else... something soft and sensual. He drifted away while conspiring ways to work around the prenup he'd signed.

URGENT POUNDING on the door jolted them both from a hard slumber. It seemed they had naturally gravitated towards each other in their sleep—her curled up against his side, his arm clutched possessively over her bent leg. Their wide eyes met, and they bolted apart.

"Rowan Brooks, answer the damn door!" Kinsley demanded amongst more pounding. "I know you're in there!"

A fresh layer of panic slithered into Rowan's gut. She clamped her chattering teeth together while gripping the backside of Riggs's hand. "What do I do?" she frantically whispered. "Break my best friend's heart and likely cancel her wedding, or lie to her and take the fall for whatever ridiculous story William fed her in the night?"

Voice husky with sleep, he asked in turn, "Which scenario would help you sleep at night?" When she flinched, he flipped his hand around to grip her fingers inside his hand. "One step at a time, remember? You'll figure it out." Then he slipped off the sofa and eyed the set of bedroom doors. "I'll just...ah... make a quick inspection of the bedroom until she leaves—make sure everything is in proper order."

"Embarrassed to be seen with me the morning after?" she teased, her voice tight with nerves.

Eyes soft, he gave a melancholy shake of his head. "You aren't the only one with a complicated life. Trust me when I say I wish I could tell you everything too."

"Rowan!" Kinsley roared from the hallway. "I don't care if you have a Hawaiian hottie in there! Don't make me kick this door down!"

"Go," Rowan urged, frantically motioning toward the bedroom.

He held her gaze for a moment. "You can do this."

She smiled, thankful for his faith in her. It took a little edge off her vibrating nerves. As the bedroom doors closed, she rushed to unlock the front door to the suite. With the sight of her teary-eyed friend standing in the hallway, white embroidered robe declaring her to be "the bride," wide pink curlers set in her hair, massive bouquet of bright red flowers clutched in her trembling hands, Rowan's knees turned to jelly. The hallway became a giant blur as Kinsley shoved the Spider Lilies into Rowan's limp arms.

"This isn't funny, Ro! Why would you do this? How could you be so cruel on my wedding day?"

23

Riggs hadn't intentionally listened in on the friends' conversation in the next room, but there was no mistaking the urgency in Kinsley's voice when she cried Rowan's name. He had no choice but to run to them. In the suite's entrance, the bride-to-be was sprawled out on the floor, tears streaming down her cheeks as she cradled her limp friend in her arms. Rowan lay lifeless, surrounded by crushed lilies. His heart stopped with such sudden force that he feared it wouldn't start again.

"What happened?" he demanded, rushing to Kinsley's side.

"She must've passed out! I caught her before her head hit the floor!"

"Let's put her down…gently, flat on her back." He helped her lower Rowan to the floor, then brushed her dark hair away from her face and checked her neck for a pulse. He let out a stammered breath when strong, steady beats fluttered against his fingertips. It was a good start, he decided.

"This is all my fault!" Kinsley wept beside him. "I should've known she didn't really send them...she'd never do anything that wicked." She touched the arm he braced over Rowan. "Is she okay?"

"I don't know." His heart slammed so hard against his ribs that he couldn't think clearly. "Is she diabetic? Does she have any health conditions?"

"No—but she's on some meds for anxiety and depression! I don't know which ones!"

Riggs had taken first aid classes as a kid to impress Victor, but he had no idea how those medications could affect her current situation. He grasped Rowan's shoulders, giving her a firm shake. "Rowan, wake up." Teeth clenched, he shook her again, harder. "Rowan! Wake up, dammit!"

At last, she drew in a silent gasp, eyelids fluttering. "What happened?"

"You passed out." When she flexed her abdomen, intending to sit upright, Riggs slipped a hand behind her back to assist her. "Easy does it." His hand briefly massaged the back of her neck before he stood. "Stay put. I'll get you some water before I call the resort's physician." The resort didn't actually have an in-house physician, but he was confident his personal doctor would be there in a heartbeat if he were to ask for her services.

"No doctor," Rowan insisted, a touch of panic in her voice. "Please."

Riggs folded his arms and grunted, not exactly satisfied, but willing to do whatever would make her happy. "Fine, but I'm not leaving you alone until I'm convinced you're okay." If he had his way, he'd convince her to see a doctor after the wedding.

WHILE RIGGS RETRIEVED a glass of water, Kinsley dropped down to embrace her confused friend. "Rowan, I'm sorry! I should've known better!"

"The lilies..." Rowan recoiled with the sight of the red flowers scattered all around her. Her stomach cramped. Was her father free? Was it a sign that he was coming for her? Unease slithering through her belly with the stealth of a snake approaching its prey, she met Kinsley's glossy green eyes. "Why'd you think they were from me?"

"Because they came with a card that said, 'wishing you a special day full of surprises.' Your name was at the bottom." Eyes pressed shut, Kinsley shook her head repeatedly, making the large curlers slip even further down her locks. "Who would do something so awful? And why?"

Chills swept through Rowan as her entire body quivered. Maybe the flowers had nothing to do with her father. William knew everything, and he had no qualms threatening her the night before.

Riggs returned to spread the thin blanket from the sofa over Rowan's shoulders before squatting at her side and handing her a chilled glass. He eyed the lilies with a deep frown. "What's this about the flowers?"

Rowan attempted to swallow, but her throat was bone dry. How could she possibly explain how she'd fainted over something so harmless? "They have special meaning."

"And not in a good way." Kinsley huffed with a visible shiver. "We don't know who sent them."

"Who else knows the significance of the flowers?" Riggs demanded. "Who knows about the wedding?"

"Hardly anyone," Rowan told him. "I've spent most of my life keeping my association with them a secret." She inwardly winced, realizing she'd revealed too much.

Kinsley anxiously tugged at the belt on her terry cloth robe. "Um, except for the part about the wedding. Anyone who reads page six would know Will and I are getting married here."

Casting a dark look Kinsley's way, Riggs asked, "They were delivered to your room?" If Rowan wasn't accustomed to his gentle nature by that point, his sudden change of demeanor would've terrified her. He looked ready to rip someone's head clean off. With Kinsley's affirmative nod, he abruptly stood. "I'm going to need the card that accompanied the flowers."

Kinsley nodded again. "It's in the penthouse."

"I'll get to the bottom of this." He marched over to the suite's phone in the dining area with the attitude of a man large and in charge. After punching a set of numbers into the keypad, he spoke into the receiver with a voice too quiet for Rowan to hear. Witnessing his dominance made her feel confused and uncertain. She was used to him always teasing her, and making her laugh.

"Um, what was Mr. Hottie doing in your bedroom this early in the morning?" Kinsley whispered, a scandalous grin tugging at her lips. "And why are both of you still dressed in the same clothes as last night? Is that why you disappeared so suddenly?"

"I had a lot to drink. I must've fallen asleep before I had a chance to change. Riggs stopped by to check on the leaky sink in the master bathroom."

"You expect me to believe that ridiculous story?" Kinsley's brows shot upward. "A handsome hotel manager who gives one-on-one tours to select guests *and* does their maintenance calls? How convenient."

"Would you stop?" Rowan pleaded, briefly glancing over to where Riggs continued barking into the phone. "It's not like that. He insists we can't be anything more than friends. I'm starting to think it's because he has a girlfriend in either California or New York."

"That's super skeezy." Kinsley wrinkled her nose. "And you still want to hang out with him?"

Unease balled in the pit of Rowan's stomach. She desperately wanted to tell Kinsley the conversation she'd had with her fiancé nearly as badly as she wanted to protect her from the crushing secret of his ugly behavior. If Riggs discovered William had in fact sent the flowers using Rowan's name, she'd have no choice other than to tell Kinsley the truth. "I don't want that kind of relationship anyway, Kins. Even if I did, I wouldn't start seeing someone who lives almost five thousand miles away."

Kinsley eyed Riggs with another devilish smile. "Either way, that's tragic, because that man is *f-i-n-e*."

Chugging the last of her water, Rowan silently assented. Aside from the sudden change in personality, Riggs was the perfect package—just apparently one not meant for her. She never dreamed she'd discover an attractive, kind man whom she didn't have to keep her guard up when around him, and one who constantly engaged her in carefree laughter. She refused to dwell on the truth…to wonder what kind of woman was out there somewhere, waiting for her beloved Riggs to return. She eyed Kinsley's wayward curlers. "You better return to the penthouse before your stylist team has a fit."

"She's right," Riggs agreed, moving in behind them. He bent to help Rowan back to her feet, and continued to support her with a firm arm slung across her back, hand braced on her hip. Her belly tingled from the intimate proximity, despite her new qualms. "You don't have to worry, Kinsley. I'll keep a close eye on this one until you're ready for her."

Kinsley's thin arms wound around her own waist. "Did you find out who sent the flowers?"

"No, but the florist gave me the credit card number used for the transaction, and I forwarded it to the resort's investigator. She was confident she'll be able to produce a name within the hour."

Rowan tried not to fret over what the investigator would find. A simple internet search on spider lilies could quickly uncover her biggest secret. Making a sweeping motion with her hands, she inclined her head toward the door. "Go forth, Kins. You're about to be married."

Giggling, Kinsley kissed Rowan's cheek. "Okay, but you better rest up before it's your turn to get beautified. There's a mimosa waiting up there with your name on it." She moved over to Riggs, standing on her toes to kiss his cheek as well. "Thanks for taking care of my girl. She means the world to me."

"I can understand why," he replied, aiming one of his dimpled grins Rowan's way. The pulse in her throat skipped a beat when she swallowed. It was impossible to tell if he was merely being charming and polite, or outright flirting. The possibilities had her head spinning.

Kinsley started for the door, her heels punching down through the tattered lilies. "Oh. What should I—"

"Don't worry about it," Riggs told her. "I'll take care of them too."

"The sooner the better," she said.

RIGGS FELT the fight leave Rowan's body once her friend was out of sight. He steeled his arm behind her and guided her towards the bedroom doors. Although he'd been eager to see her in the pale blue bridesmaid's dress he'd spotted hanging in her closet, he was beginning to worry she wouldn't have the stamina to make it to the ceremony. "Let's get you situated in bed. I'll clean up out here, and order you something for breakfast. Any preferences?"

"You don't have to babysit me, Riggs. I'm perfectly fine now." She removed the blanket from her shoulders and started to pull away. "I have to shower, and—"

He gingerly brought her back against him, hardly resisting the chance to embrace her with a reassuring kiss. "Your body suffered a major trauma. You'll never make it through the day if you don't start it with a good, hearty breakfast." He pointed at the bed, still adorned with those damn chocolates and flowers. "Rest until your food arrives. You can shower after you're finished eating."

"There's that bossy side again," she muttered, gingerly relaxing into his side. "I'm starting to empathize with your poor staff."

"What can I say? Good friends don't let each other pass out at weddings, and stink the place up."

She allowed him to help her settle against the wall of white pillows propped against the headboard. He loved that she could be just as stubborn as she often was proper. After brushing his lips over her cool forehead, he clicked the flatscreen on and set the remote next to her before closing the bedroom doors. He didn't want her overhearing his next conversation.

THE BRIDE WORE an off-the-shoulder ivory gown with a boned bodice and puffy chiffon sleeves fit for a princess. The dainty crown nestled in Kinsley's flowing red curls matched the complicated beading sewn onto the gown's lace skirt. It was a one-of-a-kind dress created by one of New York's top five wedding designers, and Rowan decided it couldn't have been more fitting for a future Broadway star.

Her heart shattered like glass beneath the drop of a hammer as she witnessed her glowing best friend exchanging vows with the less than honorable producer, the setting sun staining the sky behind them with glorious hues of pink and purple.

As they'd lined up for the ceremony, William had shot her a smug look as if to remind her of his threat. She'd gone out of her way to avoid making any more eye contact with him ever since. Instead, she focused on the subtle off-white print embroidered onto Riggs's white linen shirt. He'd taken a seat in the back row where he could both keep a close eye on the ceremony, and discreetly communicate with staff members.

More than once, she'd caught his gaze skimming over the feminine braid woven among her barrel curls, and down to her sky blue, A-line dress that draped over her bare feet in the sand. The first time, she feared he'd noticed the princess boning and v-neck were slightly ill-fitting after she'd allowed herself to indulge in a healthy serving of the steak and lobster meal the other night without purging after. The second time their eyes connected, the desire in his honeyed gaze had been unmistakeable, making her stomach buzz with false anticipation.

When he hadn't pressed her on the subject of the

spider lilies, she'd been exceptionally grateful—especially when he stayed in her suite and took care of everything as promised, giving her enough privacy to call Detective Novak and confirm her father was still behind bars. It only somewhat calmed her to learn he couldn't have been the culprit. Someone else wanted her to suffer. But who?

Riggs had shared breakfast with her once it had arrived, and accompanied her an hour later when she was summoned by Kinsley's beauty team. After they'd completed her hair and makeup, he'd asked the stylist team to clear the room so he could report his investigator's findings to Kinsley and Rowan. The flowers had been ordered with a credit card stolen from a man who lived in South Carolina. Without obtaining a warrant to trace the phone number from which the order was placed, the investigator had reached a dead end.

When he'd relayed the information to them, the intensity in his honeyed eyes was so severe that Rowan had to look away. Even without knowing the significance of the spider lilies, he was visibly irate that someone had messed with them. Rowan feared his investigator had already uncovered the truth. Would he still want to spend time alone with her once he discovered she was the offspring of someone so vile?

There hadn't been the slightest hesitation when he'd stepped up to play the role of her hero—first after the incident with William, then again after the delivery of the flowers. Despite her reservations, nothing had ever felt as natural as accepting his protection. Knowing he'd only be in her life for another week, she finally recognized her attachment to him was becoming tragically deep.

As the resort's officiant announced "Mr. and Mrs. Halsrud," Rowan artificially smiled through watery eyes, praying her best friend hadn't married a man savage enough to have sent the flowers. She joined Drake behind the newlyweds, taking his arm with an even bigger smile. Her childhood friend looked exceptionally dapper in the slimming gray suit and sky blue tie worn by all the groomsmen, sandy hair sharply parted off to one side and recently trimmed.

"Don't do that," he whispered, squeezing her arm draped between them. "Don't give me one of those pageant smiles. I can tell you're upset."

"Not now," she pleaded through more tears. "This is your sister's day."

The wedding party and their families were summoned by the photographer for another session on the beach. By the time they'd finished and gathered around the long tables set for dinner in the same prime location as where the luau and rehearsal dinner had taken place, Rowan didn't know how she could possibly muster another smile. Needing a moment to herself, she slipped away while a group of guests fawned over Kinsley's dazzling wedding band.

She'd made it to the torch-lit path Riggs had brought her to that first night when someone snagged her arm and jerked her backwards. Colliding with a hard chest, she shrieked.

"It's *me*." Drake dragged her close against him, nearly crushing her in his arms. His breath was pungently sour. "Sorry I scared you. Are you okay?"

"I'm great." Brushing off a flicker of fear, she took a step back. Why did he continue to embrace her with the intimacy of a lover after everything she'd said? "Are you drunk?"

"I need to know if you're *really* okay, Ro." Hands on either side of her face, he searched her watering eyes as the pads of his thumbs stroked her cheeks in tandem. "Kins told me about the spider lilies that were delivered to her this morning."

Briefly closing her eyes, she detached his hands from her face. "I don't want to talk about it."

"Who *exactly* did you tell that you'd be in Hawaii for a wedding?"

"No one that isn't here, other than my old roommate, but she doesn't know about my father."

"You're sure there's no one else?"

The idea that anyone close to her would've done it was ludicrous. She'd only informed a select few for good reason. "There aren't many people in the know. Your family, my grandparents, Taylor, one of my college professors, my psychiatrists, a woman my editor sent along with me on my book tour. And I guess you can add William to the list now too, because last night he told me he knows my secret."

"What?" His head ticked with a brief shake. "Why? Under what context?"

With the palms of her hands held up, she backed away. "I can't talk about this with you."

"Why not? This conversation isn't over, dammit!" He lurched at her, digging his fingers into her elbows. Something wild flashed in his eyes. "What about the resort manager you've been cozying up to all week—making eyes at from across the room? Does that asshole know?"

The tears burning behind her eyes gave way. She couldn't catch her breath, and her heart was one beat from bursting out of her chest. "Let go of me," she warned.

"Not until you answer my question! I know you've been spending time alone with him, so don't lie to me! Did you tell him in the throes of passion, while he was buried deep inside you?" With a dark scowl pulling at his lips, he began to lightly shake her. "Why him and not me? Why aren't I good enough for you?"

"Drake, stop! You're hurting me!"

Eyes growing wide with her declaration, he released her and stumbled back. He scrubbed his face with both hands, then nervously regarded the party in the distance. "I'm sorry, Ro. I didn't mean to—"

"Forget it." Unable to face him any longer without cracking, she turned back to the resort's main building while swiping a knuckle over her fallen tears. "If Kins asks where I am, tell her I went to my room to freshen up. I'll come back down in a little bit."

24

In the privacy of her suite bathroom, Rowan splashed cold water on her face and used a makeup wipe. She felt significantly better once she'd reapplied a lighter dusting of her own bronzer, mascara, and eyeliner. The artist Kinsley hired had used too heavy of a hand, resulting in a look that had been far too close to Rowan's days of competition for her comfort.

She popped the cork on a small Prosecco from the mini bar, and stepped out onto her dark lanai while taking a swig directly from the bottle. She felt a touch of envy, imagining Riggs was rewarded with the same breath-taking view every single night. On one of their runs together, he'd mentioned the scenery never got old, but he sometimes experienced island fever. He'd also confessed he'd been orphaned, with an old friend in New York being his only family.

It was the most information he'd shared about himself since they'd met. She supposed the information had made her feel a little more connected to him, on another level.

Although her circle of friends and family had grown since she'd left Blue Bay, she couldn't help wondering if it would be easier to move far away where she didn't sense the ghosts of her father's transgressions. Then again, those same ghosts had already found her in Hawaii. Trickles of fear spilled down the sides of her neck when it dawned on her that Vanessa was one of few people in the know. They hadn't parted ways on good terms. Was her own mother diabolical enough to taunt her as punishment for allowing *The Devil's Daughter* to be published?

Watching the shimmering moon cast a magical glow over the splendid island, the conversation with Drake repeated in her mind. His anger and jealousy had triggered yet another panic attack. Until then, he'd been among one of her few safety nets. She was beginning to think there was no one she could trust.

A brisk knock came from the suite's front door. The hand was heavy, ruling Kinsley out as her visitor. She feared it was Drake, or worse yet, *William*. Sighing, she lifted the chiffon skirt of her dress and padded barefoot across the hardwood floor to peer into the hallway. Flutters erupted throughout her belly when beautiful honeyed brown eyes peered back through the peephole.

With only a slight hesitation, she disengaged the lock and opened the door to let Riggs in. "How did you know I was here?"

"Kinsley heard you'd gone to your room. She asked me to check on you." As he breezed past her, his youthful grin stilled her heart. His white linen shirt was accompanied by tan dress shorts and bare feet. Something about the familiarity of his casual style took her breath away. She'd never considered any man as beautiful as the one she'd met all those years ago, when they'd both been younger and she'd been more naive.

Something clicked deep inside her soul. Whatever it was about him called to her in a way that was too complicated to put into words.

When the door shut behind him, she snagged the collar on his shirt, drawing him dangerously close. His jaw flexed, eyes darkened. Their twinned heavy breaths were the only sound aside from the gentle lull of waves spilling from the open lanai door. The idea that she might be forcing him to do something wrong fizzed with his hardy, masculine scent. Girlfriends back home be damned—she didn't want to leave the island without the delight of tasting the man who'd shown her kindness and compassion at every turn.

His gaze flickered down to her parted lips. "Rowan...you, in that dress...Christ." His fingertips gripped her hips, hard enough to leave marks, and his eyes darkened. She drew in a ragged breath in anticipation of his lovely lips finally finding their way to hers. "You have no idea how badly I wish I could swoop you into my arms, and throw you down on the bed in the next room." On a deeply discontented sigh, he released her. "But I can't."

RIGGS CHARGED towards the mini bar. She was too fucking irresistible in that pretty blue dress. Especially once she'd cleaned her face to expose her freckles. When her lips had become temptingly close, the urge to call Chelsea on her cell phone and end it for good had made his fingertips throb. But it would've been an asshole move, unfair to everyone involved. And it very well could've resulted in devastating consequences.

He had to clear his head and calm his dick. With

his back to Rowan, he tipped back a travel-sized whiskey in one swallow and closed his eyes, savoring the harsh burn. "We better get back to the reception before Kinsley starts to suspect—"

"My father is the SLS killer."

The pit of his stomach roared with unease. "What—?"

"The Spider Lily Stranger…Jonathan Rivers." Jaw clamped tight, she stepped closer. "My real name is Sienna Rivers. I changed it after my father's arrest… when I moved to Blue Bay to live with my aunt. That's why those lilies upset Kinsley. That's why they had such a profound effect on me."

"Holy shit." Dropping down into one of the white leather chairs flanking the kitchen's island, he ran a trembling hand through his hair. He wanted to believe she was crazy, only creating a wild tale to gain his sympathy, but he knew better. Rowan wasn't the type. He realized it was the thing from her past she'd mentioned that kept her awake at night.

He remembered hearing stories of the SLS killer when he was younger. The monster from Brooklyn had brutally strangled dozens of women across the country throughout more than a decade-long killing spree. "Holy shit," he muttered again.

Her eyes skated across the suite. "I wanted you to

know the truth in case your decision not to sleep with me is because you think I'm unhinged, or unstable. I mean, I can't say with uncertainty that's not the case, but my therapist says the truth is far more complicated."

Baffled by her reasoning, he stood and strode back to her. "That's not at all what I was thinking." He framed her weary face with his hands. She was as beautiful as anything he'd seen. And so delicate. "I suspected you'd been through something dark and ugly...something that had changed you...made you afraid of your own shadow, but—Christ, Rowan." Unbearable rage swelled inside his throat. He wanted to throw something heavy across the room and watch in satisfaction as it shattered. "Did he ever...*hurt* you?"

"No. He never even tried—not physically anyway. He hurt me plenty in other ways." One of her hands rested over his frazzled heart. "He's the reason I'm afraid you're the only man I'll ever trust." The way she searched his expression, he assumed she was hoping to see a sign of reluctance. A chance that he'd give in.

"So the book you wrote—"

"It started out as a way to deal with my emotions, but it was accidentally sent to the wrong person. Somewhere along the way I was convinced to turn it into a fictionalized version of the truth. I'm beginning to think it was a serious mistake."

Nodding with understanding, he toyed with the silver charms dangling from her wrist. "You were wearing this the day we met. Is it from him?"

"No. I wouldn't still be wearing it if it were." She slipped her arms up around his neck, causing a wave of pleasure to shimmer over his skin. "Please, Riggs. Give me the pleasure of being with you." Her enticing lips lingered a stuttered breath away. "Just this once."

A muted groan rumbled against his Adam's apple. He was done for. She was literally going to kill him if she didn't stop pleading. "You're making it nearly impossible to say no." He pulled her arms down, gathered her hands inside his, and brushed his lips over her knuckles. "My decision has nothing to do with you. In fact, I'm one heartbeat away from giving you what you want. But I'm in too deep to start something with you right this moment."

Her lips formed a heart-wrenching smile. "Are you married?"

"Do you really think I would've spent all this time with you this week if that were true?"

"Fiancée?"

"That's why I told you upfront we could only be friends." Releasing her hands, he berated himself for pulling her into an impossible situation. "I can't be with you until I'm a hundred percent available. It wouldn't be right *or* fair."

Her wet eyelids fluttered. "Do you love her?"

"Never did, never will," he answered without a shred of reluctance.

She released a strained laugh. "Then why are you *with* her?"

"It's complicated…I doubt I could explain it right now without sounding like a royal asshole, and I really don't want to taint your sainted view of me."

"I don't understand." Tears swarmed in her pale gray eyes, emblazoned with suffering. "Why would you ask someone to be your wife if you didn't feel a profound connection to her?"

"Sometimes I'm not sure how I ended up on this path. I guess not all relationships form out of love." Capturing one of her enticing curls between his fingers, he sighed. He could only imagine the immense pleasure he'd get from combing his fingers through all of those curls at once, and burying his face in their silky strands. "After everything you've told me, it's only fair if I'm more candid with you, too." He held back a discontented sigh. "I'm not actually the manager of this resort."

Suddenly pale, Rowan clutched his forearm. "Then who—"

"I own it. It's only one of many properties I own across the country."

"That's some secret." A nervous bubble of laughter escaped from her lips as she released her grip on his arm. "Wanna trade?"

"I would if I could." He rubbed circles against her warm, freckled skin, wishing he had something more reassuring to say about her situation. "I don't like to flaunt my wealth, and I don't enjoy spending money on material things. I'd rather hang out on the beach with a board under my arm. But for some reason Victor thinks it's better if I wear clothes and act civilized."

"As surprised as I am to hear you're rich, I'm still not actually *that* surprised. At least the part about you being modest. You don't wear designer labels, you hardly ever wear shoes, and your watch cost you well under a hundred. I'd only be surprised if you drove anything less than ten years old."

"Don't let my fleet of Bentleys hear you say that." Chuckling, he adjusted the silver watch on his wrist, recalling how he'd purchased it from a shady street vendor with his first significant paycheck from Victor. He'd worn it every day since as a reminder of how far he'd come. "Am I that transparent?"

"No. Not at all. I was raised by a mother with principles the exact opposite of yours." She bristled. "But that's a horror story for another day."

The intensity from that morning returned to his gaze. "Ro, if you want to know who sent Kinsley those flowers, I have the resources to make it happen."

"I don't know." He detected a flash of unbearable pain and fear pass through her eyes before she turned away from him. "Let me think about it."

He gripped her shoulders, waiting until her gaze returned to his. "I can't stand knowing someone out there got their rocks off trying to scare you. What if it's someone carrying a serious grudge? What if they decide to do something again?" He bared his teeth like a wild dog. "Something...much worse."

A rather weak, unconvincing smile spread over her sweet lips. "Next time I'll be more prepared. No more fainting...I promise."

She wasn't fooling him. She was still afraid, and it killed him to know the horrors she faced. As if it had a mind of its own, his hand swept several curls over her shoulder. His fingertips lazily dusted over her delicate skin. It was useless to try to stop himself from consoling her now that she'd exposed her soul. "I'm sorry I didn't tell you about my position with the resort sooner. I had to make sure you weren't another gold digger. I've met my share over the years."

"Like your fiancée," she assumed in a bitter tone. Her lips puckered like she'd swallowed a sour grape. Beautiful *and* smart as hell, he mused. Even flawed, she was perfect. "Is she here, on the resort? Have I met her?"

"She lives here, yes, but she spent the week in Kauai." He kissed her knuckles while meeting her frustrated expression. It was getting harder to resist the beautiful eyes beckoning him to do more. "I'm going to ask you to trust me, Rowan. I now understand why it isn't something you're able to do easily, but I'm asking you to trust that I won't hurt you." He bent down, touching his forehead to hers. The strong sexual current running between them made it seem as if there was another person in the room. "Trust that I'll find my way back to you...one day soon."

"Soon isn't enough. I don't think I'll survive if you walk away from me."

With a deep chuckle, he drew her into his arms.

She fit against him too easily, too perfectly. It was as if they'd crossed paths for that very purpose. "You will survive, because you're stronger than you know, and I'm not walking away." Warring against the pull in his gut, he held his lips against her forehead for a beat longer than he should've allowed. "We better get you back to your best friend before my resolve breaks."

25

Following a short, fitful night in which Rowan caught almost literally no sleep alone in the suite's massive bed, she knocked on Taylor's door as the island warmed with the rising sun and the song of tropical birds filled the air. Her aunt's hair was still pinned behind her head, although in complete disarray, and coal black mascara smudged around her sleepy eyes. In sharp contrast to the whimsical dress adorned in jewels sporting shades of peacock green and blue that she'd worn to the wedding the night before, her favorite nightgown was badly wrinkled, and its once vibrant blue color had faded to a dull gray.

"Aunt T, you look—"

"Save your breath," Taylor said, waving a hand over her head. "I caught a glimpse of all this fabulousness in the hallway mirror." She paused to hack into her arm with a deep, barking cough. When finished, she held a hand over her chest. "I think all those tiki torches at the reception got to me."

Rowan passed through the doorway. "You've been coughing a lot since we left New York. It's starting to sound worse. Maybe you caught something."

"Or maybe all those years I smoked like a fool in my teens and early twenties are finally catching up to me." Taylor began plucking bobby pins out from her mess of brown curls. "I'm surprised to see you up already considering we just called it a night a handful of hours ago. What's got you going so early, kiddo?"

"There's something you should know." Her heart felt heavy. She hoped her aunt could help lessen her burden as she had countless times before. "Several things, actually. I wanted to tell you about them earlier, but I didn't want any of it to spoil your memories of Kinsley's day."

"Do any of these *things* involve the handsome prince running this resort?"

Winding her arms around herself, Rowan let out an exhausted breath and nodded. Her aunt usually had a way of seeing right through her. It was a relief to know some things didn't change. "Let's order breakfast and mimosas. It's going to take awhile to tell you everything, and you're going to want a strong drink when I'm done."

Taylor swatted a hand through the air. "Screw the orange juice. Just order a bottle of champagne. This sounds serious."

While they waited on the lanai for their platters of fresh pineapple and omelets, Rowan relayed most of her conversation with Riggs the night before. She chose not to share his secret about the resort, knowing he'd gone out of his way to conceal his connection. "I should've known better than to think someone like Riggs could actually be mine, and assume he didn't already belong to someone else. Why else would he have been so insistent that we remain friends?"

With a deep frown that creased the loose skin around her eyes, Taylor bent forward on the lounger to take her hand. Rowan felt a pang of sadness when she recognized her aunt had aged at an aggressive rate, appearing decades older since she'd first taken Rowan in. She wondered how much of that had been due to her own plight.

Taylor heaved a scratchy breath. "First of all, how could you possibly believe you weren't worthy of him? Even after all these years...sweetheart, I can't understand how you still don't recognize how special you are."

Rowan ducked her chin. "I'm not perfect."

"No one is, sweetie."

"Riggs has to be close."

Grinning slightly, Taylor crooked an eyebrow. "Except he's holding back something to do with this fiancée business."

"I feel foolish for falling for him."

"He's shown you boundless kindness and compassion. I'd say falling for him was out of your hands." With a gentle laugh, Taylor leaned in to hug her niece. "If you feel deep in your heart that you can trust him like he asked, I'd say it'd be worth the wait. He seems pretty amazing. The fact that he refuses to pursue you while he's engaged to another woman speaks volumes."

They were interrupted with a knock and a voice announcing, "Room service!"

"We're out on the lanai!" Taylor called back.

Keona, the youthful Polynesian staffer who had served Rowan every day since her arrival, rolled a cart into the suite. It contained their breakfast and a vase filled with freshly cut tropical flowers. Rowan was able to identify every one after Riggs had spent the week teaching her the island's different species.

"Good morning, Mrs. Brooks, Ms. Brooks." Smiling in a toothy grin, he plucked a white envelope off the cart and handed it to Rowan. "Please let me know if there's anything else I can do for you beautiful ladies this morning. Enjoy your meal. *Aloha!*" With a slight bow, he left the room.

Rowan's name was scrawled on the heavy linen envelope in a thin black marker. She felt the weight of her aunt's curious stare as she pried the flap open. *Riggs Forrester* was embossed on a square piece of cardstock bearing a watermark of the resort's logo, and he had scribbled "sometimes manager" underneath. She giggled under her breath.

In the same marker and penmanship used to write her name on the envelope, the note said:

SORRY I COULDN'T STAY *with you after the reception. I hope you found peace in your sleep.*

Enjoy these flowers as a reminder of this past week and all that's to come.

I've been called away to business on the Big Island for the day, but I'll find you later tonight.

Please don't forget everything I said.

Soon.

. . .

WARMTH SPREAD through her heart when she recalled his promise to her: *"Trust that I'll find my way back to you...one day soon."* She never would've pegged herself as a romantic before meeting Riggs. But now...

"You're *swooning*," Taylor whispered in a scandalous tone.

Cheeks growing hot, Rowan stuffed the note back inside the envelope. "The flowers are from Riggs."

"I figured as much." Taylor turned away to muffle another cough. "Let's eat, then we'll drink while you tell me the rest."

Taylor consumed the bulk of the champagne, eyes wet, as Rowan painstakingly explained every last detail of the flower incident, as well as her conversations with William and Drake.

"Oh sweetie," she began once Rowan was finished. She wiped at her tears with a despondent look. "That's perfectly awful. I can't imagine who would do such a thing to you and Kins."

"I called Detective Novak to confirm my father was still in prison, and there hadn't been some kind of hiccup in his appeal." A deep shiver ran over her skin when she imagined her father stepping back out into the sunlight for the first time, that vacant look frozen on his face. "And I don't want to think my mother would be that merciless, but I can't stop my thoughts from going there. She was so angry about the book."

"I can't stand the idea of that being true."

"Me either."

Taylor settled back against the cushioned lounger, and cast a regretful glance out at the gentle waves lapping over the sand. "Your mom has changed her colors so many times since we've met. I don't know what to expect from her anymore. She was once so carefree and happy. I wish you would've known her back then, Ro." Her eyes returned to Rowan's, filled with pain. "I don't recognize the woman who forced you into competition, or came to your graduation harboring all that misplaced anger toward you. I'm starting to believe she became a bitter person once she suspected your father was sleeping with other women…before she knew the brutal truth. Perhaps that's where the need for control over your life came into play. That could very well be what broke her spirit."

Rowan nodded, having heard a similar theory from her therapist in Blue Bay. She wondered if Taylor had begun seeing Dr. Walters as well. "What about William? Do you think he could've sent them as retribution? After he hit on me the other night, then showed his true side, I don't know what to believe. Do I dare tell Kins what happened?"

"I'm not—" Taylor heaved another deep breath, sending her into a coughing fit. She grabbed the white linen from her lap and held it up to her lips. When she pulled the linen away, it was stained with blood.

"Aunt T?" Concerned, Rowan ran to her. "I'll call the doctor."

"No doctor, Ro, please. It's just—"

Clutching her chest, her aunt collapsed onto the lanai floor.

THE RESORT'S in-house nurse was a local woman with a wide mouth, prominent cheekbones, and luxurious long black hair braided down her narrow back. She wore a flowing dress adorned in a hibiscus print, and several hundred dollar wedged shoes. The only thing to give her profession away when she walked into Taylor's room was the stethoscope slung around her neck.

"I'm concerned with what I'm hearing. Paired with the blood, it's suspect."

Rowan gripped her aunt's hand. "Suspect of what?"

"It's too early to say at this point. I'm going to put in a request for the local clinic to fit you in as soon as possible for X-rays and tests."

Nodding, Taylor seemed to take the news in stride. Her expression showed no sign of concern whatsoever. Rowan, however, was sick with worry. Although she was close with Steph and Andy, her aunt was her rock. She couldn't stand the idea of losing her.

"How long until we know something?" she asked the nurse.

"It will depend on their lab's workload." The nurse stood and patted Rowan's shoulder. "I wish I could give you a definitive answer." Her dark eyes shifted to Taylor. "I wish you well, Ms. Brooks."

Standing abruptly, Taylor threw her a tight smile. "May I speak with you for a moment in the hallway?"

"Of course." The nurse nodded in Rowan's direction. "*Aloha*, Miss Brooks."

"*Mahalo*," Rowan replied.

Taylor's tight smile turned to Rowan. "I'll be back in a flash."

With the soft click of the suite's front door

behind the two women, Rowan reached for her cell phone, wishing she had thought to get Riggs's number the night before. She needed his comfort, even if just hearing the false promise that everything would be okay.

She sensed her aunt knew whatever was wrong, it was serious. She was on pins and needles by the time her aunt rejoined her on the lanai. She shot to her bare feet, ready to tackle her aunt with a hug. Surely she'd be okay. "What was that about? What's going on, Aunt T?"

Lips bent with a sad smile, Taylor closed her eyes. "Sit down, sweetheart. There's something I have to tell you, too."

PART 3
STORMY INTERLUDE

"Pain is certain, suffering is optional." -Lachlan Brown

26

Riggs scowled out at the Pacific Ocean from the open wall of his villa, feeling a kinship with the tremendous waves pounding into the rocks, and the dark sky rumbling with flashes of lightning. It had been an entire month since Rowan had left the island prematurely, without bothering to leave a note or say goodbye. Kinsley and William had moved on to their honeymoon reservations on Kauai the morning after their wedding, and the rest of Rowan and Kinsley's family members had left the resort early along with Rowan, citing a personal emergency. There wasn't anyone left to speak with that would know Rowan's whereabouts. If he hadn't been in such a damn hurry to meet with his lawyers to discuss the process of voiding his prenuptial agreement, he wouldn't have missed her departure.

He'd obsessively dissected their last conversation, over and over. He'd tried calling the phone number used to reserve Rowan's suite at the resort, only to discover it had been disconnected. He also tried her aunt's number, but those calls went directly to voicemail, without fail.

Kinsley had been considerate enough to return his call from Kauai a few days later, but only to explain it wasn't her place to tell him Rowan's business. "If she wanted you to know what's going on, she would've called the resort and asked for you or your number," she'd said.

"Please, Kinsley. I'm worried sick about her. She must've told you there's something going on between us."

"She also told me you're with another woman."

"Technically, yes. But I'm working on that."

A harsh breath had shot through the ear piece. "Riggs, I'm sorry. You're not going to change my mind on this."

"The night of your wedding, she told me about the lilies...the connection to her father...Jonathan Rivers."

There had been a dramatic pause. Then, "No shit?"

"We discussed the idea of digging a little deeper

to find whoever sent them. If someone has hurt her again...*damn it,* Kinsley! I have to know! Can you at least tell me whether or not she's okay?"

"She's far from okay, but again, that's not your business." After wishing him well, Kinsley had ended the conversation. Hearing Rowan was "far from okay" had only made things worse, and prevented him from sleeping more than a handful of hours at a time.

In the weeks since she'd left, he'd thrown his focus into carefully ending things with Chelsea and managing the resort. But he was growing more restless with every minute that ticked by with ruthless agony. He'd set an alert on his phone for any news related to the SLS killer, and was dismayed to learn the son of a bitch had a chance of getting released because of DNA technicalities.

Grumbling under his breath, he stepped away from the open wall of his villa and placed the call to New York he'd been eager to make. "Victor, how are you?"

"Everything okay, son? You sound...dismayed."

Things were far from okay all around, Riggs mused. "Is it alright if I disrupt your wild bachelor parties and come spend a night with you in the city?"

"You're asking permission to stay in your own penthouse?" Victor let out a hacking laugh. "Must be something serious."

"Remember the woman I told you about?"

Victor hummed in a teasing tone. "The lovely one you wished you would've waited for instead of foolishly attaching yourself to Chelsea?"

"Guess I can expect you to rub that in my face until the end of time." Riggs let out a gruff chuckle. "Something's going on with Rowan, and she won't return my calls." His stomach seized with another surge of worry. Why had she cut him out of her life? Had she already forgotten about his promise, or written it off as meaningless? "I'm going to Blue Bay to look for her."

"I see. What will you tell Chelsea?"

"I was hoping you wouldn't mind playing along if I claim you've fallen ill again."

"That depends. What's wrong this time? Are the angels of death at my doorstep?"

"I think we both know it won't be angels that come knocking for you, old man."

Victor laughed with an abrupt wheeze. "You know I'll always have your back, son. Even if you were to confess you're a closeted axe murderer."

The irony made Riggs wince with the force of a

sucker-punch. "I just need to take care of some things here, then I'll catch the first flight out."

THE COMMUNITY of Blue Bay was quaint and charming, matching the laidback personalities of both Rowan and her aunt. Riggs suspected the small stretches of cobblestone streets came alive in warmer weather, but appreciated the quiet after spending the better part of a year on a busy island. Following the directions from his phone, he parked the rented midsize sedan in front of a picturesque cottage with a small shed built in the same style of architecture out back. Its cedar shakes were in need of maintenance, but the property was otherwise appealing with vibrant begonias planted throughout, and whimsical yard decor that included glass wind chimes and metal pinwheels. The other houses in the neighborhood were nearly all modern monstrosities of glass and metal, making the cottage even more unique.

Sliding out of the sedan, he felt an instant chill with the 15 degree difference from Maui. He made his way past an older model black Jeep and a shabby silver Volvo from the '80s parked in the driveway.

The flash of a powerful light caught the corner of his eye. He glanced around the side of the cottage, discovering a stone lighthouse several hundred yards away on the edge of a half-moon peninsula. With an abundance of little square windows and a worn facade, he understood how Rowan had been inexplicably drawn to the sleepy community as a child.

The sound of a feminine gasp took his breath away. "Riggs?"

He spun around, heart lurching in his chest with the sight of the woman he was certain was meant to be his. She stood on the cottage's front step in a lightweight peach sweater and white jeans that sagged at her waist. Her dark brown hair curtained her face, limp and lifeless. Even with a fading tan from her time spent in Maui she was white as a sheet. Her cheekbones were more prominent than before, and the skin surrounding her clavicle puckered from recent weight loss. He was convinced she'd blow away with the slightest breeze. As he held her shadowed stare, he reminded himself he was intruding and she might not be as receptive as he'd like.

"Why—*what* are you doing here?" she asked with a baffled shake of her head. Her voice was hoarse and wavered with uncertainty.

Moving toward her with hesitant steps, he attempted a grin. "I thought we'd finish your surfing lessons." The look she gave him was so broken that the raw desire to hold her in his arms broke through, forcing his feet to pound the lawn until he was able to gather her in his arms. "What happened?" he whispered into the thick of her hair. Her frail body trembled against him as she let out a whimpering cry. With the absence of her usual lilac fragrance and the force of her fingers clawing at his back, he wasn't satisfied that she'd been unharmed. She was hardly more than a bag of bones. "What's going on with you?"

"It's my aunt T." She leaned back, her expression broken. "She's…dying."

ROWAN SLOUCHED on a stool beside Riggs at the kitchen island, fascinated by the way his Adam's Apple bobbed with every sip of the coffee she'd brewed. She'd had plenty of nightmares since abandoning Riggs, but seeing him in her aunt's kitchen made it feel as if she'd been immersed into the lovelies of dreams—the kind where shadows and monsters couldn't reach her.

When she'd discovered him in her aunt's driveway, she'd been sure her fragile mind had been playing tricks. Something about him was all wrong. The grin he gave her earlier was lacking both dimples and its usual charm, and the bags beneath his eyes were nearly darker than her own. It was as if a cloud of gloom hung over his shoulders. He wore a long-sleeved t-shirt in her favorite shade of turquoise bearing a surf company's logo, and slightly torn, faded blue jeans. When her eyes had shifted down to his battered skater sneakers, it had almost brought a smile to her face. She couldn't believe he'd worn shoes long enough to break a pair in.

She refused to let the tears building behind her eyes spill. "I can't believe you're really here."

He set the cup down after a minute and slipped a hand behind her neck, tangling his fingers in her unwashed hair. "Tell me everything, starting with why you left without explanation and haven't called since."

Embarrassment filled her cheeks with heat. She must've looked a mess. She couldn't remember the last time she'd bathed. "I can only deal with so much," she began, leaning into his strong hand. "I had to shut you out completely, or I wouldn't have had the strength to deal with my aunt's diagnosis."

She wound her fingers around his wrist, drawing from his strength. "The day after the wedding, she told me she'd been diagnosed with lung cancer. She didn't want to 'ruin' Kinsley's joy, and planned to tell us when we returned home.

"But then she started coughing up blood, and her oncologist told her she needed to come home right away. The cancer has spread—it's everywhere." She closed her eyes for a moment, enjoying the sensation of his fingers massaging her scalp. Tears finally trickled over when she looked back at him. "They think she has three weeks left to live, max."

His honeyed eyes softened, mirroring her heartache. "Rowan, *baby*, I'm so sorry. If I'd known, I would've come back here with you, and you wouldn't be facing this alone."

Hot jealousy licked at her core, turning her voice bitter. "What about your fiancée?"

"She doesn't matter. I'm here for the duration. I don't plan on leaving as long as you need me." His fingertips stroked up and down her neck. "Where's Taylor now?"

"At the hospital." She winced with the memory of leaving her aunt tucked beneath a thin blanket, surrounded by half a dozen blinking and beeping machines. Taylor had insisted that she go home and get some real sleep. She'd spent the prior night curled up in an uncomfortable chair at Taylor's side. "She fell two days ago and hit her head. They're giving her fluids and watching for signs of a concussion. She doesn't like to eat, and it's made her so weak." Her heart wrenched, overcome with guilt. Her aunt had done so much for her over the years. She was doing a poor job of returning the favor. "I don't think I can help her on my own any longer."

"What about hospice?"

"I don't have the heart to make the call." She felt a rush of shame, knowing her reasoning was selfish. "It makes this all feel too...real."

"I'll do it for you." He dropped a kiss on top of her head and rose from the stool, heading toward the refrigerator. "First you're going to eat something."

Her stomach rumbled with deep, unbearable pain. She'd been good about eating while in Hawaii, while *with him*, but she'd neglected her stomach ever since her aunt's fateful news. Andy and Steph hadn't been able to convince her to join them for regular meals. "I'm not—"

He shot her a stern look over his shoulder. "Are you really going to waste your breath by arguing with me?"

"So bossy," she grumbled.

"If you think this is me, being bossy, you ain't seen nothing yet." Returning his gaze to the contents of the refrigerator, he made an exaggerated noise of disgust. "On second thought, I'm taking you out. We'll grab food suitable for consumption on the way back."

She watched as he closed the door and took an inventory of the cupboard shelves. Despite her sorrow, her chest became a little lighter. He'd traveled a mind-boggling distance to check on her, and she knew he'd keep his promise to stay as long as she needed him. The only problem was that she couldn't imagine a time when she'd never *not* need him.

27

After they grabbed club sandwiches at a little cafe down the street, Riggs purchased several hundred dollars' worth of groceries with Rowan trailing behind like a zombie. Back at the cottage, he drew her a hot Epsom salt bath and put the groceries away while she soaked her weary muscles. He then made good on his promise to arrange for Taylor to return home with hospice. For dinner, he grilled steaks and vegetables on the back patio. Rowan cuddled beneath a blanket at his side, gazing at the lighthouse while sharing stories of her aunt's late husband. When she gingerly picked at her steak the same way she had with her club sandwich earlier, he began to worry she'd become anorexic.

Once dishes were put away, they sat together on

Taylor's deep white couch to watch a Jason Sudekis comedy. Rowan fell asleep on his chest long before the final credits rolled. He shamelessly enjoyed the situation for a good half hour before carrying her to bed and tucking her beneath the covers. He didn't bother with her pajamas as she had already slipped into a loose fitting t-shirt and cotton shorts. Besides, he didn't want her to think he'd take advantage of her in the situation. He returned to the couch where he only slept a handful of hours. He was too concerned about Rowan to rest.

The next afternoon, hospice moved an electric hospital bed into the living room, and Taylor returned home with a middle-aged RN. Nurse Betsey, an ash blonde of average height and slightly overweight, possessed a spirited personality that set both Rowan and Taylor at ease.

The weakened state of Rowan's aunt rattled Riggs, giving him a deeper understanding of the situation. He did his best to stay out of the nurse's way while performing his own version of nursing in bringing Rowan back to good health.

The first full day of Taylor's return, Rowan was exhausted after the nurse had discussed methods of caring for her aunt and her different medications.

That night she slept in Taylor's bedroom, and sent Riggs into hers. He decided her room was cute and whimsical, and he enjoyed thumbing through her mammoth collection of books when he couldn't sleep. It was logical someone enchanted by a wide range of stories would want to become an author. He couldn't wait to report his findings back to Victor, knowing Rowan would hit it off with him from the start. He drifted off into a hard sleep with her scent heavy in the air and sheets.

A week passed. Then two. Some days, Taylor was lucid and engaged in short conversations. Once she even joined them for a quick round of rummy. Other days, Nurse Betsey had to increase the dosage of morphine to manage her pain, and she was too sleepy to do much of anything. Steph and Andy were invited over for a brief visit on a handful of the good days. On occasion, Riggs heard the quiet murmurs of Taylor and Rowan's conversation, and did his best to give them privacy. He held Rowan whenever the days became exceptionally hard.

Rowan also experienced both good days and bad. There were times Riggs swore he was dealing with a young child, having to make bargains with her in order to get her to eat healthier portions. He practically dragged her out of the house every morning for casual walks around the neighborhood, knowing she didn't yet possess the energy to resume her usual running routine.

Nurse Betsey detected Riggs's frustration, and shooed them out of the house on day 15. "Taylor wants the two of you out of her hair," she explained, playfully holding her hand beside her mouth. "Don't shoot the messenger, but apparently you're cramping her style." They all knew she was being facetious as Taylor had been sleeping all morning.

They ventured through downtown Blue Bay where Riggs convinced Rowan to stop for double scoops of chocolate and mint ice cream. He had remained a platonic friend since his arrival, as it was what Rowan needed to get back on her feet, but he felt a little tinge of hope for their future as they strolled along the sidewalk, enjoying their cones while hand-in-hand. As if on a proper date.

Outside the library, Taylor spotted a flier with a picture of a white West Highland Terrier puppy. Tears swarming her eyes, she plucked the paper off the pole and read it aloud. "Eight month old puppy for adoption…owner passed away unexpectedly. Blue is potty trained and child friendly. Serious inquiries only." She gripped Riggs's forearm. "Oh, Riggs. He looks exactly like the Westie Taylor had when I was little. She adored that dog. I had to convince her to put him down while I was in college." Lips quivering, she looked up at him. "At least they'll be reunited soon."

THE FOLLOWING MORNING, Riggs woke early and decided to throw muffins from a box into the oven while doing laundry. He tiptoed past Taylor, only to discover she was as alert as he'd seen her since he'd come to Blue Bay. Although her skin was blotchy and her breaths were shorter than ever, her eyes twinkled in the faint dawn's light spilling through the cozy little room as she held the oxygen mask over her nose and mouth.

"Good morning...handsome," she sang, lowering the mask to her lap. The motor of the hospital bed quietly whirled as she sat upright. "Suppose I could...talk you into...getting me a glass...of ice?"

"Good morning," he replied, bending to kiss the top of her head. "And of course."

"You truly...are a...prince, Riggs...Forrester." As

he started for the kitchen, she heaved a throaty breath filled with phlegm. "I suppose it's time...for the two of us...to have a talk...regarding your...intentions with...Ro."

Riggs held a glass beneath the refrigerator's dispenser, lips pressed together as he watched a shower of ice tumble down. He'd suspected there would come a time when Taylor might request a serious conversation, and he didn't want to explain to a dying woman how the process of ending his engagement in order to be with her niece was in the hands of his lawyers. When the glass was full, he returned to her, holding it within her reach. She removed a chip and circled it around her lips.

"Are you...in...*love* with...her?"

"Get right to the point, why don't you?" he teased with a grin.

"Not...a lot of...time...left." She attempted a stern look, but it turned into an equally bright grin. "Don't...distract...me...with those...sexy dimples."

He sandwiched her exceptionally cool hands between his, holding her hazel stare. In the time it took to travel to Blue Bay, he had come to the realization that he was ready to risk everything to be with Rowan. He was certain that could only mean one thing. "I haven't found the right time to tell her with all that's going on, but I'm certain that I do, in fact, love her. I'm pretty sure I have ever since the night we were reunited at my resort. Hell—it probably started the moment I first saw her laying on the beach in California, red as a lobster." He gave her hands a gentle squeeze. "I plan to stay by her side for as long as she'll have me."

"If you...break her...heart...both my Jason...and I...will come back to...haunt your ass...only not in a...friendly ghost...kind of...way...more like...horror movie...style...climbing walls...and shit."

Chuckling heartily, his eyes stung with a rush of unshed tears as he regarded the wedding picture in a silver frame on the table at her side. Beneath a storm of bubbles, a younger Taylor in a white dress embraced a thick-necked man in a New York City Police dress uniform. Their smiles were equally toothy, and sheer joy shone through their eyes. It was unfair they'd both lived an abbreviated life, Riggs thought. He sensed Taylor didn't have long, and dreaded Rowan's reaction to the death of someone who had been her world. "I know she's fragile...and exceptionally special. I'll do everything in my power not to hurt her, and protect her from whatever shit-storm her father left behind. I promise I'll give her the best of everything—the best of *me*."

"Yes." Taylor's eyes closed. "And help her...find her...purpose."

"I will. I promise." He silently wondered if Rowan's true purpose had something to do with finding him...*loving* him. "You don't have to worry about Rowan, Mrs. Brooks."

Just then, Rowan padded barefoot into the living room, rubbing her eyes. In a white cotton tank top and shorts pajama set with a tiny blue polka dotted print, hair wild and straight around her freckled face, Riggs wished he could open his eyes every morning to that exact sight. She was raw and stunning in the first light of day. He was especially pleased to notice she'd put on a few pounds—enough that her cheeks had resumed their usual healthy glow, and she no longer resembled a walking skeleton.

"What are you two conspiring out here?" she muttered, bypassing them for the coffee maker.

"I'm...hungry," Taylor told her. "Suppose...you could...whip up some...crepes?"

Rowan whirled around with wide eyes and a beaming smile. "Really? You're hungry?"

Taylor nodded with an equally bright smile as she reached for the oxygen mask. Rowan turned her smile onto Riggs, making his heart squeeze with glee. Instead of reminding her Nurse Betsey said there would be good days in the end, and it didn't mean Taylor was getting better, he returned her smile. He only wished there was a way he could reverse time for her, knowing it was undoubtedly about to get worse.

TAYLOR PASSED on a Saturday evening amid a violent thunderstorm, half a week past her initial prognosis. Nurse Betsey had warned them the end was near once Taylor stopped eating and slept two days straight. Watching Rowan hold her aunt's hand as she took her last breath was the hardest thing Riggs had ever done.

The 50-something funeral director arrived within the hour, sharply dressed in a business suit and polished shoes. Despite the late hour, he relaxed in a chair across from Rowan, answering her questions and concerns with an ease that suggested there was nowhere else he'd rather be. Bob had known Taylor well, and showed extra care in preparing to remove her from her beloved home. Riggs followed him outside to the sleek hearse in the driveway, standing outside the breadth of the director's umbrella.

"I'm taking care of all the arrangements," he told Bob, slipping him a Blue Heaven business card bearing his personal cell phone number. "Anything Rowan requests is fine by me."

Bob glanced down at the card caught between his fingers. "That's kind of you, Mr. Forrester. Taylor was lucky to have had you in her life. Rowan too."

"I'm the lucky one," Riggs said, shaking Bob's hand. "Thank you for showing Rowan kindness. You're exceptionally good at your profession."

As the hearse pulled away, Riggs's smart phone buzzed with rapid fire inside his pocket. He sprinted beneath the protection of the garage roof and retrieved his phone. He'd missed half a dozen calls from an unlisted number, and Richard Wong, the capable employee he'd appointed to watch over the Hawaiian property in his absence, had sent a string of urgent texts.

YOU NEED TO CALL ASAP
    FBI HERE WITH WARRANT
    REQUESTING YOUR PRESENCE
    THIS ISN'T GOOD, BROTHER

. . .

RIGGS WAS sure the ground had fallen out from beneath his feet. He had never engaged in illegal practices with any of his properties, and had absolutely nothing to hide. Still, worry niggled at the back of his mind. Something serious was going down.

28

Between conference calls with the FBI and his resort staff, preparing arrangements for Taylor's memorial service, and tending to Rowan's broken heart, Riggs was spent beyond measure. The agents he spoke with hadn't been pleased when he refused to return immediately as they demanded, but he wore them down and they'd eventually agreed he could wait until after the service to fly back.

He was glad he'd still been around when, on the morning of the service three days later, a single spider lily arrived from her father. He'd included a short note offering his sympathies. A delivery of Gerber daisies arrived from Rowan's mother shortly afterwards. She'd also included a short note offering her sympathies for not being able to attend.

Although Rowan seemed unfazed, he sensed she was relying on her ability to merely appear that way. Since coming to Blue Bay, he'd come to understand she was an expert at faking her true feelings whenever she was expected to put on a brave face. He hated that he wouldn't be around to help her properly cope, and ensure she continued to eat regularly. The timing of the cluster-fuck in Hawaii couldn't have been worse.

Hours before the service was scheduled to begin, Rowan watched on with a dazzled look as Riggs packed his suitcase. She was a vision of beauty with her hair in meticulous curls that spilled down to the middle of her back, fluttering cobalt blue dress that reminded him of butterflies. He could barely glance in her direction without getting uncomfortably hard. It didn't seem appropriate to be turned on while she was in mourning.

He flashed her a toothy smile, eyebrows wiggling. "A few weeks ago, I could've stuffed you inside here along with everything else."

"I still don't understand," she said, tragically unfazed by his attempted humor. "Why would the FBI think you're involved in money laundering?"

"That's an excellent question," Riggs grumbled.

He had his suspicions, starting and ending with Chelsea's father. He'd convinced himself the powerful banker was desperate enough to get his daughter off his hands that he'd fabricated the bogus charges as a way to punish Riggs for dumping her. When he'd filled Victor in on the situation, he had wholeheartedly agreed, and immediately began reaching out to his contacts with the bureau. He promised Riggs he'd clear his name as soon as humanly possible.

With an angry huff, Riggs snatched Rowan's hand, pulling her down to sit next to him on her childhood bed. Stomach in knots, he studied her elegant face, the waning gleam in her colorless eyes, the slight tremble of her precious lips. She was taking Taylor's death far better than he'd imagined, but she'd become anxious once he announced he had to leave. He tucked a soft curl behind one ear, enjoying the way her crystal earrings dangled from her small lobe and caught in the sunlight from her window. He decided he'd buy her a set of diamond earrings for Christmas.

"Change your mind—come back to Maui with me tonight." Warning himself to stay in control, he dragged his fingertip along her dainty jawline. "I'll get lonely without someone to boss around and force-feed my subpar cooking."

With a small shake of her head, her shoulders dropped. "I can't, Riggs. I've been ignoring my editor for too long already. We're meeting tomorrow to discuss a second book deal."

"Tell them you're unavailable, but could manage a video call. Better yet, I'll call and tell them I've kidnapped you…stuffed you inside my suitcase."

Her lips flattened. "The bossy thing can be charming at times, but this is my career we're talking about. I can't blow it off to start some whirlwind romance."

Frowning, he continued to trace the outline of her jaw. They had yet to share a kiss, but he was so deeply in love with her that he wasn't sure he could restrain himself much longer. "Is that all this is to you?"

"No." She hooked her hand over his arm, meeting his gaze with confidence. "That's not at all what I meant. I—"

"I'm in love with you, Rowan."

A rush of tears pricked the whites of her eyes. "You are?"

"How could I not be? Have you met you?" With a soft chuckle, he feathered the pad of his thumb over her sinful lips. Every single time he'd watched her eat, he'd yearned to taste them. "I can't exactly pinpoint when it started, but I can assure you the way I feel doesn't have an expiration date. I'm also not taking any refunds, so better get used to it."

A soft cry fell from her parted lips. The glow inside him grew into hot embers as he gripped her lovely face with one hand. Sliding his other hand over her lower back, he yanked her closer, unable to resist the need to touch her one second longer. Months of frustration disappeared when their mouths met in a frantic caress of heat and hunger. He was all at once unable to think straight—unable to *breathe*—with the tangle of their tongues and the gentle press of her lips against his.

He worried he was moving too quickly for someone who had been through considerable trauma, but the thought fizzled once her slender fingers wound inside his hair and she held him close. She returned the kiss with the same fervor, same want. His resistance melted with the urgent slide of their bodies. Eager to explore her warm skin and silken curls, his hands were everywhere at once. Her muscles were lean and rigid beneath his touch, her limbs long and slender.

"I want you," she breathed heavily against his lips. "I've wanted you for so long."

No further coaxing was required. He quickly slipped the straps of her dress aside, allowing his mouth to freely taste her supple body. Touching her was exactly what he'd needed ever since the day she'd left the island. He'd craved the connection for so long, wanting to show her exactly how he felt whenever she was near.

Her breathy gasps with every flicker of his tongue and suck of his lips fueled him to continue on, removing her lace bra and cupping the glorious swells of her naked breasts. Every smooth dip and gentle bend of her was so pure, so innocent. He was certain she'd never seen the inside of an operating room. The extreme way she reacted to his every touch, he was begging to suspect she'd also never known the gentle hand of a lover.

After a long round of breathless kisses and fervid strokes, he removed his shirt and kicked off his pants as she reached back to ease the zipper down on her dress. There was a moment where it stuck, and they both laughed in a nervous sound when he stopped to help her, tangling his watch in her hair in the process.

Finally she was gloriously naked on her back, full bottom lip held between her teeth as she gave him a timid look. "There's something you should know. I've only been with one other man this way, only it wasn't exactly like this—not really. We'd been dating for a short time, and—"

"This isn't an opportune time to discuss old lovers, sweetheart." His stomach churned as he ran a fingertip over her chin. "Unless you're hesitant because this other man hurt you, I don't want to hear it."

Pinkness spread over her cheeks. "It wasn't like that. I merely wanted to tell you I'm...ahhh...a little inexperienced at this kind of thing. I was intoxicated, and—"

He silenced her with a gentle caress of his lips against hers. "I'll show you the way."

He took his time investigating the tender curves of her body, enjoying the quiver of her belly when his hand traveled beyond her hips. She arched against the sweep of his fingers, sliding her legs against the mattress and pleading his name with a sharp whisper. Every brush of her body against his was hell on his control. He continued his relentless search, relishing in the soft noises falling from her swollen lips, and the desperate scratch of her short nails against his back. When she came apart for him, body becoming rigid then limp as a noodle, head tipped back and mouth stretched wide, she released a half-cry that sounded slightly more surprised than satisfied.

Her words were slurred when she muttered between kisses, "What'd you just do t'me?"

The veins in Riggs's neck twitched with a small flare of anger. Had the other man she'd been with failed to bring her to climax? What kind of clown had she dated? He vowed to always take the time to pleasure her first before worrying about his own needs. It had been one of the highlights of his lifetime to watch her come undone with his touch.

He kissed and caressed her back to life, feeling slightly amused when she finally responded to the scrape of his teeth against her nipples. Although eager to bring her over the edge a second time, he had to fight to keep his shit together once she tugged him free of his boxer briefs, and wound her fingers around him, guiding him inside.

Eyes wide, he arched his hips back. "Whoa! Fingers off the trigger, Annie Oakley! You only get one shot at this—at least for now."

Eyelids flipping open, her beautiful gray eyes

pleaded for him to continue. "If you're clean, I'm on birth control to regulate my periods. Please, don't make me wait any longer."

Victor had taught him never to go bare with a woman, and he had never contracted anything. He'd also never made love before then, and never wanted to sleep with anyone else again after Rowan. With another searing kiss, he squared himself above her and sunk down with a garbled moan. She met his every stroke with breathy pants and a tighter grip of her fingers into his hips, encouraging him to thrust deeper.

He didn't know it could feel so right to be intimate with someone. He wondered how he'd survived all his life without her up until then. He'd never experienced the kind of satisfaction that nestled deep inside his soul with their connection. Embarrassingly enough, the dizzying sensations were profound enough to bring an abrupt end to their lovemaking.

"Jesus Christ, Rowan." He shuddered against her, burying his face in the crook of her neck, inside the heavenly nest of her hair. "Ho-ly *shit*. I'm gonna need a minute to regain my sanity."

Bodies still entwined, skin slick with sweat and breaths staggered, his fingertips lazily swept across her freckled shoulder as she rested her head over his heart. Exactly where she was meant to be. He wondered if the euphoric lift of his heart and stomach equaled the sensation birds experienced when soaring high above the clouds. He was in awe they'd finally given into their desires after fighting them for so long, but also felt guilty it had happened the same day she would scatter her aunt's ashes. "Are you alright?"

"Are you serious?" Her voice sounded a little deeper, thick with passion. "I didn't know sex could be like this." Her hand gingerly stroked over his belly. "When can we do it again?"

He laughed hard enough to bounce her head against his abdomen. "I finally understand why Jack Johnson wrote a song about making his wife a prisoner in bed, only letting her up to make banana pancakes. But we should clean up. Steph and Andy will be here soon, and I wouldn't want Steph walking in and shooting you envious looks for the rest of your life."

The heat of her sigh tickled his chest. "This might sound weird, but I can't stop thinking how happy Aunt T would be right now." She let out a small giggle. "She threatened to haunt me if we didn't hook up soon, said they'd be keeping a close watch on us from across the bay."

A surprised cackle rose in his throat. "Let me guess…by 'they' she meant Jason too?"

She leaned up to meet his humored gaze with a puzzled expression. "How'd you know his ashes were scattered by the lighthouse too?"

"She said they'd both come after me 'horror movie style' if I broke your heart—but the threat was unnecessary." He crunched his belly to kiss her forehead. "Come join me after you've met with your editor. I'll make all your travel arrangements—ones significantly more comfortable than the inside of a suitcase."

When she remained quiet, he feared she was having second thoughts about what they'd done. He untangled his legs from hers in order to lean on his forearm and study her expression. She held her bottom lip inside her mouth, eyes glossy. He gently pulled her lip free with his finger before stealing another tender kiss. "What's going on in that beautiful head of yours? Calculating the formula for world peace? Solving the age-old mystery of who let the dogs out?"

Her eyes slid away from him. "What about your fiancée?"

"That's as good as done. Her father's army of idiots…they added a clause to the prenuptial agreement stipulating that Chelsea would be awarded with every single property I own if I were ever to leave her for another woman. I think her father was that desperate to pass her leaching ways along to some other poor schmuck. That's why I'm uneasy about this mess with the FBI. That's why I've been cautious since I met you. As far as she knows, I've been staying with Victor in New York this whole time."

Her graceful lashes fluttered over her cheeks. "It would've made things a little easier if I'd known what was going through your head."

"I didn't know how to explain it before without sounding like a materialistic jerk. But it was never about the money, Ro. I couldn't stand by and let her steal what Victor had given me—everything I'd built with his gift."

"Do they know about me?"

"I don't think so. But I can't shake the shitty feeling her father is behind this money laundering scheme."

"Maybe it'd be for the best if I stayed away while you handled the situation." With a vacant look, she squeezed his arm. "I wouldn't be able to live with myself if I were the reason you lost everything."

"Even if it were to happen, it still wouldn't be

your fault. And besides, my staff knows to be discreet. If you were to ask any one of them about the time I lost my swim trunks and board to the reef while surfing, and had to walk past dozens of hooting construction workers with only my hands to cover me, my employees would ask if you're nuts, then laugh at the memory later in the privacy of their homes."

She giggled. "Did that really happen?"

He made a face. "Are you nuts?"

She giggled even harder. Like a young school girl. He yearned to make her laugh in that carefree way every single day for the rest of her life. "What about Chelsea? Is she still living on the island?"

"Last I heard she's in Honolulu. I don't think she'd have any reason to check in on me now."

"Give me some time to think about it, okay?" She rolled out of bed, bending to brush her lips over his one last time. "One step at a time, remember?"

His eyes tracked her naked body closely as she somewhat timidly crossed the room and headed into the bathroom across the hallway. He suspected she didn't know she possessed the body of a supermodel, the grace equivalent to that of a bonafide princess. She was exquisite in his eyes. One of a kind. And she was finally *his*.

Regret and displeasure nagged him down to the bone with the reality that he'd be thousands of miles away by morning. He didn't know how he'd carry on without her now that he'd become connected with both her soul and her body.

29

Early evening, after the tasteful send-off of Taylor's ashes at the foot of the lighthouse while surrounded by family and friends, Rowan clung to Riggs in her aunt's driveway. He'd made her feel exposed and vulnerable in the best way imaginable. Between the complication with his fiancée and the distance separating them, she never dreamed they'd reach that point of intimacy. She'd almost cried out that she loved him in the midst of it all, but decided it was best to protect her heart until she knew for certain the sentiment was real.

Sleeping with Riggs had been a completely different experience from her drunken encounter with Koby in college. She finally understood how people could become addicted to sex, and why some couples were unable to keep their hands off each other. If Riggs hadn't been forced to leave, she imagined they would've spent endless days holed up in her bedroom, only getting up to make those banana pancakes like he'd mentioned. She was willing to give up just about anything in order to experience another toe-curling release created by the thoughtful man encased in her arms.

It would've been easy to cave to the nagging ache in her belly and agree to leave with him, but she held her ground. She owed it to herself to prove she could survive if he were to change his mind, and never return. For all either one of them knew, it might not work between them anyway. They hadn't discussed the logistics of carrying on an extremely long-distance relationship.

On one of Taylor's last good days, she'd informed Rowan that the cottage had been transferred to her. It was her wish that Rowan would, at the very least, keep it as a vacation home to enjoy with her future family. Whether or not that future involved Riggs, Rowan swore she'd honor that wish. But she couldn't envision herself making a permanent move to Hawaii. It seemed like the kind of dream meant for someone else—someone with a happier life. Without any other plans set in stone, she intended to make the cottage in Blue Bay her primary residence until something changed. If they were meant to be together, they'd find their way back to each other...eventually.

"There's still room in my suitcase," he whispered into her ear. "I'd probably just have to swap out a few pairs of underwear so you'd fit."

She breathed out a small giggle, wishing things were different and she could carelessly indulge in his humor. "I've decided I won't be joining you in Maui, Riggs."

Head tilted back, his expression became heavy with dismay. "You say that like traveling inside a suitcase cramps your style."

"You have business to attend to out there—you'll be busy with the FBI. And I need time to settle in... time to heal. If things go as planned tomorrow, I'll be busy writing my next book."

"I know Maui is disgusting to look at, but staying there might inspire a word or two."

She worried she was breaking his heart, and he was using humor to mask his pain. "How about we make a deal?" With a sweep of her eyes committing his handsome face to memory, she stood on her toes and wrapped her arms around his neck. "If the situation with the FBI gets dicey, and you decide you need me by your side for support, I'll come to you."

He wet his lips and his gaze darkened. "What if I simply need you in general?" He angled his mouth closer to hers while his fingertips trailed along the back of her arms. "What if I need this sexy body… these beautiful lips?"

She drew him back down to her for a sultry kiss. When their lips reluctantly parted, she pressed the side of her face against his. "Remember the promise you made to me that night in my suite?" she whispered against his ear. "Soon will just have to wait a little bit longer."

The reality of her situation sunk in as she stood alone in the driveway, watching until the tail lights on his rental became pin dots against the darkening sky. Although both Drake and Kinsley had offered to spend the night in the cottage, she'd told them she'd rather be alone. Her relationship with Drake still remained uneasy, and Kinsley had brought her new husband along. She didn't have the energy to face either of those scenarios. It was enough she'd be forced to ride into the city with all three of them in the morning.

Snuggled beneath one of her aunt's crocheted

blankets, she settled on the couch and watched old video clips Drake had recorded of their families over the years. She shed silent tears through every scene involving Taylor, knowing she'd be all alone in the cottage with memories of her aunt everywhere she turned.

An hour later, it was as if Riggs sensed her despair when his name popped up on her phone with a text.

GO TO YOUR FRONT DOOR. *I arranged for a sharply dressed man to keep you company while I'm gone. Don't let him hog the bed.*

WITH A CONFUSED BURST OF LAUGHTER, she raced to the door, fueled by curiosity. It was just like him to plan something thoughtful, although she couldn't imagine who he'd sent to keep her company. When peering outside, she was only able to see the top of a white-haired woman's head on her front step. She opened the door to a 60-something year-old woman with a trendy hair cut, dressed in a red raincoat and tan slacks, a purple reusable bag slung over one shoulder. She was glancing down at a cellphone in one hand while holding a dog leash in the other.

Rowan nearly fell to her knees. The end of the leash was clipped to the collar of a white Westie Terrier sporting a cobalt bow-tie.

The woman slipped her phone into her pocket. "Rowan?"

"Riggs did this?" Rowan whispered, bringing a hand up to her mouth.

The woman's thin lips parted with a flash of snow-white dentures. "Your boyfriend made a sizable donation to my mother's church in her memory. He was so perfectly charming that it was hard to say no, even though I knew nothing about you. But you look responsible enough, and your home is quite lovely. Plus your boyfriend assured me you'd owned a similar dog in the past." The woman handed Rowan the leash and the bag from her shoulder. "This is Blue. He's a good boy, but my husband and I are far too busy to take on a pet. There should be enough food in there to last him a few days. I kept his favorite toys, too. He slept with my mother at night, so I'm afraid I don't have a dog bed to offer."

"Hi, Blue." Rowan set the heavy bag down by her feet and bent to greet the little dog. His tail thumped through the air excitedly as he perched on her bent knees and eagerly licked her chin. With a youthful giggle, she scooped him into her arms and held him close. He had the same clean scent as her aunt's last dog, and he was just as cuddly.

Although she was beginning to suspect she was falling in love with Riggs long before that moment, she fell in love with him all over again.

MANY HOURS LATER, with Blue curled in the bed at her side, Rowan woke to a peculiar sound. She blinked against the darkness, straining to listen. It might've been hail, but with a glance outside it clearly wasn't raining. Still, it sounded like pebbles pinging against glass.

Rushing through the living room, she felt a sudden chill when passing over the exact spot in which Taylor had taken her final breath. Her heart gave a sudden jolt. Would the feeling go away with time, or would she always sense her aunt's presence? Perhaps she was only being paranoid.

She peered out the set of windows overlooking the backyard, and spotted something blowing around near the entrance of her aunt's studio. Her eyes caught the movement of something red.

Blue was suddenly behind her, barking insistently. With a squeak, she slapped her hands over her erratic heart and let out a bubbling laugh. "Shhh, buddy! You scared me!"

The dog didn't stop as she began to open the door leading out to the patio. She almost didn't open the door once shivers slowly trickled up the length of her back, erupting inside her head. She wanted to trust her instincts and crawl back into bed, but needed to prove there wasn't a real threat the way her psychiatrists had taught her over the years.

The lawn Riggs had recently mowed was cold and damp on her bare feet as she hurried across the yard. The familiar lull of the ocean's waves and the flicker of the lighthouse were of little comfort as she approached the studio and opened the door.

Every last drop of blood drained from her extremities. Hundreds of red spider lilies had been scattered throughout the building. In the center of the studio, a small handwritten sign taped onto her aunt's crafting table read: *Until we meet again*.

THE MORNING after her aunt's memorial service, Rowan woke with a start, unable to shake a nightmare involving her father and spider lilies. Then she felt the dog's rough tongue lapping her face, and the events of the evening came rushing back with sickening clarity.

Moment after she'd discovered the lilies, she'd snapped out of her shocked state and went to prompt work in removing the evidence. If the Lewises were to catch wind of what happened, they'd certainly relay the information to Riggs, and he'd turn back around. She couldn't let him risk losing his business or going to jail in order to play the role of her hero yet again.

Once the sign and flowers were collected inside a garbage bag, she stored them inside a corner of the studio until morning when she'd make a trip to the city dump. Once again, she'd been unable to deny that either Drake or William could've staged the flowers. It would've been convenient enough for either one of them to sneak over once the sun had set.

After reading a text from Riggs, saying he'd landed in Honolulu and missed her already, she tossed her blanket aside and let the dog out the back door. She felt the burn of anger deep inside the pit of her stomach when she imagined someone creeping through her yard in the middle of the night.

When she spotted Steph heading her way with a smile that didn't quite reach her eyes, her heart raced to a frantic beat. Had Steph seen someone in the night? She quickly scanned the area around her aunt's studio for any lilies that might've gone astray.

"Good morning, kiddo!"

"Morning, Steph."

Blue woofed once and pranced in her direction with the enthusiasm of a miniature pony.

"This must be Blue!" Steph bent down to greet the happy dog, giggling when he flipped over to his back. "He's even friendlier than Scotch!"

Rowan shook her head once. "Wait. You already knew about Blue?"

Scratching his belly, Steph grinned up at her. "Riggs asked our advice on whether we thought this sweet boy would be a help or a burden to you. He even arranged for us to watch him while you meet with your editor today."

Of course he did, Rowan thought with a mental eye-roll along with her smile. The guy was working overtime to become sainted.

Steph slowly stood, eyeing Rowan with caution. "How'd you sleep last night?"

"Okay," Rowan lied.

"Andy thought he heard someone outside in the middle of the night." Stuffing her hands inside her jeans pockets, she shrugged. "I told him it was probably just a rumble from the thunderstorm that hit north of here."

"I heard it too."

"Did Riggs make it back to Hawaii okay?"

"He sent me a text from Honolulu."

"I'm sure you're going to miss having him around."

Sensing Steph was fishing for more information, Rowan simply nodded while glancing down at her feet. She wasn't ready to share her relationship status with him while it was still so painfully new and their future was unclear.

"Well...I guess I'll head back inside and finish cooking breakfast. You're welcome to join us before you all head into the city. Bring your new little man along whenever you're ready. Kins is dying to meet him."

As Rowan watched her walk away, she vowed to find the person responsible. It had been one thing to be harassed while away in Hawaii, but it was quite another for someone to come after her on the evening of her aunt's service while she was sleeping in her own bed. She refused to let the experience of re-settling in Blue Bay become overshadowed by whatever bastard was intent on watching her cower. She refused to let them frighten her any longer. She was done playing victim to their twisted games.

30

The ride to New York with the Lewis siblings was filled with long stretches of awkward silence once Rowan made it clear she wasn't up for conversation. She was relieved when Drake at least acted normal while sitting alongside her in the back of William's Mercedes. It was almost as if their kisses and argument in Maui had never happened. She played with the idea of announcing her discovery in the studio in order to gauge William and Drake's reactions, but decided she didn't want Kinsley stuck in the middle. She'd find a different way to confront them separately.

On the bustling sidewalk outside the twisted glass skyscraper where Rowan's publisher was housed in the middle of downtown Manhattan, cold fall wind swirling around their skirts, Kinsley embraced her tightly. "Love you, sis."

"Love you too."

"Call when you're finished with your meeting, and I'll arrange to have a car bring you to our place. We'll crack open a bottle of wine from Kauai, and relax until it's time for dinner. I made reservations for just the two of us. I figured you could use a little girl time in the city after this brutal month." Her voice lowered. "Besides, I want all the deets on your time with Riggs! The way you two were constantly touching each other yesterday—"

"Come on, sweetheart," William hollered through the open passenger's window. "We're blocking traffic." When his eyes briefly connected with Rowan's over Kinsley's shoulder, he threw her a tight-lipped grin and waved. "Good luck in there, *Rowan*."

Rowan's stomach dipped and twisted with the venom hidden beneath the surface of his sentiment. It didn't take a stretch of the imagination to conclude he might be her stalker.

Backing away, Kinsley's lips touched her cheek. "Yes, good luck! Be sure to play hardball when they pitch the offer for the new book. Remember, you're a bestseller now!"

Rowan nodded mockingly. "Yes, I remember. Thanks again for the ride."

"Go get 'em, tiger!" Drake called out from the back window.

"You've got this!" Kinsley cheered while sliding into the front seat. She waved wildly out the window as they pulled away from the curb.

Rowan took the elevator to the twenty-fifth floor and checked in with the young, dark-haired receptionist perched behind a glass and metal desk. The space was bright and modern with a mix of brick walls and iron windows that framed the Chrysler Building. The heels of Rowan's peep-toed shoes clicked loudly against the polished white marble floor, echoing in the open space as she took a seat on the sleek leather sectional in the waiting area.

She removed her wool coat and smoothed the skirt of her black dress, taking a mental inventory of the subjects she'd be willing to write about. She was done with horror and murder, and hoped for something lighthearted. Maybe a romance. Her cheeks warmed when she thought of making love to Riggs. After the profound experience, she finally felt qualified to write on the subject.

She was only seated a handful of moments before her editor's secretary led her to the same conference room where they'd made the deal for *The Devil's Daughter*. She'd never been at total ease with the editor assigned to her by the publishing house. Daren Hinks was a small, older man with a smooth bald head, beady eyes, and a foul odor that clung to his fair skin. Plus he told awful jokes. When she entered the bright conference room adorned with brick walls and iron chandeliers, she was relieved to see Daren flanked by Ginny Roberts, her literary agent, and Ann Kester, the woman who had accompanied Rowan on her nationwide book tour for *Devil's Daughter*. On second glance, she realized both women appeared uneasy.

Daren was the first to shake her hand, cloaking her in his stench. "Good to see you, *Rowan*. Once again, we were sorry to hear about your aunt. I do hope the service went well."

Glancing wearily at the women, she responded with a small nod. They each flashed her the kind of forced, unnatural smile that she'd give judges in her early days of competition as they took turns shaking her hand.

Daren pulled a rolling chair out, motioning to her. "Have a seat. Is there anything we can get you? Water? Coffee? Tea?"

"No thank you." Her eyes locked with Ann's as

she lowered down to the black leather seat across from her, coat draped over one arm. Something was amiss, and she had bonded with the woman after one of her breakdowns enough that she trusted Ann…to a point.

Sliding forward on her seat, Ann's eyes jumped down to the stack of paper sitting in front of her. "Before we begin, I'd like to clear the air about something." She glanced upward, holding Rowan's confused stare. "None of this was my doing."

Discontent slithered through Rowan. She had a sickening suspicion why Ann would make such a declaration. Her heels tapped against the industrial carpet. "Have you changed your mind about a second book?"

"Do we *look* crazy?" With an overly-toothy smile, Daren picked up his stack of paper, and gently tossed it across the table to her. "This meeting is all about opportunity, Miss Brooks. An opportunity to share your *true story* with the world."

"My *true* story?" She glanced down at the stapled stack of paper with unbearable heat spreading down her neck. The proposal was titled, *"The Devil's Daughter II: The Exclusive TRUE Story of the SLS Killer's Daughter."* Her eyes snapped back to Ann's. "What did you tell them?"

Clutching the same string of pearls she'd worn every day of Rowan's tour, Ann gave a firm shake of her head. "I promise, Rowan. I didn't tell a soul."

"Your identity was leaked to a reporter this morning," Ginny explained with an air of disappointment. She was normally a friendly woman, with beautiful brown skin and the thickest black hair Rowan had ever seen, but she appeared annoyed when her dark amber eyes bore into Rowan's. "They called me first, asking for a comment to go along with the article he's intending to print." She practically snarled as her eyes narrowed. "Is it true? Have you been lying to us this whole time?"

Rowan's lips opened with a response before she snapped them back shut. The room was spinning, and her queasy stomach threatened to spew. "What reporter?" she wheezed. "When's the article going to print?"

"Does it matter?" Daren chortled, clamping his hands over his knees. "This is your chance to join the ranks of other famous authors who have shared their unique experiences with serial killers—like Ann Rule and Michelle McNamara! It's rare the public gets a glimpse of what it was like from someone with your up-close point of view! This is the age of serial killers. Everyone's obsessed! We're sitting on a gold mine, Ms. *Rivers*, and you're the prospector with the power to give the green light!"

Dragging in shallow, uneven breaths, Rowan slowly began to rise from the chair. Her coat dropped over her feet on the floor. "There's been a... mistake." Desperate for their help, her eyes volleyed between Ann and Ginny. She gripped the edge of the glass table, willing herself not to faint. "Please, *someone*...give me the name of this reporter. I need his number...address...anything!"

"Somebody, do something!" Ann pleaded, bolting to her feet. "She's going to pass out!"

No I'm not, Rowan thought stubbornly, staggering toward the exit. Daren called out for her to come back, and Ann pleaded for her to wait.

She caught her breath in the hallway before bolting toward the elevator doors. Both her peaceful way of life and her blossoming career would be over if the truth came into the public eye. They would claim she was "deceitful" and "money hungry" for crafting her father's story into a work of fiction. She imagined her mother standing over her, arms crossed, sharp *tisk* snapping against her tongue. *You should've listened to me*, she imagined her mother saying. *You did it to yourself.*

The part that she couldn't live with, the thought

that would keep her awake at night for weeks on end, was how her father would react to her big reveal.

Once on the sidewalk, on one of the busiest streets of the bustling city, she threw up into a garbage can.

LATER THAT EVENING, when she returned one of Kinsley's many missed calls, her friend demanded to know why Rowan had stood her up. Rowan didn't have any idea how she'd made it all the way back to Blue Bay from New York. She'd forgotten her coat in the conference room, and didn't remember anything after she stepped outside. When she'd changed out of her dress, she'd found a train ticket in the pocket. Her blood ran cold. She'd learned about dissociative fugue while in college—a rare psychiatric abnormality in which a person experiences temporary amnesia—and began to fear she'd completely lost her mind.

"Kins, they knew," she said, glancing out the front set of the cottage's windows. She was convinced the residents of Blue Bay would come after her with figurative torches at any moment. "They knew everything."

"What's going on?" Concern raised Kinsley's voice an octave higher. "Who are you talking about?"

"My editor...my agent. They said a reporter contacted them, wanting a comment on my true identity. They're planning to expose me as the SLS killer's daughter."

"Oh...*shit*. Are you sure?"

"They wanted me to write an autobiography."

A scraping noise washed over the ear piece, and Kinsley's voice became muffled. A deep voice volleyed with hers for a full minute before she said, "Ro, sweetie, I'm sending mom and dad over."

"Please, no. I don't want to talk to anyone right now."

"Then can I call Riggs?"

"No!" She jammed her fingers inside her curls, realizing she was even starting to sound insane. With a calming breath, she gripped her cell phone a little tighter. "Please don't call Riggs, Kins. I realize he'll find out eventually, but he's tied up for a few days, and can't be bothered. I'll tell him on my own time."

"Alright. But I'm still sending mom and dad over to be with you. I don't care if you stay there or sleep in my old bed, but I don't want you to be alone when the news breaks. You've already been through a lot this week. Taylor wouldn't want you facing this on your own."

"I'll be okay," she promised, fingering the bracelet Kinsley's parents had given her the night of her 12th birthday. Although she hadn't believed in the sentiment of things ever truly being okay after the night of her father's arrest, she willed herself to make it true.

Again, her thoughts returned to William. He had given her another smug smile right before she'd met with her publisher. He had to have been the one who leaked her identity to the reporter. She'd never had the opportunity to ask for Taylor's advice on how to approach Kinsley with her suspicions. Maybe it was time to disclose everything to his new in-laws. She knew Andy was already leery of William's relationship with his daughter. Maybe he'd hear her out.

By the time Andy and Steph came over, armed with a bottle of sparkling wine, a frozen pizza, and her new dog sporting a red bow-tie, Rowan had managed to calm somewhat. *One step at a time,* she heard Riggs telling her. Once Steph threw the pizza into the preheated oven, she sat with Rowan on the couch, and Andy poured them each a glass of wine.

With Blue perched on her lap, she accepted the glass Andy offered, and told them the details of her meeting.

Steph squeezed Rowan's leg. "I'm sorry, sweetie. The timing isn't great. But since you were little, Taylor talked to you about the possibility of this happening some day. I'm confident you're strong enough to ride out whatever storm is coming. Taylor was, too." She leaned in to scratch behind Blue's ear. "Are you sure that woman from your book tour didn't tell them?"

Shrugging, Rowan scratched Blue's other ear. "I don't know what she'd have to gain."

"Probably a nice fat bonus," Andy muttered before taking a healthy gulp of wine.

"But why would she wait this long?" Steph asked him.

The confession that she suspected William was behind it all stung Rowan's tongue as she finished her wine. What if she was wrong, and she only managed to wedge more hard feelings between Kinsley's husband and parents?

"This wine is running right through me," Steph said, starting for the bathroom. She pointed to a stack of envelopes on the kitchen island. "Oh, I forgot. Ro, I grabbed your mail." She did a little dance. "I'll be right back! Don't talk about anything until I return!"

Rowan lifted her empty glass. "Want another?" she asked Andy.

"Hell yes," he answered, downing the last of his drink. He handed his glass to her before removing his glasses and wiping them on the edge of his t-shirt. "Steph's right, you know. You're a strong young woman. Whatever comes out of this, you'll survive it with your head held high."

Her insides shook a little as she released Blue onto the floor. "I hope you're right."

She carried the empty glasses into the kitchen, setting them on the island so she could sort through the small stack of mail. With the sight of her aunt's electric and cable bills, she realized she'd have to transfer everything to her name. She dreaded calling to make the changes, knowing people would soon recognize the name Rowan Brooks in an unfavorable way.

The last piece of mail was a plain white business-sized envelope, addressed to "Miss Rowan Brooks." Her eye first caught the rubber stamp impression, declaring it had been mailed from a state correctional institution. As she read the return address, her hands trembled uncontrollably, knocking one of her aunt's precious handmade wine glasses down to crash on the tile floor. The sound of it shattering into a dozen pieces fell deaf on Rowan's ears.

She'd received a letter from her father.

Unlike the rest of the world, he already knew her new name.

31

The three carat diamond earrings burned a hole in Riggs's jeans pocket as he nudged the rental's accelerator a little more. It had been over a month since he'd left Blue Bay, and he was fucking angry. Angry at the FBI, angry at Chelsea and her conniving father, and most of all, angry with himself. The nightmare had begun because he'd allowed Chelsea to seduce him all those months ago. If he'd seen her for what she really was and had told her to take a hike, he wouldn't have wasted so much time away from Rowan.

He would've preferred to have bought an engagement ring instead of the earrings, but he sensed Rowan hadn't been herself ever since the weaselly bastard of a reporter had called her out to the world.

He wasn't going to push his luck by asking her to marry him at the wrong time.

They'd been deep in the middle of the FBI's audit of the resort when his phone had chimed with an alert on the SLS killer. He'd roared so loudly in anger that he frightened the female agent assigned to work with him. Forgetting about the time difference, he'd sprinted out of the conference room and called when Rowan had been asleep. "We figured this would happen one day," she'd said between yawns.

The way she'd brushed it off didn't sit right with him. "I'm coming back there."

"The FBI has cleared you?"

"No, but—"

"Then there's no reason to come back. I'm fine, Riggs. I promise."

Her voice had been too cold, too void of emotion. It continued to sound that way whenever he called to check in with her every day that followed. She always had an excuse not to answer his video calls, and always returned them with a regular voice call. He was certain she was putting on a brave facade, but it wasn't fooling him.

When he pulled up to her cottage in Blue Bay the evening of December 20th, the lawn was covered in a light dusting of snow. Every other house in the neighborhood was adorned with lights and holiday decorations. Rowan's remained dark except for a light in the living room and a sad little wreath on the front door. He shouldered his overnight bag, peering into the little red coupe with California plates parked next to her Jeep in the driveway. The back seat appeared to be filled with men's clothing. His pulse quickened as he approached the front door. He hadn't told her he was returning. He'd wanted it to be a surprise. Now he was starting to regret the idea. He hadn't considered she might already have company. He couldn't even begin to think why a man from California with an entire wardrobe in the backseat would be staying with her.

His heart rocketed to the ground when a younger guy with a headful of chin-length, curly brown hair and pipes the size of small trees opened the door. He wore long gray skater shorts and a standard surfer shirt like the kind he'd worn himself on the California beaches. He didn't want to assume the worst of Rowan, but Riggs couldn't deny the man with deeply tanned skin and bedroom eyes would be exceptionally attractive to women. A little smile tilted the man's lips. "What's up, man?"

Before Riggs could make himself form an answer, a little white dog in a red and green plaid bowtie appeared at the man's feet, barking like Riggs was there to rob the place. He had to laugh. At least he'd gifted Rowan with the fierce guardian. "Hey, Blue."

The guy let out a stoner's laugh. "You know Ro's dog?"

"Yeah, I do. Is she home?"

"My lady's takin' a bath, bro." Smirking, he wiggled his eyebrows. "Can I give Ro a message?"

A roar stuck in Riggs's throat. The guy was too massive to fight, but there wouldn't be anything that could stop him from being reunited with Rowan. He charged past the man, ramming into him with his shoulder.

"Hey!" the guy yelled behind him. "Who do you think you are, bargin' in like that?"

I'm her man, Riggs thought as he marched toward the bathroom. The cottage was in complete disarray, resembling a fraternity with empty beer cans, dirty laundry, and pizza boxes scattered throughout. It even possessed the funky odor of pot. Riggs couldn't help feeling responsible. While he'd been focused on his business, no one had been around for her. His anger simmered a little more. How the hell had the Lewises let her fall so far?

The bathroom door was unlocked. He threw his shoulder into the door as he turned the knob. A young blonde with a joint held between her cherry red lips sat in the tub with bubbles up to her chin. Her forest green eyes widened on Riggs, and a coy smile fell upon her lips. "Hey there, sexy. You here to party?"

"Bro!" the curly-haired guy shouted from right behind him. "You some kind of perv? I told you my lady's in here!"

Teeth bared, Riggs whirled around and gripped the kid's t-shirt with a fist. "Who are you? Where the hell is Rowan?"

WHEN KINSLEY SWUNG the massive steel door open to their multi-million dollar apartment in Tribeca, her face flushed with guilt and her eyes grew wide. She wore a navy kimono, and her red hair was fastened in a pile on top of her head. "I wanted to call you, I swear."

Riggs felt his lips curve with a snarl. "Where is she?" he demanded.

On a heavy sigh, she waved him in. "Come on. I'll explain everything."

Eyes skimming over the luxurious furnishings, he was unable to register anything, except for the fact that he didn't see Rowan. "Where is she?" he repeated.

She reached into a tall cabinet over a hightop bar in the living room, retrieving two crystal whiskey tumblers. "She's at an all-night diner down the street, writing on her laptop," she called over her shoulder. She opened a stainless steel door beneath her and grabbed a silver bucket. "She goes there whenever William and I are home."

His outrage grew as she calmly filled the glasses with ice, then poured a dark liquid from a matching crystal decanter. "What's the name of this diner?"

"Unclench your jaw before you give yourself TMJ, and get your fine ass over here for a drink." She held up one of the glasses, eyebrows lifted. "You're going to need it."

He stormed over to accept the glass, and took a generous swig. The single malt scotch spread like fire down to his stomach. "Start talking."

She walked around the bar and perched on a stainless steel barstool at his side, pulling her robe a little tighter. "Real talk? Rowan's a mess." When Riggs scowled, she held up her manicured hand. "Like I said, I wanted to call you. But she didn't want you to know everything that was going on, because she knew you'd come back. She told me you could lose everything if you did, and said she wouldn't be able to deal with the consequences if that happened."

"I knew something wasn't right the day I called her about the article." He released his drink onto the bar's granite top, and dropped his face into his hands. How could he not blame himself for not being there when she needed him most? He gave a vigorous scrub of his cheeks, and swiped the scotch back for a bigger gulp. "I should've listened to my gut. I should've come back that day."

With a shake of her head, Kinsley waved her hand between them. "That's old news. I mean, yeah…the national fallout from that wasn't great, but she did fairly well—even when the media went nuts with it. But no one around Blue Bay seemed to care. They still treated her the same whenever she was out and about, if not with an added touch of kindness. But her book sales skyrocketed the week after it all came out, and hit the bestseller list a second time. Can you believe it?" She paused, taking a dainty sip of her scotch. "You'd be proud of how well she did at first."

"At first?" He clenched, then promptly unclenched his jaw. "What happened?"

"She got a letter in the mail from her father."

That bastard, he thought. He'd already done enough damage to his daughter. Why couldn't he have left her alone? His spine straightened. "What'd it say?"

"Mostly that he was proud of her for becoming a famous author, and living her best life even after he'd messed with her future." She set her drink on the granite and heaved a sigh. "It wasn't so much *what* it said as the fact that he knew she'd changed her name."

"How?"

"No one knows, but she's convinced he's the one who told the reporter, because his letter arrived on that same day. She thinks he has a connection on the outside, doing his dirty work. She thinks he's the one who keeps sending her the spider lilies."

"*Keeps* sending?" Fingers tightening around his glass, he snarled. "She's received more?"

Kinsley lowered her head, glancing up at him through the thickness of her dark lashes. "The night of Taylor's funeral, after you left, someone filled the studio behind the cottage with dozens of them."

"Son of a bitch!" he roared, wheeling around. The pressure in his chest imploded. He'd tear her old man apart for hurting her. "I never should've fucking left!"

"Please don't break that glass! The set was a wedding present from my in-laws!"

He glanced down at his hand holding the crystal glass, unaware he'd been prepared to chuck it across the room. He turned back around, setting it on the bar.

"The letter did a number on her head, Riggs—especially after she decided it was time to read the *other* letters he'd sent when she was little...the ones her mom had given her at her college graduation party. She started calling my dad all hours of the night, saying someone was in her house. She started to worry she was constantly being followed around Blue Bay. My parents tried to stay with her as much as their schedules would allow, but we all agreed it was best to have her come stay with me for a while since I'm between gigs. She doesn't seem quite as afraid here in the city. I mean did she at first, but she's making real progress. A few weeks ago, she wouldn't have gone to the diner by herself after dark. I think she feels safe here because she doesn't think her dad knows where I live."

Frustrated tears burned the edges of his eyes. "You should've called me, Kinsley. I would've given everything up to prevent this from happening."

"I know. I'm sorry. But she was so damn

adamant. She can be so headstrong…stubborn. I was afraid she'd never speak to me again if I betrayed her."

His fingers twisted the earring box around in his pocket. "Who's the stoner responsible for trashing her cottage?"

Head thrown back, she released a tinkling laugh. "That's Wren, a kid she met at the shelter she volunteered for in college. He's a good kid…for the most part. He graduated last spring, and decided to take his girlfriend on a road trip. I guess they went to Blue Bay, looking for Rowan, and they ended up liking it so much they're going to stick around for a while. He's looking for a job there, so she's letting him crash there until she gets back on her feet. He's also watching Blue since our super doesn't allow pets." She gritted her teeth. "How bad is it?"

"I gave him a good scare. He wouldn't tell me anything—who he was, or why he was there. Just said to call you. I told him I'd be back soon, and the place better be cleaned up."

A metallic sound came from the front door. Kinsley popped up from her seat and gripped his wrist, emerald eyes frantic. "Riggs, in case that's her, you better prepare yourself. She has *really* changed since you left."

The massive door burst open a moment later. Riggs's heart stilled when a shaggy-haired blonde shuffled in with a laptop bag crossed over her chest. She was as underweight as she'd been the first time he'd gone looking for her in Blue Bay. In a ripped pair of jeans, a rocker T-shirt beneath a black bomber jacket, and dark aviator sunglasses, she was totally unrecognizable. He supposed that was the point. She was hiding.

Reluctantly, he started for her, stopping within a few feet of the near stranger that reeked of booze. "Ro?"

"Hey, hot stuff." Staggering toward him, she flipped her glasses up to the top of her head and squinted. Her eyelids were rimmed with black makeup, and the whites of her eyes were bloodshot. "Don't I know you?"

32

Warm sunlight cut through Rowan's eyelids like a million tiny razors. She'd spent another night pounding drinks at The Randy Irishman, a pub one neighborhood over. Only this time, she'd continued to drink until she'd become out-of-control wasted with a bunch of guys out celebrating a financial windfall of their startup. She was certain she'd consumed enough that Kinsley would see past her guise of writing at the diner. She couldn't remember coming home after, which was fine by her. Anything to keep the nightmares away.

Groaning, she rolled onto her side and reached for a blanket to cover her pounding head. Her hand connected with a large, hairy skull. A bloody scream ripped through her throat.

"Christ, Ro," a man's voice growled. "It's me."

Her stomach dropped. Riggs was in her bed.

She bolted upright, aggressively rubbing her eyes with her fists. When she opened them, he was still sprawled out next to her in a pair of boxer briefs, deeply tanned limbs a stark contrast to the white sheets. His body was even more beautiful than she'd remembered from the one time they'd slept together. The pull in her belly begged her to explore his glorious skin.

She glanced down at her own body, anxiously fingering the charm bracelet around her wrist. She still wore the vintage Fleetwood Mac T-shirt from the night before with nothing more than a thong. Without question, she knew Riggs wouldn't have so much as touched her when she'd been out of it. She also knew by the bulge in his briefs that he enjoyed seeing her half-naked.

Crippled with shame, she curled into herself and covered her body. She had really let herself go since he'd left. She couldn't imagine what he thought of her cropped blond hair, and she imagined the hangover taking residence in her head made her appear horrendous.

"What in the hell are you doing here, Riggs? How did you find me?"

"I called Kinsley after I nearly flattened the beefy

surfer in your cottage." He sat up, scratching at his wild hair while giving her a dry look over his bare shoulder. "*She* decided it was time to fill me in."

Although she doubted he wouldn't have actually tried hurting Wren, she felt a pinch of guilt for inadvertently putting them both into the situation. "Why aren't you in Maui?"

"Victor was able to convince his contact with the FBI that it was all a set-up. They arrested Chelsea's dad, and cleared me of all charges." She turned to watch as he stretched his arms up toward the lofted ceiling. The accentuated muscles in his back and biceps flexed like a work of art. He swung his gaze back to her with a dimpled grin. "Why aren't you in Blue Bay?"

Everything inside of her turned to mush with his grin. She dropped her chin to her bent knees, wishing she could disappear. "It's a long story."

"Kinsley already filled me in." His smirk became cynical. "So your serial killer dad has been brought up to speed on your identity, and everyone knows you're his daughter. Big deal. Are you really going to let it ruin your life?"

Her eyelids fluttered with disbelief. She'd never witnessed him being so blunt with her or anyone else. But then a jolt of rage slammed into her. How could he dismiss what had happened? "You weren't around when shit hit the fan! You don't know what it's like!"

The muscles in his jaw twitched. "I wasn't around because you chose to keep me in the dark. And you're right, I don't know what it's like. But it still doesn't give you the right to go off the deep end. Everyone's dealing with some kind of shit, Ro. It'll only change you if you let it." He jumped off the mattress and swiped a long-sleeved t-shirt off the floor. "Get in the shower, and get dressed. We're leaving in twenty minutes."

"If you think you can go back to bossing me around—"

He silenced her with a sharp look. "I sure as hell can, and you can bet your hot little ass I will. Kinsley may have let your bullshit slide while you were here, but I'm not going to stand back and watch the girl I love disappear." After wiggling into a pair of jeans, he returned to the mattress and crawled—*stalked*—toward her on his hands and knees. The intensity in his honeyed eyes was breathtaking. She braced herself as the pull of desire liquified her limbs. She didn't have time to pull in a breath before he planted a deep, intense kiss on her lips.

As much as she wanted to push him away, her

body sparked to life, craving more. She hadn't allowed herself to miss him just like she hadn't allowed herself to play the part of a helpless victim. She knotted her fingers inside his wild hair, needing him closer. Needing more of him. She'd been a fool not to ask for him to come back sooner.

His lips were off hers much sooner than she would've preferred. "Brush your teeth, too." He wiped his mouth on his forearm, grimacing. "Your mouth tastes like ass."

With a sly wink, he promptly exited the room, leaving her unsatisfied and achy. She continued to stare at the closed door for a full minute, lips parted.

AT THE SHOOTING range five city blocks from Kinsley's, a man with shorn hair used a large gun to destroy a human-shaped target in the booth next to Rowan and Riggs. Once finished, he grinned over at Rowan. "Ma'am."

Adjusting the headphones they'd been issued at the front desk, she turned back to Riggs. "Why are we here?" she blurted.

"I'm putting control back in your hands." With the barrel aimed at the target in the distance, he positioned her hands around the weapon. "Literally."

He quickly walked her through the basic features of the pistol in his hand and the logistics of firing it. "Don't put your finger on the trigger until you're ready to shoot."

"How does a surfer know so much about guns?"

He straddled her from behind, arms braced over hers. "When I was a kid, my mom died of a heroin overdose. I had to learn how to fend for myself on the streets."

"*What?*" It was the first time he'd shared anything about his mother. He'd never so much as hinted that he'd been raised in a dangerous environment. She tried turning to him, wanting to comfort him somehow. "Riggs—"

He nudged her back around and kicked her feet wider apart. "They tried to put me in different placements, but I decided it was better to be on my own. I slept with a knife under my pillow." With her cocooned against him, he adjusted her grip on the pistol. "By the time Victor found me living on the streets and offered me a job, I was scared of my own shadow...just like you. He taught me how to shoot a gun so I'd be less afraid, and know how to protect myself."

She blinked rapidly, drying the tears building behind her eyes. "I had no idea."

"That's because I don't walk around, feeling sorry for myself." The flutter of his lips against her ear halted her breath. "You're going to aim at the target's head by looking through the sight with your dominant eye, other eye closed, and line up the top of the front sight with the rear sight."

She followed his directions, slightly unsure she was doing it right. "Got it...I think."

"When you're ready, take a deep breath and hold it. You're gonna squeeze the trigger, but don't move anything else. Hold your stance...be still. You can release the trigger after you've taken another breath. Make sure you point the gun at the floor before you make any other movements." He stepped away. "Whenever you're ready."

Her heart hammered in her chest. The gun felt heavy without Riggs supporting her hand. It also felt powerful. "Aren't you going to stand by me?"

"Always. Just not right this second." He let out a soft chuckle. "Go ahead, Ro. You've got this."

On a deep inhale, she resisted the urge to close both of her eyes when she squeezed her pointer finger over the trigger. She felt a slight recoil in her arms as the bullet fired, missing the target's head by less than an inch.

"Not bad, ma'am," the guy one booth over said. "First time?"

She relaxed her arms, making a point to aim the gun at the floor as Riggs instructed. The corners of her lips lifted with a proud smile as she turned to the man. "Yessir."

"Oorah!" he cheered. "Get some! You'll be a sniper in no time!"

Chuckling, Riggs wrapped her in a side hug. "You may look like a young Stevie Nicks after a bad bender, but you're as badass as Sigourney Weaver in *Aliens*." He kissed the corner of her mouth before gently bracing her shoulders and turning her back to the target. "Let's keep going until you're completely comfortable. Then we'll move on to self-defense."

As Rowan prepared to shoot a second time, she couldn't stop smiling.

VICTOR WILSON WAS ABNORMALLY handsome for someone in his eighties, reminding Rowan of the smooth old guy in the tequila commercials. He wore dress slacks and a white collared shirt unbuttoned halfway with tan penny loafers, and a fedora that suited the broad lines of his face. It was funny how she almost saw a little of Riggs in the sparkle of his eyes and the playful tilt of his lips, even though they weren't related by blood. He welcomed her into the modern penthouse with open arms and a kiss on each cheek.

"You're even more lovely than my boy had described," he told her with a ridiculously wide grin.

"You should've seen her *before* her recent makeover," Riggs teased, nudging her waist as bypassed them for the wet bar.

Shame heated her cheeks as she dipped her chin. After getting sweaty from a private Judo class at a gym near Kinsley's apartment, they had gone back to shower and change. Although Riggs had said she was dazzling in one of Kinsley's fluttering white party dresses, and she'd put real effort into her hair and makeup, she could only imagine what Steph would have to say about her hair once she returned home. Hopefully her pseudo mother could fix the hack job, and restore its natural shade of strawberry blond.

"Fetch us a beverage, Riggs," Victor told him, sounding much like one of Riggs's bossy modes. "We'll be back in a moment." Then he hooked his hand through her arm, leading her away. "I hear in addition to recently becoming an established author, you have a passion for reading as well. I'd like to show you my collection."

As they passed the wide terrace, her eyes scanned over the city's dramatic skyline and stopped on the Empire State Building. She'd visited the observatory once, with both of her parents. Before their lives had become so complicated. She missed the time they'd spent in the city, on the rare occasions in which her life wasn't tainted by pageants. As a little girl, she'd dreamed of living in a glamorous penthouse in the heart of the city.

Nerves rattled her stomach as Victor neared the master suite. She suspected the invitation was an excuse to speak with her alone, maybe even lecture her on how immature she'd been. But her fears were instantly soothed by the thousands of books lining the walls of the most elegant bedroom she'd ever stepped foot inside. She bypassed the oak ladder and ran her fingertips along several of the books' spines, breathing in their ancient scents. "This is amazing."

"Riggs had these shelves built for me, even though he knew my stay in his hotel wouldn't last forever. Perhaps they weren't really for me after all.

Maybe somewhere in the depths of his soul, he knew he'd fall in love with a bibliophile one day."

Dipping her chin, she eyed him bashfully. "Do you believe in soulmates?"

One of his shoulders lifted and dropped. "I believe in destiny. I think the person you're meant to be with comes into your life with the stealth of a violent storm...makes you question everything... changes your reality." He smiled with a faraway look. "Sometimes it takes someone considered ordinary in the eyes of others to do extraordinary things that revolutionize your world."

She felt her answering smile all the way down to her feet. "That's deep, Mr. Wilson."

"It's Victor to my friends and family, my dear. And that's probably a quote I once read somewhere." He moved in front of her, frail hands placed on her shoulders. "I do hope you'll become a permanent part of Riggs's family someday. I've been all he's had for so long, and the most he's ever been able to call me was a cherished friend. I've never known him to be so elated...lighthearted. I've also never seen him fret over anything the way he worries about you."

"I messed up. I should've told him I needed him here, with me. I was too proud...too afraid to admit I couldn't face this on my own." She lowered her head, wanting to shield him from her watering eyes. "He's always been good to me…no matter what. I'm not sure I deserve him."

Victor tipped her chin upright with his finger, forcing tears to streak down her cheeks. His wrinkled face was stern, and his eyes were kind. "Your father put you through a great trauma, dear child. I imagine it's hard to reach out to a man when you've been so deeply betrayed by the most prominent male figure in your life. Be kind to yourself, Rowan. Be patient. Riggs understands what it's like to feel betrayed by the people who brought you into the world. I'm certain fate brought you two together for a reason. It's up to you to give that reason a purpose."

All at once, she was reminded of the conversation she'd had with Taylor the night she learned her father would spend the rest of his life in prison. They'd been sitting in the cottage kitchen, watching the light from the lighthouse pass over the bay. *"Whenever things get too hard, I see that light and I think of my Jason. He believed the purpose in our lives is what we create for ourselves."*

An idea came to her right as Riggs cleared his throat. He leaned against the doorway, arms and ankles crossed, feet bare. "If you two are finished conspiring to run away together, there's a thirty-year-old bottle of German wine breathing in the other room."

Victor wiggled his white brows, rushing from the room. "Sounds like it needs a little mouth-to-mouth."

Rowan wiped a knuckle over her eyes before meeting Riggs's brow crooked in question. In a black sweater and black jeans, brown hair combed back, she found him completely irresistible. The ache in her chest that she felt was all she needed to know. She was truly, deeply in love with Riggs Forrester. In that instant, as she looked into his honeyed eyes, she knew without question that she would one day make him her husband.

33

Gathered around the polished black penthouse table, the three friends dined on Cesar salads and Mediterranean shish kabobs prepared by the hotel chef. Victor told stories of his wife and childhood with the skyscrapers of downtown Manhattan winking scandalously behind him. It was a romantic setting, even with the presence of the man who'd essentially raised him. Riggs wasn't sure what words Rowan and Victor had exchanged in the privacy of his suite, but they'd become as chummy as he'd predicted. She'd touch his shoulder when he made her laugh, and he had a certain look of satisfaction whenever glancing in her direction.

It had been a major relief when Rowan had sprung back to life so effortlessly once he was around. When she'd stumbled into Kinsley's apartment the night before, he'd feared he would be forced to drag her off to rehab. Although he missed her long, sensuous curls, he was becoming somewhat fond of the short blond shag after she'd showered and added subtle waves. In fact, it was exciting to think of what it would be like later, when they were alone in the guest bedroom, when he had a chance to strip her—

"Earth to Riggs!" Victor sang with a bemused smile. "I said goodnight, my boy."

Shaking his head, Riggs shoved away from the table. "Sorry." When he stood he glanced Rowan's way, pleased to see the glow in her cheeks. "Guess I was distracted."

"I imagine I know why," Victor answered with sarcasm. The two men embraced with loud claps on each other's backs. Victor gripped his elbow before he could let go, and whispered, "Don't ever let her go, son."

"I don't plan to," Riggs whispered back.

Victor stepped around him to hug Rowan. "Goodnight, my dear. It's been a real pleasure—one I expect to experience again…real soon."

"I'll be back," she declared, smiling at Riggs over his shoulder. "Thank you for a lovely evening, Victor."

Victor drew away, holding his hand beside his mouth. "This one's a keeper," he said to Riggs.

As he left the room, Riggs swiped their wine glasses off the table and eyed Rowan. The dress she'd borrowed gave her an angelic look, even if it was a touch too big for her shrinking frame. He hoped the progress of getting her back into shape would go quicker than last time, because he had big plans for that body and wasn't sure his patience would last. "Grab your coat. I'm refilling these, and we're going out on the terrace."

"Yessir," she grumbled, padding barefoot to the front closet and muttering something under her breath about his "bossy ass."

He filled their glasses, grabbing another bottle of wine, and ignited the concrete fire pit on the terrace. Gazing over the dramatic city skyline with the warmth of the fire cutting the chill out of the brisk December air, he appreciated the golden glow of the city's grid of skyscrapers. Not everyone was so fortunate as to have the best of everything. He could take residence there, in California, or in Maui. But even as someone who was raised on the West Coast, he was drawn to the magic of Manhattan. And knowing Rowan had grown up in New York, he hoped she'd enjoy spending time there just as much. When he'd first purchased the property, he'd stood in the same place with complete awe, wishing there was someone else who would appreciate the spectacular view as much. When Rowan stepped out beside him, bundled in Kinsley's woolen peacoat, he knew he'd found that someone.

She set one forearm on the concrete ledge and gazed down at the city with a breathy sigh that came out in a white puff against the cold air. "Sometimes I still think of this as my home." Then she held out his coat, draped over her other arm. "Put this on before you catch a cold."

"Yes, *boss*." With a deep belly laugh, he pulled the coat over his arms and hauled her against his side, delighting in the sound of her surprised squeak. She wrapped her arm around his waist and angled into him, staring up into his eyes while dragging her finger across his jawline. Beneath the new look she was still as soft as ever inside. The vulnerable look in her colorless eyes tugged at his heart. "I'm sorry, Riggs. I'm sorry I didn't call...I'm sorry I let you down. I didn't intend to let it go this far."

He nudged her hand away from his jaw, lacing their fingers over his stomach. "It hurt like hell to see what you'd done to yourself—getting drunk and neglecting your body all over again...shit, Ro. For a minute I was scared I'd have to send you away to get sober. And I hated that you fled your aunt's cottage...left Blue behind. But you should be apologizing to yourself—to *Taylor*. She would've hated seeing you that way, living in fear."

Tears shone in her eyes when she nodded. "I don't want to live in fear anymore."

"I'm hiring a private investigator to keep an eye on the ins-and-outs of your father in prison. He can give us a heads up if there's anything unsavory headed your way. But Jonathan's behind bars, Ro. He can't physically hurt you. He can live rent-free inside your head all he wants, but only if you allow it."

"I'm hoping my psychiatrist will help me come to terms with that." She huddled closer, tucking her head against his chest. "There are other things I'll need to work on. I'm sure you've noticed I don't exactly have a healthy relationship with food." Shivering, she wrapped both hands around his waist. "I've never told anyone this before, but it all started years ago when my mother made me believe my weight was a serious problem. I obsessively counted every inch, every calorie. If I didn't win at pageants, it was because I was too fat or too lumpy."

A boulder dropped inside his gut. He couldn't imagine she'd ever been overweight. Even so, she was a damn kid. He nudged her chin back with his knuckle. "You were in pageants?"

Eyes aglow, lashes fluttering, she flashed her teeth with a quick smile. "You have no idea. As far back as I can remember, competitions were my life until I went to live with my aunt. My bedroom in Brooklyn was overflowing with trophies. Vanessa Rivers didn't raise a loser."

All at once he understood her constant need to put on a good show. She'd felt extreme pressure to be the best for the first half of her life. "Christ, Ro. That explains that awful smile you give everyone when you're upset, and the way you sometimes handle situations like you're under a microscope." He hated that for her. He wanted to meet her mother only for the chance to let her know she'd been a shitty mom. He bent to kiss the tip of Rowan's dainty nose. "Can't say I'm surprised to hear you'd won so many trophies. I can't imagine there was ever a day when you weren't breathtaking."

She snorted. "You'd be surprised. I'd spent so many years trying to be perfect that it was hard to let it go. I suppose this little rebellious stage was my way of doing that." Her eyes vacantly skated across the skyline. "I wasted so much time chasing perfection that I didn't know how to let myself be happy."

His fingertips unintentionally dug into her back when he hugged her a little tighter. "I can't tell you how much I hate that. You're as close to perfect as a person can get—*especially* when you're not trying. You deserve to be happy, Ro. You have a kind heart... a generous soul. It's time for you to put everything aside, and figure out what truly makes you happy. If it's writing, focus on that. I'll take care of everything else. If it's something other than writing, I'll help you figure out whatever else it might be."

She squeezed him back, setting her head on his chest. "You know, something Victor said before dinner made me remember how I once thought I'd figured out my purpose in life."

One of his hands cradled the slender nape of her neck. "Which is?"

She leaned away to look up at him again. "Working with traumatized children." Passion lit her eyes as bright as the skyscrapers beyond. "When I volunteered at the shelter in San Francisco, I felt like I could really connect with them—kids like Wren and Stormy. I'm sure it's because I'd been through something similar myself." She shrugged in a shy way that reminded him of the quiet, proper girl he'd met on Del Mar Beach. "I want to open a shelter...in Blue Bay. I know there wouldn't be much for clientele within the city limits, so we could offer to transport kids from the city. We could use the profits from *The Devil's Daughter* as seed money."

Something tugged deep in his belly. "Who's this 'we' you speak of?"

"I figured you'd want to be involved, since you've been in their situation too." Her smile stretched her cheeks, making her eyes twinkle with excitement. "I don't know where we'll end up living one day, but I definitely hope we can spend summers in Blue Bay. It's what Taylor wanted when she left me the cottage. We could hire someone to run the shelter once it's up and running. Maybe if it's successful enough, we can open similar shelters in other locations—the same places you own hotels. Here, Maui, Del Mar."

Grinning, he brushed his fingertips along each of her curved lips. He was able to fully comprehend how he had fallen so hard, so fast. She was smart, and sexy, and compassionate. And god knows he loved that she was willing to spread her wings at his side. "There's that mention of 'we' again. And what's this talk of my hotels?" He bit back a foolishly happy grin. "Are you inserting yourself into my life?"

"I don't plan on spending another day away from the man I love."

His breath caught, and his heart tumbled into his ribs. "You—"

"I *love you*, Riggs Forrester." She shifted around to stand directly in front of him, expression serene when she took his face in her hands. She was a vision of beauty on a normal day, but seeing her against the skyline he adored as she confessed her love for him was indescribable. The tug inside his chest produced a deep sigh, rumbling against his throat. "I've loved you for a long time now. I was just too afraid to admit it. And now I want to start a new life with you."

He pulled her into his arms and captured her mouth with his. She clung to him, meeting the swirl of his tongue and stroke of his lips, spreading heat through him with the force of a volcano. He lifted her into his arms, gliding through the terrace doors with their mouths still connected, and blindly navigating his way into the guest suite. With the door closed behind them, he deftly peeled her dress and undergarments off, skimming his fingertips over every inch of the lovely body he'd so desperately missed. She arched into his touch with stuttered breaths, recklessly yanking at his sweater, his jeans, his hair. Anything within her reach.

"You'll always be perfect to me," he whispered into her ear.

"I need you, Riggs. I'll always need you." She framed his face, eyes dark with desire. "And right now that need runs painfully deep." She kissed him again, desperate and urgent. Full of unspoken promises, fueled by a never-ending appetite.

He had every intention of drawing it out, of pleasuring her as many times as she could physically take. But the claw of her fingernails and vibration of her naked body against his groin was more than he could handle. *More. He needed more.* It was a primal sensation. One that was unmistakably raw and driven by blind passion. And since it had been so long since he'd had her, he would take and take until she had nothing left to give.

He set her down on the high bed and allowed himself to let go, to show her how much she'd been missed. How much he cherished her...her body. He swore he'd never let an obscene amount of distance separate them ever again.

He had every intention of marrying her just as soon as he was certain she was emotionally healed, and ready.

PART 4
TIDES TURNING

"You're always one decision away from a totally different life." — Mark Batterson

34

The opening of the Brooks-Forrester Shelter for Youth was as grand of an affair as the residents of Blue Bay had ever experienced. The two-story building had taken nearly eight months of construction, and another three months to finish the preparations for its first residents. The results of Rowan's vision and determination were phenomenal. The contractor had taken extra care to match the charm of the community's oldest structures, making the white clapboard building appear as if it had been there for years. There was a state-of-the-art gym, a theater room, a bright mess hall, and enough custom-built bunks to sleep dozens of boys and girls from all walks of life. It had been designed with a nautical theme, generating a feel that was more relaxing than institutional.

Rowan was most proud of the well-stocked art

studio, due in large part to the supplies Taylor had left behind. She'd kept a few things in the cottage studio that were close to her heart, like the pottery wheel and the supplies they'd used to make soap. There were too many mediums for Rowan to use on her own, especially when her time in Blue Bay would be limited once the shelter was up and running.

In the year since the idea of the shelter had first come to light, Rowan and Riggs had struggled to create a routine that suited them both. Although they both made great sacrifices in order to stay together, they rarely argued. They traveled so often that there were times Rowan would wake with a jarring start, and become confused by her surroundings. Riggs and Blue had become the only consistency in her daily routine, and the sight of them at her side would immediately give her peace.

On her birthday, her father had sent her a spider lily and a card, but for the first time in her life, she didn't care. She had Riggs and a wonderful future to look forward to—she wasn't going to let the past control her.

The night of the shelter's grand opening celebration, Rowan hustled from room-to-room with her stilettos in hand, ensuring that everything was in proper order. The building would soon be bustling with friends, family, and community members casting their first look at what she had *almost* single handedly created. The diamond earrings from Riggs swung from her earlobes like a clock pendulum as she peered around every nook and cranny. She'd put so much time and effort into the opening that she wasn't sure what she was looking for, or what could possibly be out of place. She only knew she wanted everything to be perfect.

"Shit...there's that word again," she mumbled, patting the elegant knot in her strawberry blond hair.

Inside the gym, where round tables with white linen tablecloths had been meticulously decorated under Harlow's direction, her eyes began to water. She'd poured her heart and soul into the creation of the shelter, and she could hardly believe her idea had become a reality.

An arm hooked around her waist, bringing her up against a warm, hard body. "I've never seen anything so *absolutely* stunning," Riggs rasped into her ear. "And I'm not talking about the party set-up."

She spun around, belly ablaze with the sight of him in a black three-piece suit. She'd fantasized about their wedding many times over the past year. Sometimes they'd be barefoot on the beach, others they would be posing against an ancient cathedral in a foreign country. Never, *ever*, had she imagined he'd be so unbelievably handsome when dressed to the nines. Flutters erupted inside her chest when he adjusted his black tie against his crisp white shirt, flashing the knockoff watch he'd worn since he was a homeless teenager. Perfection was a word she was no longer allowed to use, but there wasn't any other way to describe the man who had stolen her heart.

She wrapped her arms around his neck, heart as light as air. Their love for each other deepened with every time they fed into their passion, and at times like that, she was unable to stop herself from claiming what had become hers. Rising on her bare toes, she pressed her red-stained lips against his ear. "Take me somewhere private, handsome. Better hurry before our guests start to arrive."

Devilish grin pressed to his lips, he gripped her hand and whisked her away. She burst into deep belly laughter when he led her into the closet where the sporting good equipment was stored on long iron shelves.

"You said to hurry," he told her, closing the door. "This was the closest thing I could think of."

Swallowed by total darkness, she knew the frantic beats of her heart had nothing to do with being afraid. Their mouths found each other without fail. His fingers read her body like a book written in braille, meant only for him. He hiked the silky skirt of her black beaded dress up high on her hip, nudging her thong aside to stroke and knead her in exactly the way she needed in order to experience a blissful release. It was almost unfair how attuned he'd become of her body and her sexual needs. He never let her so much as touch him until she'd been satisfied.

He covered her mouth with his as she climaxed, continuing to kiss her until her feet were planted back on the ground and her body resembled something other than a wet noodle. She giggled against his lips when trying to release the button on his pants. "Sorry, I don't know what I'm doing with the clasp on these trousers."

"Hold on, I'll get the light."

She shielded her eyes, knowing the fluorescent bulbs would be harsh. The charm bracelet Steph and Andy had gifted her as a child tickled the bridge of her nose. With a steady hum, the lights flickered on over their heads.

A moment later, Riggs asked, "Is that better?"

Hunger burned in the pit of her belly with the sound of his voice. She wondered if there would ever be a time where the need to be with him was anything less than urgent. Tongue sweeping over her lips, she slowly removed her hand and opened her eyelids.

Riggs was down on one knee, black velvet box perched in one palm.

"Oh, Riggs," she whispered, holding a shaking hand against her lips. She'd been expecting a proposal, just not in a closet, surrounded by gym equipment. The situation was imperfectly right.

"This wasn't exactly where I'd planned to do this, but the opportunity seemed as good as any." His dimples slid into place. "I wanted you to be glowing like this when I asked you to spend the rest of your life at my side."

"Wasn't that already the plan?" she teased, blinking the moisture from her eyes.

"Of course, but I wanted to make it official." He opened the box, revealing a dazzling, princess-cut solitaire diamond, set on a slender platinum band. Rowan knew very little about precious jewelry, but the modest size of the stone was exactly right. She wouldn't have wanted anything flashy, and neither would he. "Rowan Brooks, you're the love of my life. I've never questioned that, and I never will. Marry me. Be mine forever."

A set of tears raced down her warm cheeks. "I already am."

KINSLEY SNORTED at Rowan's side. "You two better go somewhere private before this gymnasium bursts into flames."

Dipping her chin, Rowan tore her eyes off of Riggs. Since he'd proposed, her head hadn't come down from the clouds. Part of her wanted to scold him for shaking her up before the most important night of her life, even though it had been ridiculously romantic. Even while surrounded by basketballs and tennis rackets.

With a hefty sigh, Kinsley brought her glass of champagne to rest between her breasts where her sparkling red gown dipped to her navel. Only Kinsley could make something extremely sexy appear elegant, Rowan mused. "I've been so horny ever since I kicked William to the curb. Would you please do your sister a solid, find me a handsome bachelor tonight? He doesn't have to be as fabulous as Riggs, although that would be a tremendous bonus."

Whenever Kinsley mentioned the divorce, Rowan still felt a lingering touch of guilt for not giving her friend a heads up the night before their wedding. She often wondered if the heartbreak of having to cancel their wedding would've been better than the heartbreak that came with finding William in bed with a twenty-year-old understudy. But Riggs had convinced Rowan it had been best to let their relationship take a natural course without her involvement.

Rowan giggled. "Sorry, but I don't know of any bachelors here aside from Drake."

"Gross." Kinsley scrunched her nose. "At least Harlow is taking full advantage of that."

They both watched as Drake, in a gray suit and tie, said something to make Harlow grip his arm and laugh with her head tipped back. Rowan's old college roommate rocked the black pantsuit she'd chosen to wear, knowing she'd spend the evening having to direct guests and caterers. Rowan couldn't remember a time she'd seen either of them so deeply into someone of the opposite sex. She never would've thought of introducing them to each other when Harlow was living in Boston. Now that she'd recently moved to New York, Rowan supposed something between them was fair play.

Rowan continued to study the room from afar. Steph and Andy huddled with her grandparents who'd flown in the night before from California with

Stormy in tow. It pleased her to see the four most important adults in her life with bright smiles, chatting like old friends. Wren and his girlfriend, Gillian, sat at a table in the corner with Stormy. Rowan had routinely sent Wren and Gillian to check on the shelter's progress. They'd found an apartment just five blocks away in downtown Blue Bay, and she had hired them both to work for her at the shelter on the condition that they passed frequent drug tests. At the rate Wren had been going while she'd been holed up in Kinsley's apartment, she worried his extreme partying would interfere with his future.

Seeing her loved ones all looking elegant gave her a zap of excitement. The next time they'd be gathered in formal attire would likely be for the wedding.

With thoughts of marrying Riggs, her eyes frantically scanned the large crowd of professionals, donors, and locals until she spotted him near the stairway leading up to the stage, shaking Victor's hand. She imagined from Victor's toothy smile that Riggs had just shared the news of their engagement.

A lump of pride lodged in her throat as she watched Riggs climb the stars and remove the microphone from its stand. He powered it up, saying, "Excuse me, ladies and gentlemen. May I please have your attention?" The din of the crowd slowly died down along with the upbeat music playing over the gymnasium speakers.

"It's a real pleasure to see so many familiar faces in the crowd tonight. I want to personally thank you all for coming." His gaze effortlessly found Rowan's in the crowd, and a dimpled grin popped into place. "Not only is this a celebration of the sweat and tears the lovely Miss Rowan Brooks has put into providing a safe haven for troubled teens to enjoy this charming community, it's also a celebration of the *true* union behind the Brooks-Forrester Shelter for Youth. Ladies and gentlemen, Rowan has gifted me with the unbelievable pleasure of agreeing to become my bride."

The crowd erupted in applause. Rowan's cheeks burned hot as she blew a kiss to Riggs, and the classic song *God Only Knows* by the Beach Boys began to play. She let out a light giggle—she wouldn't have expected any other selection from her forever surfer boy at heart.

Gasping beside her, Kinsley snagged her left hand to gape at the new diamond. "I *knew* it! You little minx! You've been acting as giddy as a school girl all night!"

From the stage, Riggs motioned for Rowan to join him. "Come here, beautiful."

The crowd began to clap along to the music, some chanting her name. She crossed the shiny planked floor with a lifted chin and a graceful smile, mindful to keep it as natural as possible even though the pressure of speaking in front of everyone weighed heavily on her squared shoulders. Riggs met her at the top of her steps, pulling her close for a chaste kiss and a brief hug. "I love you, Ro. You've made me a better man."

Behind him, Rowan watched the crowd part for a set of caterers carrying a large tiered cake with sparkling candles. As they neared, her fingers dug into Riggs's back. "My god," she wheezed. "*No.*"

Red spider lilies covered every inch of the cake. It was impossible to determine the color of the frosting underneath, if there was any. And when they lifted the cake a little higher, red liquid dripped onto the floor beneath it.

Blood, Rowan thought, feeling her knees weaken.

35

The gymnasium hadn't erupted in chaos. Riggs decided it was because many of their guests wouldn't have known the significance of the flowers—at least not immediately—and not everyone had been given a proper look. Hell, he'd barely caught a glimpse of it himself before Harlow's eagle-eyes had noticed Rowan's horrified reaction. She'd bolted through the crowd with ease, calmly steering the caterers and the disturbing cake back out the gymnasium doors.

Arm braced around Rowan as she lifted the microphone to her lips, he winced. She was throwing the crowd one of her bullshit pageantry smiles. "Thank you everyone. We truly appreciate your support."

He plucked the microphone out from her grasp. "There's been a change in plan, folks. If you would please gather in the hallway outside the gymnasium, your tour guides for the evening will divide you into groups, and the next portion of our evening will begin."

Wren and his girlfriend exchanged confused looks with each other and the other employees who'd been told the tour would take place after dinner. But with Riggs's firm, encouraging nod to Wren, they soon sprung into action.

"Why would he do this?" Rowan whispered. She'd gone stiff as a board since seeing the cake. He gave her serious credit for not reacting in a way that would've frightened their guests. "Where did the blood come from?"

Jaw clenched, he grunted with a non-response. He prayed it was something other than blood, even though the droplets left behind looked legitimate. Rowan was convinced her father had been the one harassing her since Kinsley's wedding. Riggs was terrified it was someone else. Someone with a much deeper agenda. How in the hell had someone snuck in despite the thorough screening process he had required of everyone on the catering staff?

Their friends and family all seemed to sense something was amiss. The Lewises and Rowan's grandparents threw looks of concern at the stage beyond the departing crowd as they reluctantly started for the hallway as instructed. Riggs accompanied Rowan down the steps where Harlow waited, lips pursed and dark eyes bright.

"What's going on?" she demanded, eyeing the red trail left behind by the cake. "Is that *blood*?"

Raw irritation ticked through his eyes. "How'd that damn cake get in here?"

"I-I don't know," Harlow stammered. "Everyone on the catering team had been thoroughly vetted like you requested. I personally cleared every employee, and ran the names by your investigator. It doesn't make sense."

"Take Rowan to the office," he told her. It was one of the few rooms in the building built to survive extreme lockdowns. The windows were bulletproof, and the walls were made with reinforced concrete. He'd decided if Rowan was going to spend excessive amounts of time with troubled kids—some who would've been taught to use violence to get their way—she needed a safety plan. His eyes snapped back and forth between Harlow and Rowan. "Use the security bar, and don't let anyone in until I get there."

Nodding enthusiastically, Harlow wrapped an

arm around Rowan's waist. "Good plan. My purse is in there—with my gun."

"Mine too," Rowan said. While she wasn't necessarily keen on the idea of shooting someone, she'd become familiar enough with the weapon that it provided a sense of comfort. She gripped Riggs's bicep. "Where are *you* going?"

"I'm going to get to the bottom of this. Someone must've seen something. That fucking cake didn't walk in here on its own." He slipped his hand inside the thick of her beautiful curls, cradling her head. "And I'm calling the cops. Someone's blood was on that cake. Whoever is stalking you has taken it up a notch. This is no longer a harmless case of harassment." He bent down, touching his forehead to hers. "Be careful."

"You too."

He brushed his lips over her, then released her. As he watched Rowan hurry out through the side gymnasium door, his heart clenched in fear with the idea of losing her after all the obstacles they'd overcome.

THEIR RUSHED breaths pinged against the polished concrete floors and freshly painted white walls as Rowan hurried alongside Harlow through the complex network of hallways. The possibility that Riggs was right, that someone other than her father was behind everything, soured her stomach. If it wasn't Jonathan, then who? Drake had been within her range of sight nearly the entire evening. Had William returned to get his revenge? Was there someone else in her life that she shouldn't have trusted?

She tried to brush her worry for Riggs aside. She'd watched him strap his ankle holster on before the party, and knew he was capable of taking care of himself. But separating from him still didn't feel right.

As they approached the freshly installed row of office windows, Rowan flicked a finger over the light switch inside. The glass reception counter and brand new computers in the hub behind it flashed bright beneath the fluorescent glow, sending a chill through Rowan. The chemical smell of new carpet and paint churned her stomach. She spun back around to Harlow. "We should go back."

Eyes briefly closing, Harlow shook her head. "No,

ma'am. Your man wanted your fabulous ass in here, where it's safe."

"I have a really bad feeling about this. Whoever messed with that cake could still be *here*. On the property. It's no longer someone just messing with my head. If that really was blood, someone is hurt."

"Let the police worry about that."

Rowan's gaze flipped back to the countertop banking the three computers. "My purse is gone."

Harlow dashed behind the receptionist's counter along with her, teeth gritted as they frantically searched through drawers and cabinets. "Damn it! Mine too!"

Just then, the lights went out all around them. The windowless office was nearly as dark as the closet had been. Rowan's pulse skipped against the hollow of her throat.

"*Hell* no," Harlow seethed, all at once grabbing Rowan's arm. "Don't you have emergency lights in this place?"

"I thought so...I mean, I thought the general contractor said something about needing to install them in order to comply with codes."

"I should've worn the pantsuit with pockets," Harlow grumbled. "At least one of us would've had a cell phone."

Rowan slipped her hand down Harlow's arm and connected their fingers. "Let's go back the way we came. There are windows—it won't be as dark."

"You heard what I said about your man wanting you here where it's safe?"

"I know, but he also wouldn't want us stumbling around in the dark. And someone has *both* of our handguns. We need to warn him."

"Okay, fine," Harlow agreed with a reluctant sigh. "But if Riggs chews me a new one later, you'll owe me a date with your hot neighbor."

Laughing, Rowan maneuvered back out of the office and led Harlow into the hallway. She walked at a clipped pace, eager to return to Riggs. Behind her, there was a soft flicker of a narrow light.

Harlow gasped, "Holy shit! What are *you* doing here?"

Rowan whirled her head around. A moment later, she was sent into complete darkness.

RIGGS SCRUBBED his hands over his face and leaned back against the kitchen's stainless steel island, impatiently waiting for the police to arrive. He'd briefly spoken with the four employees present to cater the event, and had learned "the new guy" had been in charge of the cake. When he'd pushed them for a name, no one could provide one. One of them had described the man as being in his thirties, muscular, and handsome, long brown hair pulled back into a nub of a ponytail. He had arrived in the company van with the cake an hour earlier, wearing the company's uniform and claiming he'd taken the place of the employee scheduled to make the delivery. No one had heard from the missing employee.

The chase doors separating the kitchen from the mess hall noisily flapped behind him. He removed his hands from his face to find Drake standing before him, brows furrowed. "What the hell's going on? What was with that cake?"

He'd recently begun to warm up to the kid who'd grown up next door to Rowan, acting as her big brother, and appreciated his concern. "There's been a breach in security. Someone put Spider Lilies on the caterer's cake. And I'm pretty sure it was dripping with blood."

Red blossomed over Drake's feature. "Whose blood?"

"Not sure of that yet, but one of the caterers scheduled to be here is unaccounted for. I sent the rest of them into the hallway to wait for the cops to arrive, so they can repeat everything they told me."

Drake's stormy eyes scanned across the empty kitchen. "Where's Rowan?"

"I sent her and Harlow to the office until we know more. It's safe there—they're both armed."

"Have you checked in on them?"

"I planned to head over there as soon as the police arrived."

The lights flickered off, shrouding them in total darkness. With a start, Riggs snarled. Somewhere down the hallway, a faint chorus of surprised cries echoed from the guests, followed by a deep voice—likely Wren's—telling everyone to stay calm.

Riggs cursed when the emergency lights didn't activate. Someone had cut the power.

He snagged his cell phone from his trouser's pocket and activated the light. "Let's go," he told Drake. "I don't have a good feeling about this. Whatever sick fuck is trying to rattle Rowan is escalating to the next level."

Without arguing, Drake trailed after him. They sprinted through the hallways, the twinned pounding of their shoes against the cement floor matching the ragged beats of his heart. His mind dragged him through Hell and back tenfold, fearing Rowan had been hurt.

Just yards from the office, they discovered Harlow in a pool of blood on the floor. While Drake called for an ambulance, Riggs found Rowan's treasured charm bracelet discarded at Harlow's side. He released a gut-wrenching roar.

THE RUMBLING sound of ocean waves pounding into land brought Rowan back around. Pain shot through her temples. She moaned. A band of soft cloth was tied around her eyes. Her hands were bound behind her back with what felt like a plastic tie, and she was propped against something cold... unforgiving. Gravel dug into her backside and freezing wind bit at her bare limbs, causing her to violently shiver. She could feel the material of her dress still in place, but she was outside without shoes or a coat. Where was she? Why did the water sound so close?

She felt a hot breath falling over her face before the deep rumble of a man's voice breached the silence. "There you are, beautiful. It's been a long time."

A tremble passed through her entire body. She *knew* that voice. "Who's there?"

Fingertips grasped the cloth over her eyes, yanking it down to her neck. A moment later, she was staring into intense, mossy green eyes.

He squatted on the ground in front of her, elbows balanced on his knees. Like a burglar, he wore a black sweatshirt, black work pants, and faded combat boots. His black hair was much longer, down to his shoulders, and a thick goatee covered his broad face. She noticed the edge of a new tattoo that started beneath his hoodie, and crept up one side of his neck. But the broad strokes of his thick jaw and chiseled cheekbones were unmistakable. In any other situation, she may have found him more handsome than before.

Confusion muddled her brain. "Koby?"

The wicked glint in his eyes was terrifying when he laughed with a harsh sound. "Here I was worried you would've forgotten all about me, now that you agreed to marry that rich surfer." He ran gloved fingers over her frozen cheek. "But I guess you never forget your first lover, do you sweetheart?"

36

Rowan's frantic mind was still unable to connect the dots. How had Koby found her, and why? After all those years, was he still that bitter about their breakup? Jealous of Riggs?

"What are you doing *here*?" She strained to look past him. A sudden, intense light flashed above their heads, casting a spotlight over the houses in the distance—her aunt's and Lewises included. "Why are my hands tied? Why are we at the lighthouse?"

"So full of questions." Huffing, he dropped down to sit on the rocks in front of her, casting a look of inconvenience. "You want the long story, or an abridged version?"

The wind's iciness chattered her teeth when she attempted a smile. "How about we go to my place across the bay, and you can tell me over a warm cup of coffee?"

"Aw, look at you." He twirled something in one hand that gleamed in the lighthouse light as it made another pass above them. "All vulnerable and shit, but still prim and proper, offering to play hostess to the man who knocked you out and dragged you away from your fancy party. Guess you'll always be a beauty queen."

She pulled in a sharp breath, moving her legs closer to her chest. It was the first time she realized they weren't bound like her hands. Her skin was painfully cold to the point of becoming numb. "What'd you say?"

"Oh, I know all about you, *Sienna*."

No big deal, she told herself. Nearly everyone had read about her in the past year. "Koby, *please*. I don't know what this is, or what you're angry about, but I'm going to freeze to death out here."

"Then I suppose I better start talking." He lifted the silver item to scratch a patch of skin beside his goatee. *A hunting knife.* "You and me have a connection that began when I was a kid. My parents weren't ever married. I was given my pop's last name, and lived with my mom in Oceanside. My old man only came around every now and then, usually just to throw money at us when it was time to pay the bills. I wasn't always the best kid. I stole some shit, skipped class to surf and ride dirt bikes with the older kids, mostly harmless stuff. Never anything that would put my mom in danger. Because my mom was my world...my everything. Do you remember the name Dawn Fredrick?"

Whatever heat remained in Rowan's face vanished. "She was one of my father's first victims."

Koby pointed the tip of the knife at her. "Bingo! Seems we have ourselves a beauty with brains, too!"

Tears leaked from the corners of her eyes as the facts of his story came to light. He'd been the one to discover his mother's lifeless body. He was the one she'd once felt a kinship with. "Koby, I'm so sorry. That must've been—"

"Not finished with my story!" he snapped, jabbing the knife into the ground beside her head. Rowan jumped with a loud wince. "Dawn was a pretty lady, a lot like you. Only she didn't live a life of luxury like you and your momma. So when a seemingly smart, handsome man with blond hair and pale blue eyes started coming around, she was easily charmed into believing he was a *good* man. One who wanted to take care of us. She never imagined her eight-year-old son would find her naked, strangled body sprawled on her bed on a Saturday morning. I guarantee she never aspired to have her son spend the rest of his childhood in abusive foster homes."

"Oh, Koby..." she whispered, tilting her head. More tears trickled down her frozen cheeks. "I can't imagine what that must've been like for you."

"It was hell, sweetheart. And when that FBI lady called to see about you visiting her grave, I was the one she talked to. I watched you cry over my momma's grave in San Francisco. At first I was merely fascinated with you—you were an untouchable beauty, like the kind of girls in the movies. You moved like someone famous too. I followed you around for a few days...watched you go into your grandparents' mansion, watched you hang out with your future fiancé that day on the beach...watched you enough to know you lived a charmed life. When I realized you were headed out of town, I wrote down your license plate number and had a hacker friend of mine get your aunt's name and address in Blue Bay."

Everything inside Rowan froze in terror. She couldn't believe he'd known who she was for all those years. Why had he waited so long to do something? What was he intending to do? Pain shot through her ice-cold hands as she attempted to wiggle free from the plastic around her wrists.

"I continued following you around after you moved to California for school. I had every intention of hurting you once you moved out of your grandparents' place. Then I met you on the beach that day, and decided you weren't just pretty, you were sexy as hell. I decided to get to know you a little better, thinking maybe we'd have some sort of connection because of our parents. Thinking maybe I'd break your heart...maybe mess with your head a little. Then you broke up with me out of the blue, and that's when shit got hairy. I tried getting your attention, hoping you'd run back into my arms. Then I found out you'd written that book, so I sent you and your friend those lilies the day of the wedding and your aunt's funeral to remind you of all the damage your father had done."

"How could I possibly forget?" she snapped. "Every single day of my life I'm reminded one way or another of what he'd done!"

The veins in Koby's neck stood out as he yelled back at her. "Yet *somehow*, you must *forgotten* all the pain he caused, because you went ahead and published that *bullshit* story, making a profit—"

"That's not what that was, Koby! I swear to you!

The money I made off that book all went toward the shelter! I wanted to help kids like you and me!" She took a minute to calm herself before attempting a small pageant smile. "That book was a mistake...it never should've been published. I'm sorry if it hurt you and brought up feelings about your mom's death."

"You think your empty apologies mean shit to me? You think they're going to bring her back, and undo what your father did? *She's gone, you bitch, and your father took her from me!*" Eyes wild, he plucked the knife back out of the ground, frantically tapping the tip against her bare knee. She couldn't feel it. She couldn't feel anything. "What do you say you and me go for one last swim, for old time's sake? I almost drowned you the first time, you know. But then you kissed me, and I decided I'd get to know you a little better. And by god, I never thought I'd get to know you in the biblical sense."

Since she'd only angered him before when trying to argue, she decided to try reason. "It's too cold to go into the water, Koby. Please, take me somewhere warm."

He sprang forward, jerking her arm from behind her. Icy panic closed her throat. She fought him, kicking and screaming. "Please, don't do this, Koby!"

He pulled her up to her bare feet, knife in hand.

"No! Please!"

Spinning her around, he yelled, "Don't fight me or I'll slip up and cut you!"

When she realized that he was cutting her free, she held her breath. The knife slid through the plastic bind, releasing her hands. On an exhale, she kneed him in the groin and leaped away as he groaned behind her. She raced toward the lighthouse with the speed of someone who'd been running 3-5 miles with her boyfriend several times every week.

"Come back here, you bitch!" he roared from close behind. "I'm not done with you!"

She knew she wouldn't make it off the peninsula before he caught up. Something compelled her to go inside the lighthouse, even if it only promised a dead-end. She swung the door open and slammed it back shut with Koby less than a few yards behind. It was eerily dark inside, but her eyes caught on a broken board at her feet. She lodged it beneath the door's lever, and began to climb the rickety spiral stairway. The metal teeth on each step cut into her frozen bare feet as she ascended toward the lantern room. Koby pounded on the door at the base of the stairwell, encouraging her to run faster with every howl of her name. She was surprised to discover the cobwebs had been cleared away, and the inside wasn't as cluttered as she'd remembered as a little girl.

When she reached the top, the cold wind whipped the icy tendrils of her hair around her face. She gripped the metal railing in her rigid fingers, desperate to find someone in the light cast by the lens behind her. The railing creaked and groaned inside her grip, having weakened from the salty air. There was a quick jerk in her stomach when she realized she was trapped.

Koby burst out from the stairway door, whites of his eyes even larger than before. He'd gone feral with rage. Lips curled back in a sneer, he lifted the knife when he started for her. "It's time you pay for your old man's mistakes!"

"What he did to your mother has nothing to do with me!" she cried, all at once believing the words to be true. A surge of strength and bravery swept over her. She thought of her Aunt Taylor and Jason, and knew they wouldn't want her to give in without a fight. She sideswiped Koby's strike as the Judo instructor in New York had taught her, and threw her shoulder into his side. He let out a bellow as he lost his footing, and broke through the rusted railing. Rowan watched with her heart in her throat as he propelled over the edge, grabbing a piece of the broken metal. Dangling hundreds of feet in the air, he cried out again.

It wasn't in her nature to watch someone die. She stretched out on her belly against the cold metal walkway, extending her arm. "Koby! Take my hand!"

"I like that plan," he sneered, reaching for it. "We can die together."

Their fingers connected momentarily before Koby jerked back suddenly, losing his grip on the metal. Fear and grief pounded through her heart as she watched him sail through the cold air, crashing into a pile of rocks. She held her breath, waiting for him to move. He remained lifeless.

Turning away from the gruesome sight, she released a startled cry. She hadn't wished him to die. He'd been mentally disturbed. She wanted to think he could've been saved with medications and therapy. But when he'd so unexpectedly jerked back, it was almost as if he'd been pushed. With the piercing wail of an approaching siren, she leaned back against the concrete and closed her eyes with thoughts of her aunt.

37

The harsh rattle of the metal bars sliding open behind them set Riggs's teeth on edge. The building was unnaturally cold, haunted with sounds of distant shouting and the odor of stale sweat. When Rowan crushed his hand beneath the stainless steel table with a sense of urgency, he wanted to shout at the guards to let them out. The visit to the secure prison in upstate New York had been Rowan's idea, created just days after Koby had attempted to kill her, and it had been championed by her therapist. Riggs had vehemently disagreed with any plan that put his future wife in the same room as a cold-blooded killer, and tried convincing her for weeks to cancel.

He'd begun seeing a therapist himself. Ever since the night they'd found Rowan half-frozen on top of the lighthouse, the icy fingers of panic would slip beneath his skin whenever she was out of his sight. He was still livid with himself for sending her away that night when he should've kept her within an arm's length. He'd been relieved beyond words that both Rowan and Harlow had only suffered minor bumps to their head after being knocked out. They could've ended up dead like the unfortunate caterer who'd been in the wrong place at the wrong time, and had sacrificed his blood for Koby's sick agenda.

The chance to back out of Rowan's plan dissolved once her father appeared before them. A quiet noise vibrated against her throat when she gripped his hand even tighter.

Jonathan's wrists were cuffed and chained to a leather strap secured around his thick waist. His orange uniform stretched tight against his bulging muscles. Riggs was rattled by how normal the hulking man appeared, and how many of his features his daughter had inherited. He was relatively attractive, but the deep lines jutting from his eyes and crossing his forehead gave him a hardened look. Otherwise, he could've been any elderly man on the streets of Manhattan.

"My sweet baby girl," Jonathan rasped, looking fixedly at his daughter. "My Sienna. You're all grown up."

Rowan's lips trembled, all at once tight and colorless. "I'm no longer that little girl."

"I can see that." His gray gaze shot over to Riggs. "Who's this joker?"

Riggs ground his teeth together with his guts screwed into unyielding lumps. Rowan didn't want her father knowing her business, and had begged him to remain impartial to their conversation. He struggled against the need to declare he was the only one man who had ever properly loved his daughter. He wanted to throw himself over Rowan, to protect her from her father's frighteningly hard stare. "None of your business."

Rowan's voice crackled with emotion as she held her father's gaze and spoke. "I've come here with one simple request: don't ever contact me again. We may still be related by genetics, but the daughter you knew no longer exists. I'm done feeling guilt over what you did to all those poor women. Stop sending me letters. Stop trying to insert yourself into my life. You've ruined countless lives, but I won't let you ruin mine any longer." Rowan stood, pulling Riggs along with her. "I'm glad you lost your appeal."

A dark sneer spread over Jonathan's lips. "All this time, and that's all you have to say to me?"

"No," Rowan decided. She didn't so much as

glance over her shoulder when she added, "Fuck you."

Riggs bit back a belly-laugh as they exited the cell, wishing like hell he could pull her into his arms and kiss her soundly. He'd never been so proud of her as he was in that moment. She'd been working overtime with her therapist since Koby had attempted to kill her, and was finally in the right headspace to give a middle finger to her father and the demons that had chased her ever since she was a little girl. He intended to make her his wife as soon as humanly possible.

THE MORNING of Rowan's 25th birthday the following February, she woke in their Maui villa feeling as refreshed as ever. The nightmares had ceased since they'd gone to visit her father, and the shelter was up and running without any hitches. She stretched her bare limbs against the luxurious sheets, breathing in the fresh tropical air, and silently giggled with the feeling of a wet tongue on her nose.

She snuggled Blue for a minute and scratched behind the sweet dog's ear before releasing him onto the floor at her side. "Go potty," she whispered, knowing he was trained enough to find his own way. He'd effortlessly adjusted to their life on the road, and was even starting to look like a local with the colorful fern-print bandana she'd found while shopping in Lahaina.

She turned to her beautiful husband-to-be and was greeted by his gloriously naked body and a dimpled grin. He'd begun wearing his wavy brown hair in longer sweeps that accentuated the fierce lines of his jaw, beckoning to her fingers. "Good morning, beautiful. Happy birthday."

"Did I wake you?" she asked, combing her hand through a thick lock of his hair. "Was I having nightmares again?"

His brows hitched with concern. "Do you remember having bad dreams?"

"No. In fact, I remember something about you being naked...and jumping out of a cake," she teased. "I think it was a chocolate lava cake. You were all gooey, and—"

He jerked her against him, eyes simmering with passion. "I like where this dream is going. I'm already naked, and I can have a cake here in five minutes. Show me how it ends."

She lowered to take his mouth, humming in satisfaction with the teasing twist of his tongue and gentle sweep of his lips, the nimbleness of his fingers and expertise of his lazy strokes. Their lovemaking continued to exceed her greatest fantasies, and they'd both become insatiable. She couldn't get enough of his strong body, the feel of his lean muscles coiled around her. At times the sensations she felt were so overwhelming they'd bring her to tears.

After they'd both climaxed and lay tangled in each other, she wondered how long until he'd be ready to go another round. She stretched up to once again to meet his mouth, but Riggs held her back at an arm's length.

"Oh no you don't. Your first surprise of the day will be here in less than ten minutes." He swooped in for another lingering kiss before backing away, honeyed eyes alight with mischief. "Wash that beautiful ass, but keep your hair dry. Throw on the contents of the red gift box on the bathroom counter when you're done."

"Bossy SOB," she muttered, wondering what reason he'd have to give her those instructions. When Blue returned with his favorite chew toy held in his mouth, she tossed it across the room and watched Riggs march toward their closet. He plucked a pair of boxer briefs from his underwear drawer and stepped into them before reaching for a pair of shorts. She sighed dreamily. She didn't imagine she'd ever grow tired of seeing his naked rear end, even once it lost its shape and became wrinkled with age. "Wait. Where are *you* going?"

He shot a mysteriously dimpled grin over his shoulder. "Wouldn't be any fun if I ruined the surprise."

He exited the villa without so much as a kiss, leaving her to shower alone. Mere minutes after she'd exited the steaming glass enclosure and slipped into the lovely white satin thong and white terry cloth robe she'd discovered inside the package, she answered the twinned knocks on the villa's front door with Blue yipping at her side.

Kinsley and Harlow stood on their bamboo welcome mat.

"Shouldn't you two be in New York?"

They each wore the exact same white robe as her own. Curiously, neither of them had put any effort into fixing their hair or face. She leaned against the doorway, giggling. She shouldn't have been surprised to discover her future husband had been thoughtful enough to fly her best friends in for the celebration.

Harlow lifted one expertly sculpted brow. "We

got a call from some smooth rich dude, ordering a sister and a redhead."

"He's a pretty smooth talker," Kinsley agreed, bobbing her head. "He somehow convinced us to traipse through the resort, *au naturel*."

With a sudden bubble of laughter, Rowan sprang into their welcoming arms. Blue barked along happily as the three women gripped each other in a circle, giggling in varying sounds. "I can't believe you guys are here!"

"You think we'd miss your big birthday bash?" Kinsley asked with an unladylike snort. She bent to scoop Blue into her arms. "Your charming fiancé wouldn't partake in such a tragedy."

Rowan's heart soared with love for Riggs and her friends. She couldn't imagine a more perfect way to celebrate. *Not perfect*, she reminded herself as she grinned at her friends. Just...fitting. And right. "What's with the matching robes? Are we heading to the spa?"

"Not exactly," Kinsley said, turning to Harlow with a devilish grin and a nod. Harlow stuck two fingers in past her lips and let out a whistle that Rowan was sure could be heard clear over on the island of Lanai. Several beautiful women in black smocks stepped into the driveway behind them, carting large rolling bags and backpacks. The woman on the end held a cluster of white garment bags high over her head.

"You hired a beauty team?" Rowan asked Kinsley, eyes wide.

"Per Riggs's instructions," Harlow clarified.

Rowan stepped aside to let the team pass, each of them pausing to kiss her cheek. "Where are we going?"

Kinsley entered behind Harlow, passing the dog into Rowan's arms. "You're not getting us to ruin the surprise."

Curiously, the woman assigned to do Rowan's makeup used a light hand. Once she was handed a glass of champagne as the hairstylist informed her he'd merely be curling her hair in soft waves, Rowan became suspicious. They were styling her hair the exact way Riggs preferred, she thought. By the time a woman from the beauty team presented Rowan with one of the white garment bags, her pulse throbbed inside her throat. She suspected she knew what she'd find inside when Kinsley and Harlow crowded in beside her, grinning with the anticipation of a couple of kids on Christmas morning.

"Go ahead, Ro," Kinsley whispered. "Open it."

Rowan took cautious steps toward the bag,

pulling its zipper down with her breath held. The bodice of the bone white sheath dress was adorned with a sweep of lace that mimicked the shape of lilac blossoms. It spilled down onto a simple white skirt made of lightweight chiffon, slit at the knee.

She knew that dress. It had been Taylor's dress the day she'd married Jason.

"Oh, *Riggs*," Rowan breathed out through a wealth of tears.

Whenever he'd wanted to discuss the details of their wedding, she'd brushed the subject aside, saying they'd work it out with time. She'd been too focused on ending the first chapter of her life and severing her relationship with her father to give it any thought.

Kinsley looped her arm through Rowan's, sighing dreamily. "Today's the day you finally get to marry that beautiful man."

"Yeah, so your hot little ass better hurry and get dressed," Harlow added, slapping her rear. "The rest of your friends and family are waiting by the beach, suffering through this perfect weather."

Kinsley dramatically rolled her eyes and clicked her tongue as she helped the woman carefully remove the dress from its hanger. "Please. You're just eager to get back to my brother." She motioned to Rowan. "Get a move on, sister. We don't have all day."

Taylor's dress fit Rowan with hardly an inch to spare around her waist. For the first time in her life, she was within the recommended BMI for someone her size, and the dress elegantly highlighted her natural curves. She squared up in front of the full-length mirror on their sliding bathroom door to admire her backside as Kinsley closed the handful of delicate buttons beneath the V-shaped back. Everyone in the room stopped what they were doing to clap in approval.

"Your hubby-to-be sure knew what he was doing when he decided to have that dress altered," Harlow declared.

Beaming at her side, Kinsley pecked Rowan's cheek and whispered, "Taylor would've been wicked proud, Ro."

Tears slipped down Rowan's cheeks as she reached for her friend's hand and gave it a squeeze. "Thank you."

Kinsley crossed over to one of the other garment bags, unzipping it to expose a simple, floor-length turquoise dress. She dropped her robe and stepped into the dress. "Frankly, I don't know what I'm going to do with myself while everyone else fawns over their lovers at the reception. Even *my parents* were making eyes at each other on the flight here."

Across from her, Harlow was stepping into a similar dress with a band across the chest rather than the spaghetti straps on Kinsley's version. "I wasn't supposed to say anything, but Drake heard Riggs invited one of his single buddies."

"He's setting me up?" Kinsley's brows shot upward, then promptly drew down. "Please tell me he's not a producer or anyone involved with show business."

"He's not," a deep voice answered from the doorway. "He happens to be a talented landscaper."

Rowan turned into her lover, finding his honeyed eyes drinking her in with the desperation of a man dying of thirst. He wore a simple white linen shirt, and tan dress pants, no shoes. He pushed a wavy lock of his hair behind his ear and produced a grin that turned her bones to jelly.

"Okay, time for anyone who isn't a groom or bride to clear the villa," Kinsley announced. She tossed Rowan a wink. "See you at the altar, beautiful."

Blissfully alone, Rowan took Riggs's face in her hands and kissed him with strong lips until they were forced apart to catch their breaths. "Thank you for altering my aunt's dress," she panted against his lips. "I know you don't like me using the word, but it's as close to *perfect* as anything could be on the day I make you mine." She backed away, eyes suddenly wide. "Hold on. Isn't it considered back luck for the groom to see the dress before the wedding?"

"Pretty sure that rule doesn't apply in this situation." Eyes suddenly dark, his lips tilted to one side. "Damn, Ro. *Baby*. The way you look in that dress...I don't know that I can take you out there, and share you with everyone else."

"You don't have to share me with anyone—with the exception of our future children." With the most natural of smiles spreading over her lips, she giggled as he twirled her around before drawing her into his arms for a slow, delightful kiss.

Hand-in-hand, they left the villa together, and headed barefoot into the sand.

Want to receive free bonus content, sneak peeks of upcoming releases, and access to Quinn's exclusive monthly giveaways? Become a VIP reader: www.quinnavery.com/subscribe

NEW RELEASE

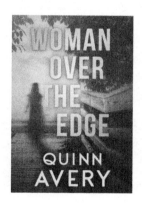

Perfect for fans of Don't Lie To Me and The Night She Disappeared, award-winning author Quinn Avery's newest book, Woman Over the Edge follows Mia's decades-long search for her sister's killer.

Mia Hughes is only sixteen years old when she loses her sister after a summer storm catapults their boat into the rocky shoreline. Only Ben, Mia's best friend along for the boat ride, is conscious after the crash. When he goes looking for help he discovers Mia covered in blood...and no sign of

Bella. With no memory of what happened before she was found, Mia spends the next twenty-two years haunted by Bella's disappearance, only to encounter a series of tragedies that she knows have to be tied to her sister...and to Ben.

Blending the non-stop action of Those That Wish Me Dead, the shocking revelations of The Couple Next Door, and the deceptive family drama of The Last Thing He Told Me, Woman Over the Edge will most definitely keep you on the edge of your seat.

QUINN AVERY is an award-winning and Amazon bestselling author who has written over 37 novels, both romantic suspense and mystery/thriller. An avid fan of the beach, a good book, and Dave Grohl, she enjoys spending her free time with her favorite people and biggest fans...her husband and children. Quinn also writes romantic suspense as Jennifer Ann.

www.QuinnAvery.com

- facebook.com/authorquinnavery
- instagram.com/authorquinnavery
- bookbub.com/authors/quinnavery
- goodreads.com/quinnavery
- pinterest.com/authorquinnavery
- amazon.com/Quinn-Avery/e/B07NLD8Q57

ACKNOWLEDGMENTS

A huge shout-out to those who keep reading my work, no matter what genre I throw out there! You guys are the best!

Thank you to the countless librarians, bloggers, and shop owners who continue to support my career. You can't imagine how much you're appreciated!

Thank you a million times to Christy Freeberg for putting up with umpteen drafts of this one, and showing excitement with every change. You've been a great friend during my biggest lows and highest of highs!

Thank you to my editor for taking this monster on, and having faith in the story!

Special thanks to Najla Qamber for being a badass designer, for always rolling with the punches, and for providing me with yet another gem!

Thank you to my sweet hubby for putting up with my sleepless nights, cooking me dinner when I forget to stop, and catching endless grief from our friends about my writing. I do have to say my heroes all each have a little of your awesomeness in them.

Made in the USA
Monee, IL
10 September 2023

42383573R00256